D0160560

MONDAY 8:07 A.M.

"YOU AIN'T GOING TO LIKE IT," SHERIFF LUTHER RANDALL SAID.

My gut knotted. "Let's do it."

Life morphed into slow motion as I followed Luther down the hallway toward Mike's bedroom. My legs felt heavy, and my shoe soles grabbed the carpet as if trying to hold me back. As if they knew what lay ahead.

My name is Dub Walker. I've worked more than a hundred homicides in my career. As an MP for the US Marines, as a lab tech with the Alabama Department of Forensic Sciences here in Huntsville, as a trainee and consultant in Quantico with the FBI's Behavioral Analysis Unit, and as a crime scene and evidence analyst on cases all over the country. I'm considered somewhat of an expert in this stuff. I've written a dozen books on these subjects, and if you do that people automatically think you know a bunch about it. Maybe I do; maybe I don't. Could go either way. It was that perception-reality deal.

I've seen angry spouses slice, dice, and shoot each other; drug deals gone sideways; murders for hire; gang massacres; Mafia hits; and a few killings that didn't fit into any pigeonhole. I've seen victims of shootings, poisonings, beatings, fires, explosive devices, and one-way flights off tall buildings. I've seen firsthand the work of serial killers who tortured, mutilated, cannibalized, and even preserved victims.

None of this prepared me for this one.

STRESS FRACTURE

D.P. LYLE

MEDALLION
P R E S S

Medallion Press, Inc.

Printed in USA

STRESS FRACTURE

D.P. LYLE

DEDICATION:

For my parents, Victor and Elaine Lyle.

Published 2010 by Medallion Press, Inc.

The MEDALLION PRESS LOGO
is a registered trademark of Medallion Press, Inc.

Typeset in Adobe Garamond Pro
Printed in the United States of America
Title font set in Cacavia01

Library of Congress Cataloging-in-Publication Data

Lyle, D. P.
 Stress fracture / D.P. Lyle.
   p. cm.
 ISBN-13: 978-1-60542-134-6 (hardcover : alk. paper)
 ISBN-10: 1-60542-134-0 (hardcover : alk. paper)
 1. Laboratory technicians--Fiction. 2. Huntsville (Ala.)--Fiction. 3. Serial murderers--Fiction. I. Title.
 PS3612.Y43S77 2010
 813'.6--dc22
                          2009041124

10 9 8 7 6 5 4 3 2 1
First Edition

ACKNOWLEDGMENTS:

A writer depends upon many people to research, to write, and to bring a story to print. This one is no different. I thank the following individuals for their time and for sharing their knowledge and support.

Dr. Emily Ward, Roger Morrison, Chris Crow, Allen Perry, Robert Bass, Glen Brown, Yolanda Tapscott, and all the wonderful professionals at the Alabama Department of Forensic Sciences. Your help with understanding the workings of your office was invaluable.

Protocol Specialist Gena Cox for the personal tour of NASA's Marshall Space Flight Center, and of course, the visit to Florida for the spectacular night shuttle launch. What a thrill.

NASA's Dr. David Hathaway, Solar Physics Group director and developer of the VISAR system, for sharing his expertise in video enhancement techniques.

NASA's Dr. James W. Bilbro, assistant director for technology, for his time and valuable discussion of the work—past, present, and future—at the Marshall Space Flight Center.

Shelly Haskins, city editor for the *Huntsville Times*, for his time and expertise.

My wonderful agent, Kimberley Cameron of Kimberley Cameron & Associates. KC, you're the best.

My editor, Christy Phillippe, for her tireless work on this manuscript.

My parents, Victor and Elaine Lyle, for their unwavering support.

And of course, Nan, who makes all this possible and worthwhile.

CHAPTER 1

SUNDAY   11:36 P.M.

He relished the moments before the kill.

When his heart thumped against his chest. When sweat slicked his skin and stung his eyes, his breathing coarse and raspy. When the muscles of his shoulders tightened and his hands tingled as if awakening. He closed his eyes and took several breaths, the night air warm and sweet. No hurry. He had time. Time to enjoy the anticipation.

Squatting behind a thick, five-foot row of hydrangeas, Brian Kurtz leaned against the cool brick wall. Its roughness tugged at his T-shirt. Inside, his victim slept. The deep, peaceful sleep of someone who thought the future held many such restful nights. Not so, Mr. Michael Savage.

Savage. He liked that name. It possessed power and passion and violence and rage. It conjured images of the old man at the Russel Erskine and the little fag over in Madison. *Savage.* They had learned the meaning of the word. Tonight the man beyond the wall would, too.

'Very soon, Mr. Savage,' he murmured.

He often talked aloud to himself, though at these times his voice sounded foreign. Tinny, flat, muffled. His pulse hammered in his ears, and the familiar rage-fueled knot expanded in his stomach. The anger wanted out. *Not yet.*

God, he loved this feeling.

He shifted his weight. The marble-sized gravel beneath the shrubs crunched softly. His shoulder shook loose a few petals from one of the ball-shaped flowers. They floated to the ground, joining others that had already taken the fall.

His plan looped through his mind for the hundredth time. Every step a crisp picture. Jump the fence into the backyard. Through the side garage door, the kitchen, and down the hall to where Savage sprawled on his bed, easy prey. The gun, the soft pop, the recoil. Then, Savage was his. The images kicked his pulse up a notch. Sweat collected on his face, and he swiped it away with the front of his shirt.

It was time.

CHAPTER 2

BRIAN LAY CURLED ON THE FLOOR OF HIS APARTMENT. NAKED. THE unpadded, wafer-thin carpet did little to soften the slab of concrete beneath. The exhaustion that always followed these outings seemed particularly heavy tonight. Even a cold shower hadn't revitalized him. He flipped over the sofa pillow he had wedged beneath his head, noticing that his damp hair had created a dark circle on its coarse fabric. He rolled to his back, stared at the ceiling, and began absently counting the tiny holes in the acoustic tiles. He lost count several times, his mind wandering to the night's events.

It had been insanely intense. The best so far. The release of his rage had been almost complete. Savage received what he so deserved.

The ringing of the phone startled him. Even though he knew the call would come, its sudden intrusion reignited his anger. He rolled to his side and stared at the phone on his desk across the room. His impulse was to yank its cord from the wall. Instead, he endured its screaming until it fell silent. Not tonight. Tonight he couldn't talk to him.

3

He settled on his back again and readjusted the pillow. He closed his eyes and was immediately crouching in the shrubbery at Savage's place again. He could smell the night air and feel the roughness of the bricks against his back. The feeling of anticipation returned. So did the ringing. *Damn it.*

Each ring pumped up the headache that had begun to gather behind his eyes. *Fuck him.* After a dozen rings, he crawled over and snatched up the phone. "Yes."

"What took you so long?"

"I was in the shower." He settled his back against his desk.

"I see." A moment of silence. He could hear the man's breathing. Slow and steady. "You did well tonight."

"How would you know?"

He laughed softly. "I saw."

"When?"

"Before . . . during . . . after. I mean it. You did well."

"I live for your approval."

"No need to get sarcastic."

"I'm not. I'm tired."

Another soft laugh. "You get some rest. Soon we'll begin again."

"When?"

"Eager, I see. That's good. I'll call." The line went dead.

He hung up the phone and stood. The pulsing in his head increased. He massaged his temples, but the headache didn't seem to notice. He moved into the kitchen, snagged a cold PBR from the fridge, popped the cap, and chugged down half of it.

A knock at the door. Then a voice. "I know you're home. I heard the shower."

It was Laranne Millonzi. She and her husband, Carl, lived in the next apartment. If she was knocking on his door after midnight, it meant that Carl was on a trip. He drove eighteen-wheelers all over the East Coast. Brian and Laranne had first hooked up three months earlier. During one of Carl's extended trips. She came over for a beer, and they ended up rolling on the carpet. He wasn't really in the mood for company, but Laranne sure knew how to relieve a headache.

He didn't bother to dress or even to pick up the towel from the floor. He opened the door.

She flashed a look of surprise and then smiled. "That should take care of the small talk."

"No talk. Let's just get to it."

She stepped inside and closed the door. She was barefoot and wore a silk kimono, short, midthigh. It slid from her shoulders to the floor. She wore nothing underneath.

The sex was quick, hot, and angry. He needed to purge his demons, and she apparently did, too. The floor, the kitchen counter, the bed, they used them all. Then he dropped into a deep sleep. He awoke just after 3:00 a.m., and she was gone.

CHAPTER 3

"YOU AIN'T GOING TO LIKE IT," SHERIFF LUTHER RANDALL SAID.

My gut knotted. "Let's do it."

Life morphed into slow motion as I followed Luther down the hallway toward Mike's bedroom. My legs felt heavy, and my shoe soles grabbed the carpet as if trying to hold me back. As if they knew what lay ahead.

My name is Dub Walker. I've worked more than a hundred homicides in my career. As an MP for the US Marines, as a lab tech with the Alabama Department of Forensic Sciences here in Huntsville, as a trainee and consultant in Quantico with the FBI's Behavioral Analysis Unit, and as a crime scene and evidence analyst on cases all over the country. I'm considered somewhat of an expert in this stuff. I've written a dozen books on these subjects, and if you do that people automatically think you know a bunch about it. Maybe I do; maybe I don't. Could go either way. It was that perception-reality deal.

I've seen angry spouses slice, dice, and shoot each other; drug

6

deals gone sideways; murders for hire; gang massacres; Mafia hits; and a few killings that didn't fit into any pigeonhole. I've seen victims of shootings, poisonings, beatings, fires, explosive devices, and one-way flights off tall buildings. I've seen firsthand the work of serial killers who tortured, mutilated, cannibalized, and even preserved victims.

None of this prepared me for this one.

Luther stepped aside and let me enter. Three lamps and the overhead light burned, yet my vision dimmed and constricted. Images raced toward me as if fired down a gun barrel. Acid surged in my stomach.

This wasn't Mike. This wasn't human. Arms and legs, bruised and fractured, twisted into some grotesque Mummenschanz. Face nonexistent. I could make out a shattered jawbone. Several teeth lay on the blood-soaked carpet. A wrought-iron poker, which I recognized as being from the living room fireplace, protruded from his abdomen.

"Told you it wasn't pretty," Luther said.

I swallowed down a wave of nausea. *Relax, you've seen worse.* That was a lie.

"What was the time of death?" I asked.

"According to Sidau, body temps, lividity, rigor all suggest somewhere between ten and one."

"Who's running the case?"

"It's a joint effort. Sheriff's department and HPD. Our guy is Scotty Simpson. For HPD it's your buddy Tortelli." Luther looked down the hallway. "Here he comes." He stepped aside and let T-Tommy enter.

Tommy Tortelli. T-Tommy to his friends. I'd known him since the fourth grade. First day of school. First day we suited up for football together. Now, at thirty-nine, he was simply a bigger version of what he had been at nine. The word was *thick*: legs, arms, chest, neck. Even his hair was thick and black. He had played linebacker. Still walked like one. A straight-ahead, no-nonsense, jump-right-in-your-chili sort of walk. At six feet, we stood eye to eye, but his 230 had me by 50 pounds.

"Ain't this some shit?" T-Tommy said.

"And then some." I felt a throbbing behind my left eye. I looked back at Mike's corpse. "I hate this."

T-Tommy clamped a hand on my shoulder and squeezed. "We'll get this fucker." He looked at Luther. "You tell him yet?"

Luther shook his head.

T-Tommy sighed. "We've got two other murders that look exactly like this."

I still couldn't swallow the thick saliva that collected in my throat. Breathing wasn't exactly easy either. I looked at T-Tommy. "You're kidding?"

"Wish I was."

"You're thinking we have a serial?"

T-Tommy stared at the floor for a brief moment and then toward the window that looked out over the backyard, eyes unfocused. "Just a theory yesterday. After this? I'd say we've moved beyond the theoretical." His gaze rose to meet mine. "At least that's the way I see it. 'Course, I want your opinion."

"HPD caught the first two murders," Luther said. "We got this one. A few days ago T-Tommy came to see me. Wanted to know if we had any similar cases. We didn't." His jaw tightened. "Until now. When I saw this . . . I knew this had to be the same guy and called T-Tommy." He massaged the back of his neck. "Scotty's setting up a task force room downtown. We have more space than HPD. They're taking all the evidence they have on the first two murders over there."

The headquarters for the Madison County Sheriff's Department, including Luther's office, occupied the second floor of the county courthouse in the middle of the downtown square. I suspected setting up the task force there had nothing to do with architecture. Simply meant Luther would keep a close eye on everything. HPD might help handle the cases, but Luther was in charge. He grabbed this case so it wouldn't get screwed up. And because he had to. For Mike. I understood.

Luther glanced down at Mike's corpse, closed his eyes for a moment, and then said to T-Tommy, "Why don't you bring Dub up to speed. I need to get back to the office. When you wrap things up here, we'll sit down and determine how best to handle the media. I'll set up a press conference for later today." He hesitated a beat and then turned and headed down the hallway.

"Let's do the tour," T-Tommy said.

CHAPTER 4

THE TOUR BEGAN OUTSIDE. TWO CRIMINALISTS CROUCHED NEAR the fat hydrangeas that hugged the front of the house. One aimed a camera at a visible shoe print and the foot ruler that had been laid next to it for scale.

"How's it going?" T-Tommy asked.

"Finished with the photos." Sidau Yamaguchi looked up and then stood. "Dub." He pulled off his latex gloves, and we shook hands. "I had a feeling they'd call you in." He waved a hand toward the house. "Sorry about Mike. Bad shit."

Sidau was the chief criminalist at the Alabama Department of Forensic Sciences. I had worked with him for six years and then as a consultant on a few cases since I left the department. I'd learned a ton of forensic tricks from Sidau.

I squatted near the print. "What've you got here?"

"Several prints here in the dirt. At the edge of this gravel. Looks like an athletic-type shoe. Should be able to grab some good casts.

Get at least a size and manufacturer."

I remembered when Mike and I put down this gravel. I shoveled it from his rusty old wheelbarrow while he got on his hands and knees to spread it beneath the shrubs. Helped hold in water, according to Mike.

I glanced toward the street. "Probably where he waited. Checking to make sure no one saw him. Where'd he enter the house?"

"This way," T-Tommy said. He led Sidau and me around the side of the house and through the gate in the hedge-covered wooden fence that wrapped the backyard. "He jumped the gate here. It was locked. Lock hadn't been tampered with. We opened it for access. We found a few white cotton fibers on the gate and on the poker inside." He looked at me. "We found similar fibers at the other two scenes."

We moved toward the garage's open side door. I examined the doorknob and lock. No signs of damage. No visible scratches. "You figure the door was unlocked?"

T-Tommy shoved his hands into his pockets and rocked back and forth on his heels. "Looks that way."

"Doesn't sound like Mike."

"Sure don't. The door from the garage to the kitchen looks the same. No sign it was worked."

We moved into the garage. I saw several of the rectangular cardboard frames Sidau liked to use around visible shoe prints. Same pattern.

"We found a couple of prints here on the concrete and a few more on the kitchen floor," Sidau said.

On to the kitchen. More rectangles.

Sidau stopped by the kitchen sink. "Killer cleaned up here."

I saw a teardrop-shaped stain on the splash behind the hot water handle. Dripped from his hand when he turned on the water. I could also see the faint purple hue of diluted blood in the crevices at the base of the handles and around the drain.

"Same type as Mike," Sidau said. "He used a dish towel to dry himself. It's outside air-drying. Found a couple of hairs on it. If they're from the killer, maybe we can get some DNA."

In the living room, nothing seemed out of place. No signs of a struggle. The sofa. The big-screen TV. Mike's lounge chair. Everything exactly as it should be. How many Saturdays had I sat here watching college football with him? How much bourbon had we consumed? How many lies had we told?

I walked to the large picture window and looked out toward the street. Yellow crime scene tape stretched across the front yard from the lamppost near the driveway to the pecan tree Mike loved so much and which served as a barrier to keep the growing crowd safely away. Couples, kids, joggers, housewives, one still in a robe and curlers, and other curiosity seekers. I scanned the faces. Was one of them the killer?

I saw Claire McBride, standing near her *Channel 8 News* van, interviewing a man. She was a tough investigative reporter. Channel 8's number one. She could get the story. If sugar was needed, she could be as sweet and smooth as warm maple syrup. Or she could melt down anybody and, if need be, drink most men into a coma.

She was also my ex-wife. Long story.

I followed T-Tommy and Sidau back down the hall to Mike's bedroom. "When do you plan to move the body?"

"Now," Sidau said. "Luther wanted you to see the scene first. I'll get the techs on it."

"And I need to chat with a couple of the guys," T-Tommy said.

After they left, I circled to the far side of the bed, searching the battered corpse for something that was Mike. Anything recognizable. My gaze settled on the USMC tattoo Mike proudly wore on his left upper arm. It looked pale and washed out and was jailed by streaks of blood. Carefully avoiding the extensive blood spattering, I examined the scene from various angles. I took a few deep breaths and swallowed hard a couple of times. *Time to get to work*, I told myself. *Stop seeing this as Mike. See it as a crime scene. Get your head in the game.* Not an easy thing to do.

The facial trauma was extensive, but I thought I could make out an exit wound through the left jaw. Couldn't be sure since the mandible was fractured in two places. If so, meant the bullet came from behind. The autopsy should tell the story.

The blood spatter pattern that surrounded the bed reflected the killer's violence. Long streaks of cast-off spatter, blood that flies off a bloody weapon when it's swung, striped the ceiling above the bed. Typical blunt-force medium-velocity impact spatters flared out from the body in a circular array. They painted the headboard, the bedcovers, the wall, the nightstand, the lamp shade, the window curtain, everything. Except for a void wedge to the left of the bed. Where I stood. Where the killer had stood. Where his body intercepted the spatters that flew in that direction.

Total overkill.

I reached down and gently touched Mike's left leg. Its coldness was shocking. I drew my hand away, but the cold lingered and seemed to penetrate my fingers. Images bounced around in my head. Mike and his wife, Mary, standing over their son in the ICU, the boy's motorcycle accident having destroyed his brain beyond salvage. The gut-wrenching decision to remove life support. Mary's deep depression and suicide. Mike's second trip in a year to Maple Hill Cemetery to say good-bye to a loved one. Mike's heart attack. His retirement from the Madison County sheriff job he loved so much. Now this.

"Jesus, Mike. Why you? After all you've been through." Tears pressed against the backs of my eyes. "I promise, old buddy, we'll find this scumbag. He won't walk. No way in hell."

I took one last look around the scene. I needed to get out of there. I had seen enough, and if not enough, all I could take in right now. In the hallway, I passed two coroner's techs carrying plastic sheets. I hated the cold, impersonal, synthetic material. Always had. I remembered when corpses were covered with blankets for transport, at least creating the illusion of comfort and warmth and respect. Silly, I knew. The dead didn't know the difference. I tried not to visualize Mike rolled inside the translucent plastic.

When I reached the living room, T-Tommy was talking to a uniformed officer. The young man nodded and walked out the front door.

"What's the story with the other two cases?" I asked.

"An elderly man at the Russel Erskine and a young guy out toward Madison," T-Tommy said. "Why don't you hustle over and see what Scotty's got set up? I'll be along directly."

CHAPTER 5

OUTSIDE NOW, ON THE FRONT PORCH, I SAW CLAIRE HAD A MICROphone stuck in the face of the housecoat-and-hair-curler woman. Her cameraman aimed his lens over her shoulder to capture the woman's animated jabbering.

Claire was a beautiful woman. Thought so since the first time I saw her. Lean and fit with waist-length red hair, a great smile, a patina of freckles over her nose, and hazel-green eyes that tended toward brown when she was tired and definitely toward green when she was angry. Or laughing. Made reading her mood a bit difficult. Looked better in the flesh than she did on TV, and that was saying a lot. She had a loyal following, her best demographic being eighteen- to fifty-year-old males. At thirty-eight, I was included in that group.

Our marriage had lasted all of fifteen months. The sex was great, the laughter better, but it just wasn't meant to be. Began during a time when neither of us was thinking clearly, me from the abduction of my sister, her from the end of a two-year engagement, and ended

16

because we worked out better as friends. She said it was a red-hair problem. That two redheads couldn't stay under the same roof very long without going at it. In truth my hair was more mahogany, the ruddiness only coming out in direct sunlight. She was a true redhead, though the shade did hop around the spectrum a bit. Today, a sort of cedar color. Our real conflicts were control issues. Each of us wanted to be the boss, especially her. No, really. The divorce was inevitable and welcome. We definitely agreed on that, so it went smoothly, and we remained close friends. Occasionally the friends-with-benefits deal.

As I approached, I heard the woman going on about how nice Mike Savage was, how she felt safe having the ex-sheriff in the neighborhood, how shocking it was that something like this could happen here, right across the street from her own home.

Claire broke off the interview and intercepted me as I ducked beneath the crime scene tape. The woman moved away, hugged her friend, another woman in a bathrobe, and began giggling about how she was going to be on TV.

"What's the story?" Claire asked.

"Good to see you, too, Claire."

"Yeah, yeah. We can do all the chitchat over a drink later. What's the story?" Claire was in work mode. That meant, don't waste her time. Get to it or go away. When I didn't say anything, she softened. "I know it's a homicide, and I know it's Mike." She touched my arm. "I'm sorry."

"Yeah. It's a tough one."

"What can you tell me?"

"You didn't hear this from me. Okay?"

"Dub, I know the game. Now tell me what you know or I'll kick your ass."

"You're so charming, how could I resist?"

"Charming, schmarming, let's have it."

I nodded toward her cameraman. "No film, no sound."

"Jeffrey." She waved a hand toward the truck. He lowered his camera and moved that way. Out of earshot. Claire thumbed off her mic, dropped it in her blazer pocket, and retrieved a pen and pad from her shoulder bag.

"Yes, it's Mike. Single victim. Murdered between ten and one. In his sleep."

She parked a strand of hair behind her ear. It didn't stay and fell along her cheek. "What else?"

"That's all I know. I got here just before you."

She gave me a sideways look. "You're holding something back." She clicked the pen a couple of times. "You know I can tell, so why try to hide it?"

I shrugged.

"And you know I can make you talk."

"What are you going to do? Kick me or screw me?"

"You wish. I'll just keep at it until I grind you down. Save yourself some pain and just tell me."

I looked back toward the house. T-Tommy stood in the living room, near the picture window, talking to a uniform. "I can give you this . . . he was shot. Probably a single shot to the head. Won't know for sure until the autopsy." I took a deep breath and let it out slowly. "He was badly beaten. Postmortem."

The pen in her hand froze in midword, and she looked at me. "I heard rumors that happened in two other recent killings. True? Any connection?"

"Don't know."

"You're on a roll now. Don't go wobbly on me."

"I really don't. I haven't seen anything on the other two cases yet."

"But you will?"

"That's where I'm headed."

"They've asked you to help?"

"Looks that way." I saw T-Tommy and the uniform come out the front door and head around the side of the house. T-Tommy had his cell phone to his ear.

"You'll keep me in the loop?"

"As much as I can. Don't want you to kick my ass."

"Wouldn't want to have to, either. But business is business."

"Love you, too."

"I know."

I nodded toward the cameraman, who now sat in the open door of the van, fiddling with his camera. "Can he do something for me?"

"What?"

"Film the crowd."

"You know I can't do that. It's illegal."

"You can't give it to the cops. I'm not part of that fraternity. You can give it me."

She hesitated a beat and then nodded. "You don't think the killer is here, do you?"

"Some like to hang around to watch their handiwork. See the havoc that follows. Maybe get close to the investigation, suggest clues, even offer to help solve the case."

"Weird." She shook her head. "I'd be as far away as possible if I'd killed someone."

"Murderers don't tend to be rational."

Claire motioned the young man over and introduced me to Jeffrey Lombardo. Handsome, with long hair pulled into a ponytail, he wore jeans and a gray T-shirt. Firm handshake. I explained what I needed.

"Be discreet," I said. "If our boy's here, he'll disappear if he knows what's happening."

"No problem," Lombardo said. "I'll give the video to Claire when it's done."

CHAPTER 6

THE TASK FORCE WAS BEING SET UP JUST DOWN FROM LUTHER'S office in the same second-floor, corner room where I'd worked the Billy Wayne Packwood case. Billy Wayne was a real beauty. Liked to capture, rape, torture, and kill teenage girls. Body count reached twelve before he was brought down. I had consulted on the case. Helped with the profile and the evidence analysis. When I entered the room, memories came at me. Images of Packwood's mutilated victims. The odor of decaying bodies. The fear Packwood spread over the city. All still sharply etched in my mind.

The room hadn't changed. Same faded yellow walls. Same metal desks and chairs. Same tired coffeemaker sat on the same wobbly wooden table. The glass coffeepot was new, but there was always a new pot. Glass had a short life span around here.

Six corkboard panels filled one wall. Two held pictures and pieces of paper, some typed, others scribbled, fastened into place with multicolored plastic pins. The photos revealed that the other two victims

21

hadn't fared much better than Mike. I knew the third panel would soon hold images of the scene I'd just left. I also knew that before this was over, most, if not all, of the other corkboards would be filled. That's the way it worked with these types of killers.

The sad truth is that a high body count helps solve these cases. One scene, even two or three, rarely offers enough evidence to identify the perpetrator. But as the horrors pile up, each scene and each victim adds another sliver of evidence that later rather than sooner sticks together enough to close the loop. When the loop does close, when the killer is captured or killed, when hindsight kicks in full force, you always . . . always . . . ask yourself why you didn't close it sooner. Why the final one, two, three, pick a number victims weren't saved. Seems like it's always that way. I hate it, but what are you going to do? It is what it is.

"Well, look who the cat dragged in."

I turned. Scotty Simpson came through the door. His premature balding made his thirty-one years look more like fifty-one, but he always had a pleasant smile, and today was no exception. "Scotty. Good to see you again."

We shook hands, and then Scotty's face turned serious. "Terrible thing about Mike. I just can't believe it."

Ain't that the truth? I pointed toward the panels. "What've you got so far?"

"One mean dude. Grab some coffee if you want, and I'll take you through it."

I poured a dose of the overripe liquid into a Styrofoam cup and took a sip. Bitter, but hot and black. Not bad for task force coffee.

Scotty moved to one side of the first panel. While he spoke I carefully examined each photo relating to the first crime scene.

Mr. Carl Petersen. Seventy-three. Retired aerospace engineer. Worked out at the Marshall Space Flight Center for twenty years. Lived alone at the old Russel Erskine. Fifth floor. Murdered June twenty-eighth. Widower. Wife died of cancer four years earlier. Kept to himself. Withdrawn and quarrelsome since his wife's death. Baseball nut. Collected cards, autographed balls, and bats. Entry was through the front door. No sign of force. Cause of death—blunt trauma. Multiple blows from an autographed Henry Aaron bat. Defensive wounds. Left arm fractured, bone protruding, bent at a ninety-degree angle. Two fractured fingers on right hand. Crushed skull. Face obliterated. Bat barrel split from the force of the blows. Killer drove it into the dead Mr. Petersen's abdomen and left it. Like the fireplace poker at Mike's.

None of this was good news.

The old Russel Erskine Hotel sat in the downtown area only a couple of blocks from where we stood. Once the city's most famous hotel, it had been converted into a retirement home. Meant Petersen wasn't a random deal. Getting in there wasn't like crawling through someone's window or walking through an unlocked garage door. And making it to the fifth floor and back without anyone noticing was the product of great skill and experience or incredible luck. With the lock intact, he either had a key—maybe an inside job?—or he was very good at working locks. Like Mike's garage door. I'm certain Mike kept everything locked. Petersen was an engineer. Bet he did, too. Those NASA guys left little to chance.

"Petersen wasn't shot?"

"Nope."

"Anything else?"

"Oh, yeah," Scotty said. "The weird part. This psycho proceeded to the kitchen for a snack."

"After all this?"

Scotty nodded. "Milk and cookies. Like it was recess."

"It was. A break between killings."

"Cooling off?" Scotty asked.

"Something like that. Once he purged his demons, whatever they are, he reverted to more normal activities. Seems odd, I know, but it's not uncommon."

"We found bloody glove prints on the refrigerator handle, milk carton, glass, and the cookie bag. Chocolate chip. Also cotton fibers in the bloodstains on the glass and on the bat. A few others on the front doorjamb. Sidau says they probably came from common gardener's gloves."

"Any DNA from the glass?"

"None."

"Anyone in the lobby that night?"

Scotty shook his head. "Not then. They've got a night guard now."

"Security setup?"

"Two cameras. Not the best quality. We did get a shot of the guy. Or at least who we believe was the guy. Came across the lobby and up the stairs. Had on a hat, so we couldn't see much."

"What time?"

"The system's clock was a little off, but best we can tell, around 1:00 a.m."

"Time of death?"

"Drummond estimated somewhere between 1:00 and 3:00 a.m."

Dr. Lou Drummond, one of Madison County's two medical examiners, worked under the direction of the county coroner, Edwin Dreyer. As with many jurisdictions across the country, Madison County used the coroner system of death investigation. An elected position, funeral-home owner Dreyer had been coroner for four terms and was odds-on favorite to win in the next election. Mainly because no one ever ran against him. Since Dreyer had no medical expertise, the state hired Drummond and his partner, Dr. Becka Cooksey, to perform autopsies, handle all the other medical procedures, and interpret most lab tests for Dreyer. Maybe not the most efficient system, but it worked.

"Mrs. Cohen, his next-door neighbor, said she heard Petersen's TV tuned to a Braves baseball game," Scotty said. "Turned it off around eleven. Next morning she took some coffee cake over, but when he didn't answer, she thought he had gone for a walk, which he did most mornings. By evening she still hadn't seen him and called the security people, thinking he might be ill or injured or something.

They used a passkey and found this."

"Mrs. Cohen hear anything?" I asked. "After the TV went off? His defensive wounds show he put up a hell of a battle."

Scotty shook his head. "Said she might have heard a thump. Wasn't sure of the time or where it came from. She did say that she often took Xanax for sleep and had had a couple of glasses of wine that night. She must have been zonked."

"She must have been in a coma." I refilled my coffee cup. It was starting to grow on me. I'd forgotten how good bad coffee could be. "Any other neighbors hear anything?"

"*Nada.*"

"Where's the video? I'd like to look at it."

"Over at Forensic Sciences."

"Anything else?"

Scotty shook his head.

"And the second murder?" I moved to better view the photos in the next panel.

"The victim was William 'Skip' Allison. Big player politically in the local gay community. Murdered July third in his apartment out toward Madison. Upstairs unit of a fourplex. Had a lover. Billy Holcomb. Exact opposite of Skip. Muscular, surly, big on tattoos. In Atlanta at time of murder. At a party with about twenty witnesses. Allison was shot with a 9 mm. Probably rigged with some kind of sound suppresser."

I raised an eyebrow. "You sure?"

"The lab boys think that some markings on the slug and the tattoo pattern suggest that."

One of the photos was a close-up of the entry wound on the left side of Allison's head. Just above and in front of the ear. A minor miracle the following trauma had spared that area of the skull. Condensed but sparse stippling collared the round, clean wound. The degree of spread was consistent with a near-contact wound, while the paucity of tattooing suggested that the muzzle was farther away. Conclusion? Could mean that a sound suppressor narrowed the spread while partially containing the burned and unburned powder that followed the bullet. Not strong evidence, but intriguing.

I massaged the tightening muscles of my neck, last night's dream and the scene at Mike's settling in. "Looks like our boy didn't stop with a clean kill."

Scotty shook his head. "No defensive wounds, so everything you see is postmortem."

"What'd he use?"

"First, one of those decorative wooden rolling pins. The blows were so violent the wood shattered, so he grabbed a brass table lamp. It was dented and bent from the force of the attack. Drummond thinks Allison was struck a hundred or more times."

My jaw tightened. "Like Mike." I drained my coffee cup and tossed it into the corner trash can. "Anything else?"

"A couple of smeared partial bloody shoe prints on the carpet. Poor substrate, so a sole pattern ID wasn't possible."

"You guys about caught up?" T-Tommy came through the door.

"Mostly," I said. "I'd like to see the first two scenes."

"Allison's has been cleaned. Turned back over to the owner. I think Petersen's might still be intact."

"It'll help if I see both."

CHAPTER 7

I PUSHED THROUGH THE GLASS ENTRY DOORS OF THE RUSSEL ERSKINE. Once the grande dame of the city, it had faltered when the center of commerce moved from downtown out to the various malls. Occupancy fell, and in 1983 it was converted into a subsidized senior apartment building. The sign above the columned entryway still identified it as the HOTEL RUSSEL ERSKINE. I hadn't been inside since I was a kid and now saw that the lobby had been restored to its original 1930s look. Spectacular. Clean and fresh with large square floor tiles and bright white walls with gray trim. A massive chandelier and marble staircase with gilded railings gave it the appearance of an old Hollywood movie set.

An attractive, middle-aged woman in tan slacks and a white silk blouse greeted us. T-Tommy introduced property manager Wilma Foster to me and then explained to her that we needed to see Carl Petersen's apartment again. Once the elevator door hissed shut and the car jerked to life, she said, "This has shaken up folks around here. Everyone loved Mr. Petersen. He was an important part of our little community."

"I heard he was a bit cantankerous," I said.

She looked at me and smiled. "A bit. But in a sweet way. He organized a book group. They met every Wednesday night. It was very popular. About thirty people showed up each week."

"Has his place been cleaned yet?" I asked.

She sighed. "I can't bring myself to do it. I haven't even been inside since . . ."

"I understand."

"Besides, it'll be a while before we can put it on the market. Things like this tend to spook potential renters."

The upstairs, as neat and clean as the lobby, smelled of fresh paint and new carpeting. At Apartment 506, Wilma keyed the door and pushed it open. It whooshed across the carpet. Needed trimming. Wilma didn't seem to notice. She took a step back without even a glimpse inside. "Just lock the door when you're done." She headed back toward the elevator.

I looked up and down the hallway. Nothing but room doors, wall sconces, and a red EXIT sign near one end. Probably the stairwell. Petersen's door looked like all the others. Killer knew exactly where he was going. Nothing random here.

T-Tommy went inside. I hesitated near the door. Where the killer had stood. Planning his entry. Was he scared? excited? Maybe a few second thoughts? Did he know Petersen was asleep? Did he have a key? If so, from where? Did he work the lock? Sweating, looking over his shoulder, fearful another resident might surprise him?

I stepped into the living room. Sealed for two weeks, it had gathered a host of musty odors. Nothing seemed out of place. No sign of a struggle. I moved past the sofa, a magazine-laden coffee table—*Scientific American*, *National Geographic*, and *Aviation Week*, that I could see—and into the small kitchen-dining area. Except for the thin layer of dust, everything appeared normal. As if the occupant might return at any minute from an extended vacation. Not going to happen. Not now, not ever.

The bedroom was another story. It smelled of violence, death, and old blood. Some of the many repulsive sensations that lived in my brain. Smells and sights and sounds that too often returned years later when least expected, dredging up memories:

The man who lost grip of his sanity, shot his wife, and then himself. Found four days later, inside their sunbaked, double-wide trailer, the stench of their rotting corpses so thick I could taste it. That had been in Sarasota, Florida.

The two floaters found a week after they were bound, gagged, and dumped in the swamp for not paying a debt to a New Orleans thug. Nibbled on by gators and turtles and fish. I had helped recover the corpses from the murky water. The feel of their bloated, mushy flesh as it slid across my fingers. Nothing feels like that.

The child that had been—

Not that one. I reined in my memories.

The bed where Carl Petersen had died was now only a frame; the mattress and box spring off to the crime lab for analysis. A section of the carpet had also been removed, leaving a concrete rectangle, haloed by dark splotches of dried blood. I saw a void pattern to the left of the bed. Where the killer had stood. Impact spatters peppered the wall near the head of the bed. Cast-off streaks painted the ceiling. Both by-products of the violence visited on Petersen. Just like Mike's.

Two bats rested in the corner, each dusted with fingerprint powder. The closet door stood open. Petersen's clothes hung perfectly spaced in a military fashion. Just what you would expect from an engineer. Two regimented rows of cup hooks dangled an array of caps from the ceiling. Atlanta Braves, New York Yankees, and several from various bait shops and garages. I then returned to the kitchen and inspected the bloodstains on the refrigerator and cabinet handles.

Leaning against the counter, I attempted to visualize how things went down. A criminal leaves behind not only physical clues—fingerprints, blood, semen, hair, fibers, all that crime lab stuff—but also fragments of his personality. Not always easy to read, and probably not overly accurate, these clues often reflect motivation. And understanding the motivation, the *why*, is what most often leads to the *who*.

Some cops and profilers claim to have a sixth sense, able to smell a crime, reconstruct it psychically. Bullshit. A good investigator keeps his eyes and mind open. Lets the evidence tell the story. Uses what he sees to draw his conclusions. Nothing prescient about it.

That's not to say I didn't create mental images of the crime. How it unfolded, what the killer was likely thinking, why he did certain things. But that wasn't psychic or clairvoyant or any other type of voodoo. It was simply experience and common sense.

For me, these images sometimes came after days of studying the evidence. Piece after piece dovetailing until only one conclusion was possible. At other times, the images appeared suddenly, triggered by something at the scene. The position of the body, a piece of furniture out of place, a crumpled cigarette pack, a tiny drop of blood. It could be something so striking that it immediately changed my view of things or so subtle that it pricked a tiny hole in my brain. Just large enough to allow an image inside, where it expanded and deepened, until it became complete.

The image I formed now was of Petersen, home alone, watching the baseball game, and then, exhausted, drifting into a sound sleep, totally unaware until it was too late. The killer, carefully manipulating the lock and easing the door open. In the quiet darkness, its gentle scraping against the carpet must have sounded like a train sliding to a halt. Once in the bedroom, he would have stood quietly over the old man, listening to his breathing. How long? Did he take time to relish the moment or strike quickly for fear that Petersen would wake up? According to what Scotty had said, his first blow glanced off Petersen's shoulder. The next two shattered the old man's arm and fingers as he defended himself. Finally, the killing blow to the frail forehead. Petersen never had a chance.

Then the killer strolled to the kitchen for milk and cookies.

True sociopathic behavior. Also the behavior of someone who knew his victim. Knew there was little danger of someone showing up unexpectedly. Knew he had time.

"How do you read it?" T-Tommy asked.

"Not the most accessible place I've ever seen. Close quarters and no easy escape route. Ballsy fucking move."

"Or stone crazy."

"That, too. His neighbor . . . the old lady . . . she lives in 508. Right?"

T-Tommy nodded.

"Hard to believe she didn't hear more than a thump."

T-Tommy locked up, and we rode the elevator down. Back in the lobby, I noticed the two security cameras that covered most of the expansive lobby area. I didn't see Wilma but found her in her office. The door was open, so I stuck my head inside. "Got a couple of questions, if you don't mind?"

She slipped off a pair of gold-rimmed half-glasses and looked up. "Sure."

"Are the entry doors locked at night?"

"They are now." She sighed. "I wish they had been that night. But we really had no reason to. This is a very safe place." She glanced toward T-Tommy and then back to me. "Or was. Everything's locked now. And we have a security guard."

"On that night, no one was in the lobby?"

"Unfortunately, no."

CHAPTER 8

GULF COAST TELEMARKETING WAS THE PRODUCT OF A NASTY divorce. Owner, Wanda Fisher, had dumped her loser husband after he humped his secretary and, with the money the courts handed her, started Gulf Coast. It began painfully small in a rented house, but over the next six years grew into a multimillion-dollar business that occupied eight thousand square feet, two-thirds of a wooden office building that sat just off Memorial Parkway a few miles south of downtown. Noreen's Flowers filled the other third. Most of Gulf Coast's footage was divided into rows of cubicles, where shifts of telemarketers took care of business.

Brian Kurtz sat in one of the cubicles and tapped the keyboard of his computer, completing yet another order form. The vague headache that had nagged him all morning now settled into a steady throb behind his eyes. In the past three hours, he had made fifty calls and closed eleven sales. Five for Mr. Foam Carpet Cleaning, four for Top Coat Painting, and two for Thompson's

Pest Control. Not a bad morning. He knew none of his coworkers could equal that. They never did.

He decided to make one more call before taking his lunch break. He adjusted his headset and dialed the next number on his list. Four rings. Five. Six. Seven.

"Yeah." The voice was gruff, impatient.

"Mr. Kushner?"

"Who wants to know?"

"I'm Brian Kurtz."

"I don't know any Brian Kurtz. What do you want?"

"I'm calling on behalf of Mr. Foam Carpet Cleaning. We're having our annual summer—"

"I don't need any goddamn carpet cleaning asshole bothering me. Why don't you shitheads leave people alone?"

"I'm sorry, sir." Brian felt his jaw tighten. "If there's a better time to call, I can—"

"Listen, asshole, why don't you go fuck yourself?"

Brian ground his teeth together. "No, Mr. Kushner, why don't you fuck yourself?" He disconnected the call.

"Brian?"

He swiveled in his chair and faced Wanda Fisher. Great. Just fucking great.

"Can I see you in my office?" Not waiting for his response, she spun and headed down the hallway.

He sat for a minute. Fuck her. Spouting orders as if she was the fucking queen or something. If she wanted to talk to him, she could do it right here. He took a couple of deep breaths to calm his growing anger. Helped some. He stood and walked toward Wanda's office. Inside, he sat in one of the straight-back chairs that faced her desk. She shuffled through a stack of pages on her desk before looking up at him.

"Want to tell me what that was all about?" she asked.

"Some jerk."

"We call them customers."

"Not this one. He was abusive and arrogant."

"Brian, we've discussed this before. Last week, to be exact." Her reading glasses perched near the end of her nose, and she peered over them at him. "You know some people can be a bit testy when we call. You're supposed to be polite regardless of what they say. You promised you would after our last talk."

Talk? It was more like a finger-wagging lecture. She, in her expensive suit, with her perfect makeup and hair, sitting here talking down to him. He wondered what she'd do if he crawled across her desk and smashed her perfect little face.

"I don't have to put up with someone calling me names or cursing at me," he said.

Wanda sighed. "I've received more complaints." She picked up the stack of papers. "A dozen more."

"From who?"

"Customers who've said you were short and rude. Even abusive."

"Give me their names, and I'll call and apologize."

"I don't think that will help." She tugged off the glasses, dropped them on her desk, and massaged one temple. "Brian, you know I like you. Know I think you're a good worker. But I can't have this. I'm going to have to ask you to leave. Temporarily. I want you to see Dr. Hublein. When he clears you, I'll see if I can take you back."

"Take me back? You're firing me?"

She took a deep breath and let it out slowly. "Let's call it a leave of absence. Just until you get things under control."

His jaw muscles ached. His teeth ached. His head pounded. "I see Dr. Hublein all the time. Once a week. He says everything's fine."

"Is everything fine?"

"Of course. Just because I don't like to be abused by some jerk on the phone doesn't mean I have a problem."

"I'll give Dr. Hublein a call."

He moved forward to the edge of his seat. He noticed she leaned back a bit. *You better be afraid, bitch.* "Why do you want to make trouble for me?"

She tapped the eraser of a pencil on her desktop. "Didn't I give you this job when no one else would? I've tried to help, and I will continue to do so. But lately . . . the past couple of months . . . you've become increasingly . . . difficult." She waved the pencil toward the papers on her desk. "These complaints . . . and other concerns from your coworkers."

"Just great. Those losers are getting me fired."

"No, Brian, I'm letting you go . . . temporarily . . . because of your behavior. Not theirs."

"Right."

"I'll talk with Dr. Hublein, you go see him, and maybe he can help."

"I don't need help."

"I'm sorry. That's just the way it has to be. Once Dr. Hublein assures me that everything is okay, we'll talk about you coming back. Until then, you'll have to leave."

CHAPTER 9

BUDDY GUY WAILED "FIVE LONG YEARS" FROM THE PORSCHE'S CD as T-Tommy and I traveled west along University Drive toward the small town of Madison. Sitting on the western flank of Huntsville, Madison was once a major shipping portal for King Cotton. Back then it was called Madison Station and consisted of little more than a commercial stop on the Memphis-Charleston Railroad. Now it was a thriving community of forty thousand.

I hung a left at Wall Triana Highway, another mile, and then right into the Madison Oaks Apartments complex. A couple of twists and turns through the parking area, and I settled the Porsche into a slot, facing the fourplex the late William "Skip" Allison had called home. Tan clapboard with brown trim, two upper, two lower, Allison's was unit B, upper right.

Getting a look inside didn't go as smoothly as it had at the Erskine.

We climbed the stairs, and T-Tommy rapped his knuckles on the door. I heard voices and movement inside, and when the door swung open, the unmistakable odor of marijuana flowed out. From Scotty's earlier description, I immediately recognized the hulk in the doorway as Billy Holcomb. Big, burly, barefoot, ragged jeans, and a cap, turned backward. His bare chest and abdomen rippled with muscles, tattoos, and thick black stubble that I recognized as regrowth from a not-so-recent body shave. Behind him stood a smaller man who looked a great deal like Skip Allison. Didn't take Billy long to find a new friend.

"What the fuck do you want?" Billy glared at T-Tommy.

"HPD," T-Tommy said.

"I know who you are. I remember the last time you came around, giving me shit. What do you want?"

"Just need to take a quick look around," I said. "Only need a couple of minutes."

He gave me a passing glance and then looked back to T-Tommy. "I'm tired of this shit. When are you assholes going to get out of my life?"

"Don't mean to bother you, Billy," T-Tommy said. "Mr. Walker just needs a peek at the crime scene."

"It's not a crime scene. It's my apartment." Billy rotated his neck. "I know my rights. I don't have to let you do jack shit."

T-Tommy smiled and shoved his hands in his pockets. I suspected it was to keep from busting Billy in the face. He never took the word *no* well. T-Tommy might look soft to those who didn't know him. He carried an extra two dozen pounds, much of it lapping over his belt, but beneath the pasta he loved so much lay the same thick muscles that made him an all-state linebacker. Who pancaked blockers and smacked down running backs on a regular basis. That would've gotten him a full ride to play for the Crimson Tide had it not been for a knee injury in the final quarter of his final game at Huntsville High School. Any guy who ever played the game knows that football breeds a level of toughness that doesn't fade. Not ever. T-Tommy was living proof.

When he was a street cop, before getting his homicide investigator shield, he had the reputation of being the first through the door. Usually taking the door, the lock, the door frame, whatever blocked his way with him. Every cop in the department asked for T-Tommy when a drug bust, or any other hard takedown, was needed.

Yet, he was one of the kindest and gentlest men I ever knew. Shirt-off-his-back sort of guy. Until some jerk . . . like Billy . . . tried to jump in his chili. Then, more often than not, it got real ugly, real quick.

"That's right," T-Tommy said. "You don't have to do nothing. That's your constitutional right. 'Course, I got the constitutional right to get a warrant. Take about a New York minute. Then we can toss this place to hell and back. Maybe drag the narcotics guys over for a look-see. I assume you have a prescription for the herb I smell? Glaucoma, is it?"

"Just fucking great. The goddamn AC's broken. We're dying in here, and you assholes come along and fuck with me."

The heat of July frays folks' nerves. Makes them a shade less hospitable. Especially someone like Billy, who probably wasn't very hospitable on a good day. And who just might have a wad of steroids and growth hormone running through his system, sparking his wiring.

"Give us ten minutes," I said. "Then we'll be on our way."

"Who are you?"

T-Tommy took that one. "He's a crime scene expert. Helping us find whoever killed Skip. You do want us to find him, don't you?"

"A little late for that, isn't it? Skip's gone."

I saw T-Tommy glance toward the smaller man, who looked past Billy at us. "I know this is a tough time for you, Billy. I can tell you're all broke up. Just let us do our job."

Billy hesitated for a minute and then stepped aside. "Don't look like I got much choice."

When I entered the living room, the marijuana aroma mixed with several others: fresh paint, new carpeting, and a chlorine cleaner of some type. The place had been overhauled. I walked to the bedroom. It was nothing like the photos I had seen. The bed was new, the carpet fresh, and the walls now a spotless gray. Still, a faint odor of blood and death bubbled its way up. Probably my imagination.

I tried to mentally overlay the room before me with the photographic images that hung on the task force room walls. Skip Allison's body floating on a bloodstained bed, impact spatters on the wall, a void pattern to the right side. No cast-off stains on the ceiling. Rolling pins didn't throw around as much blood as baseball bats.

I moved through the apartment and examined each room. Billy's friend had camped out on the living room sofa, but Billy shadowed my moves. Not so much to keep an eye on me, but rather he seemed to be curious about what I was doing.

Back in the bedroom, I leaned against the doorjamb and, as at Petersen's, attempted to visualize the killer's movements. The unlocked front door offered easy entry. Allison asleep and unaware. Here the killer wasted no time. Simply leveled the gun near Allison's temple and squeezed the trigger. The blood spatter pattern showed that Allison's head was still on his pillow when he was shot. Meant the killer didn't want to give Allison a chance to fight for his life. Meant he had planned to use the gun from jump street, not a spur-of-the-moment decision. Made sense after the fiasco at Petersen's.

The three crime scenes didn't make sense. They wormed around in my gut. A feeling I often got when the facts didn't mesh. The usual pigeonholes didn't fit this killer. His approach and entry were carefully planned. Maybe even rehearsed. He didn't simply walk in and start wailing as a psychotic, disorganized killer would. Yet, the brutality of the beatings suggested just that. The work of someone totally out of control. I couldn't get my mind around these two profiles. Not yet, anyway.

Did the killer only plan the actual murders and not what came after? Did the dead bodies before him ignite some suppressed rage and compel him to batter the corpses? A hundred or more blows to Skip Allison. Who knows how many to Mike? Did that quench his rage or simply push his madness into some dark corner where it coiled and waited? Sure looked that way. How much control did he have over his demons?

I thanked Billy. Got a grunt in return. T-Tommy and I left.

CHAPTER 10

FURY. ANGER. RAGE. THE NEED TO STRIKE OUT. TO HURT. TO harm. To kill.

Brian knew he had to get away from Wanda, from the morons who sat around him, buzzing away into their headsets like a swarm of irritating insects. He stood at his desk, fists clenched, jaws crushing his teeth until they ached. The sudden heat of the room thickened the air. A trickle of sweat slipped down his cheek. Over the top of his cubicle wall, he saw several of his coworkers staring at him.

What the fuck are you looking at?

He gripped the back of his chair, knuckles white. He wanted to hurl it at . . . what was her name? The one next to him. The big girl with wide eyes, circled by iridescent blue eye shadow. With nauseating red-orange hair, razor cut on one side, piled in unruly curls on the top of her head. With that ridiculous string of multicolored, marble-sized beads that dangled behind her left ear. Glenda something. Riordan found its way through the static in his head. That was it . . . Glenda

46

Riordan. She looked like an obese cockatoo. A terrified obese cockatoo. He could almost taste her fear. He wondered what she would look like if he . . .

Get out. Get out, now.

He slung his backpack over his shoulder and stormed out the door. Shielding the sun's harsh glare from his eyes, he climbed down the three wooden steps and walked along the walkway that led to the parking area. Two Mexican gardeners worked among a blanket of flowers to his right. One of them gave him a quick nod and then returned to pulling weeds. As Brian reached the asphalt lot, a man stepped from behind the gardener's truck. Pockmarks cratered his face, and his teeth, one upper missing, were deeply yellowed.

"Hey, buddy." His voice was raspy and diseased. He extended a dirt-stained hand toward Brian. "How about a dollar for some food?"

Brian was in no mood for street trash. "Why don't you get a job, asshole?" He brushed past the bum.

"Fuck you."

Brian whirled toward the man and through clenched teeth said, "Get out of here before something bad happens."

"Give me your wallet."

The knife appeared from nowhere. The blade lashed across Brian's forearm. Blood raced down his arm and drizzled onto the hot asphalt.

The angry white heat inside erupted. Brian screamed and swung his backpack in a wide arc, catching the man on the shoulder. He staggered. The knife flew from his hand and clattered across the lot.

A second swing struck the side of the man's head. He wavered, but managed to stay upright. Brian's fist put him down. Hard. The man's head cracked against the pavement.

Brian leapt on the stunned vagrant. Right, left, right again. Rage drove his fists into the face of the now-unconscious man. Blood flowed from his mouth and misshapen nose. The gardeners grabbed Brian's arms and pulled him away, but he muscled from their grasp. He snatched a hoe from the back of their truck.

Two women exited Noreen's Flowers and screamed a duet. Brian's head snapped in their direction. One of the women dropped a large floral arrangement. It tumbled down the stairs, spewing flowers. "Call the police," the other yelled. Both retreated into the flower shop.

Brian returned his attention to the object of his anger. He slammed the hoe handle across the man's chest and face. Two more gardeners appeared, and the four men wrestled Brian to the ground.

"Get off me," he screamed.

"*Senor. Por favor, no se mueva.* Don't move," one of the gardeners said.

"Let me go." He strained against them, but couldn't get free. "Okay. Okay. I won't hurt him anymore."

Still they held him.

"Look. I'm bleeding. Let me go."

"Okay, señor," one of the gardeners replied. "We let you go. No more fight. Okay? No more fight?"

"I promise."

They loosened their grip. Brian rose to his feet. One of the gardeners handed him a dirty rag. He pressed it to his arm to stanch the blood flow.

A police car, tires squealing and lights flashing, sped into the parking lot and slid to a stop near them. Two deputies jumped from the car, batons in hand.

"What's going on here?" the older of the two asked. He was tall, muscular, and possessed a don't-fuck-with-me demeanor. His dark eyes and hair and bronze skin bespoke his Hispanic heritage.

"That son of a bitch attacked me." Brian removed the dirty, blood-soaked rag, revealing the bleeding wound. "Tried to rob me."

The officer knelt beside the unconscious man, felt his neck, and then placed his hand on the man's chest. "He's alive. Jesus, what a mess. Hal, get the paramedics rolling." Still squatting, he twisted to face Brian. "What the hell did you do to him?"

"I told you. He came at me with that knife." He pointed to the weapon, lying several feet away. "I defended myself."

"With what? A truck?" The officer stood. "I'm Deputy Paul Rodriguez. That's Deputy Hal Oakley. What's your name?"

"Brian Kurtz. I work here." He nodded toward Gulf Coast's door.

"What exactly happened?" Rodriguez asked.

"This guy came at me with a knife. Demanded my wallet. I refused. He cut me."

"Hal, toss me the first-aid kit."

In the distance, an ambulance siren grew louder.

"I can't do much for this guy," Rodriguez said. "He needs to get to a hospital. Let me look at your arm."

Brian held out his arm while Rodriguez placed several gauze squares on the wound, securing them with two strips of tape. "That should hold until we get you to the hospital." He led Brian to the patrol car and seated him in the backseat. "You sure did a number on that guy."

"I thought he was going to kill me. That's the biggest knife I've ever seen."

"Did you know him?"

"Never seen him before."

"You wait here while I talk with these guys." He closed the car door and approached the gardeners, speaking in Spanish.

Brian felt his anger ease to a low simmer. An ambulance sped into the lot and disgorged two paramedics. They knelt by the mugger. From the backseat, Brian watched the entire show unfold before him: the medics dealing with the mugger, Rodriguez and Oakley talking with the gardeners.

Twenty minutes later the medics had finished placing an oxygen mask, an IV, and a neck collar on the vagrant, and chatted back and forth with the hospital on the radio, telling them their ETA was ten minutes. They strapped the mugger to a stretcher and loaded him into the ambulance. One medic jumped into the back and closed the rear doors behind him. The other climbed into the cab, and they sped away, siren blaring.

When Rodriguez finished with the gardeners, he used a pen to push the knife into a plastic evidence bag. He sealed it and handed it to his partner. He then walked down to the flower shop and spoke with the two women. Brian couldn't hear what they were saying, but the women were wide-eyed and animated, speaking rapidly with waving arms. He smiled. How pathetic. They would talk of this day for years to come with their perfect little families and at their mundane dinner parties. They would never return here without a feeling of dread and would look carefully around the parking lot before leaving their cars.

Finally, the two deputies returned to the car, Oakley driving, Rodriguez riding shotgun. They sped out of the lot.

Rodriguez flipped on his handheld radio. "This is Rodriguez, unit 671. En route to Memorial Medical Center with one male suspect for medical treatment."

"Roger. Do you need backup?"

"That's a negative." He clicked off the radio.

"Suspect?" Brian said. "I'm not a suspect. I'm the victim."

"The other guy looked like the victim," Oakley said over his shoulder.

"He started it. I was minding my own business, and he tried to rob me."

"Relax," Rodriguez said. "The witnesses tell the story just like you said. They saw the whole thing."

Rodriguez picked up the plastic bag and inspected the knife

inside. Brian could see that frayed black electrical tape secured a cracked wooden handle. Its rusted six-inch blade possessed a finely honed edge and remnants of blood. His blood.

"Looks like that thing's got a few miles on it," Oakley said.

Rodriguez dropped the bag in the car seat and twisted to face Brian. "This guy fits the description of a suspect we've been looking for in several similar robberies. Same MO. Same general description. We have prints from a couple of the other scenes, so we'll know if this is the guy." His dark eyes locked on Brian. "What I can't figure is, why did you beat him like that?"

That was nothing. He deserved worse and would have gotten it if those Mexican fucks hadn't been there. I should have killed the son of a bitch. "I was scared," Brian said. "I was afraid he'd get up and attack me again. I guess that made me sort of . . . overreact."

"That's an understatement. The gardeners said they were afraid of you. Took the four of them to pull you off, and you fought them all the way."

Brian knew they had been afraid. He saw it in their eyes. "I don't remember," he said quietly. "It all happened so fast. All I remember is the knife and fighting him off with whatever I could get my hands on."

CHAPTER 11

AFTER LEAVING BILLY HOLCOMB TO HIS NEW BOY TOY, T-TOMMY and I swung by Mullins Restaurant. The lot was full, as usual, but we got lucky and found a slot right beneath the restaurant's bright blue and yellow checkerboard sign. We snagged one of the yellow Formica-topped tables along the far wall. Beneath a collection of photos of old Huntsville.

T-Tommy slid a menu from between the napkin holder and the glass sugar canister that sat in the middle of the table. I don't know why. He knew what he would order. I knew, too. Best burgers in town. I had a cheeseburger, T-Tommy two—with fries and a chocolate shake. I splashed mine with a generous dose of Tabasco from the bottle I always carried in my jacket pocket. I waved it toward T-Tommy, knowing he'd decline. Always did. And he responded as always: a raised eyebrow, a grunt, and "It's your chitlins."

Tabasco. The juice of life. Constant. Reliable. The McIlhenny clan. Avery Island, Louisiana. Peppers, salt, and vinegar. That's it.

53

Aged three years in oak barrels. Same way it's been done since old man Edmund McIlhenny cooked up his first batch in 1869. Made ordinary food good, good food great, and a Mullins's burger a thing of beauty.

After we ate we paid the bill and headed over to see Dr. Lou Drummond.

The Alabama Department of Forensic Sciences sat just north of town on Arcadia Circle. It shared a long, low tan brick and concrete building with the Department of Public Safety and the Sheriff's Investigative and Patrol Offices. I had worked there for nearly six years as a lab tech. After I ditched med school. After I almost ditched everything. After Claire pulled me out of my funk and we played out our thing. After a two-year stint as an MP with the US Marines. Long story.

While there, my interests gravitated toward blood spatter and trace evidence analysis. I got pretty good at it, too. Lou Drummond, my boss and mentor, saw that I had a knack for reading evidence and for reconstructing crimes both physically and psychologically. Not sure where that gift came from. Most likely the big dose of common sense I got from my dad. Lou encouraged me to expand my horizons and helped me gain a position in Quantico with the FBI's Behavioral Analysis Unit.

After that, I consulted on difficult crimes around the country, wrote a few books—the best way to become an expert in the public's eye—and lectured frequently. From time to time I even returned to

Quantico to teach a class or two. I had also consulted on several local cases, the most famous being the charming Billy Wayne Packwood.

We found Lou in his office, phone to his ear. He wore his usual gray surgical scrubs and white lab coat. A thin, ferretlike man, with sparse hair and thick, wild eyebrows, Lou had been a medical examiner for Madison County more years than anyone could remember. A workaholic, he never seemed to go home. A fidgeter. Always on the move. Like a long-tailed cat in a room full of rocking chairs. When he spoke, his arms conducted an invisible orchestra. I had once said that the only way to keep Lou quiet was to handcuff him. Even when sitting, one leg or the other was in motion, as if he would get up and sprint out of the room at any moment. But his blue eyes never wavered. When his gaze grabbed you, it held fast. As if he were dissecting your every word.

He now toyed with the phone cord, winding and unwinding it around his finger. With a shake of his head, he hung up the phone. "My daughter." He forked his fingers through his hair. "She and that loser she dates are down in Destin. Went down on his Harley." Then he immediately changed gears and looked at me. "Good to see you."

"You, too." We shook hands.

"You went over to Mike's, I understand."

"Yeah. And the other two scenes."

He nodded. "I just finished Mike's autopsy."

Lou never wasted time. He'd only gotten the body a few hours ago and had already completed the post. "And?" I asked.

"Cause of death was the gunshot. Massive brain injury. I'd suspect he never knew a thing. All the rest was definitely postmortem."

Thank you, Jesus.

"The bullet was damaged but not too badly. Got it down in the firearms lab right now."

"Let's go over the others. What do you have on them so far?" I asked.

Lou began to pace. "Petersen died of several blows to the head. Any one of four could have been the fatal blow. Allison, like Mike, from a single 9 mm. His was to the left temporal area. Like Mike, all the trauma was postmortem.

"The blood spatters and the wounds indicate the killer is strong, right-handed, and between six feet and six-two." Lou leaned against his heavy wooden desk, drumming his fingers against the edge. "Sidau Yamaguchi tells me he probably weighs between one-eighty and two hundred pounds and wears a size ten and a half shoe. That's based on the shoe prints he found in the soil at Mike's this morning."

"No blood or bodily fluids from the killer at any of the scenes?" I asked.

"Correct." Lou lifted himself and sat on the desk. One foot began a tap dance to some internal drumbeat.

"No evidence of sexual assault?"

"None."

"The cotton fibers? From plain-vanilla gardeners' gloves?" T-Tommy asked. "The kind that can be purchased anywhere?"

"Looks that way. We're sending samples to the FBI lab. Maybe they can pinpoint the manufacturer." Lou's fingers continued their monotonous rhythm. "I'm pessimistic, but it's worth a try."

"Shoe prints?"

"Same deal. Nike sole pattern. Common style. My guy at the FBI says that'll narrow it down to a few million."

I heard the door behind me open and turned that way. Becka Cooksey entered, a folder in her hand.

"Firearms report," she said. "Same weapon used on Mike and Allison."

CHAPTER 12

"CODE TRAUMA. CODE TRAUMA." THE PAGE OPERATOR'S VOICE blared from the ceiling-mounted speakers at Huntsville Memorial Medical Center.

Dr. Charlie Beck tossed the remainder of his tuna sandwich into the trash can beside his desk. So much for lunch. He darted out of his office and turned down the main hallway of the emergency department.

"Dr. Beck, that trauma patient we were expecting just got here." Marcy Clark, the ER head nurse, hurried toward Trauma Room 1.

Charlie hustled to keep up. Entering the brightly lit room, he saw a battered and bloody man lying on a stretcher. Deborah Studen, one of the ER nurses, had already begun cutting away the man's dirt-stiffened and bloodstained clothes.

Charlie went through a cursory physical exam. The victim, obviously a vagrant, smelled of back-alley filth and urine. Insect bites, in various stages of healing, blotched his skin. Swollen and blood-caked lips surrounded yellowed teeth. Multiple contusions and abrasions discolored his face, shoulders, chest, and arms. "Vitals?"

The valve of the blood pressure cuff hissed as it deflated. "Ninety over sixty," Deborah said. "Pulse one-twenty-five. Respirations thirty-eight and shallow. 02-two Sat 68 percent on ten liters."

"Let's tube him," Charlie said.

He pulled on surgical gloves and stepped to the head of the stretcher. Marcy handed him a laryngoscope and an ET tube. He inserted the scope into the man's mouth and lifted his tongue out of the way. The carina and vocal cords popped into view. Charlie easily slipped the tube into the trachea. He inflated the balloon cuff and attached an Ambu bag. "Check for breath sounds."

Marcy pressed her stethoscope against one side of the man's chest and then the other while Charlie repeatedly compressed the Ambu, expanding the man's lungs with each squeeze. "Good sounds on the left. Zilch on the right."

Charlie rechecked the ET tube. "It's in good position. Must have a pneumo. Got a chest tube tray?"

"Right here." Marcy unwrapped the sterile packaging and placed the tray on a surgical stand.

"I'd bet on a broken rib or two and a punctured lung," Charlie said. He scrubbed the man's chest with Betadine and then inject-ed Lidocaine for local anesthesia. Using a scalpel, he deftly made a deep cut in the side of the chest between two ribs. He used a hemo-stat to spread the wound open and then, with a quick pop, pushed the instrument into the chest cavity. Blood gushed out, cascading to the floor.

He inserted a finger through the opening and probed in all directions to ensure the lung was free from the chest wall.

"Chest tube." He took the finger-thick plastic tube from Marcy and advanced it through the opening. Blood swirled down the tube into the kick bucket Marcy had rolled into position with her foot.

"Suture." He applied several stitches to close the wound and anchor the tube in place, while Marcy attached the tube's other end to a suction bottle.

"BP's up to one-ten," Deborah said.

"Great." Charlie peeled off his bloody gloves and tugged on a clean pair. "Now, let's see what else is wrong." With the patient stabilized, he went through a more extensive head-to-foot examination. "No localizing neuro signs. Hopefully his coma's just a concussion. Fractured nose and left forearm. Left orbital contusion. No evidence of internal abdominal trauma, but I can't be sure." He turned to Deborah. "Let's get a STAT CBC, SMA twenty, blood gases, and chest, skull, and cross-table lateral C-spine X-rays. Also type and cross-match for two units of blood. What's his 02-two Sat now?"

"Ninety-three percent."

"Okay. Let's get the lab and X-rays done."

Charlie dictated his operative report on the chest tube insertion while waiting for the X-rays to be completed. Twenty minutes later a tech brought the stack of films to the ER. One by one Charlie held them against the fluorescent view box. Marcy stood next to him. "No skull fracture. Neck looks okay. Two broken ribs on the right side." He nudged Marcy with an elbow. "Don't you just love it when I'm right?"

"Insufferable is the word that comes to mind."

Charlie laughed and held up another film. "ET and chest tubes are in good position." Another film went up. "Fracture of the left ulna. Who's the trauma surgeon on call today?"

"Dr. Sammons. I'll page him," Marcy said.

"And for neuro and orthopedics?"

"Samuelson for ortho and, I think, Rigel for neuro."

"Get them on the phone, too. Let's get a STAT CT brain scan."

"Dr. Beck?"

Charlie turned to see Deborah walking toward him, flanked by two sheriff's deputies.

"Doc, how's he doing?" the taller deputy asked.

"Don't know yet. Are you the officers who were on the scene?"

"I'm Paul Rodriguez. This is Hal Oakley."

"He has a couple of cracked ribs, a punctured lung, a fractured arm, and a trashed nose," Charlie said. "He's still unconscious. We have other tests to do before we know the full story. Where's the guy you arrested?"

"We put him in Trauma Room 2," Deborah said at the same time Rodriguez was saying, "We didn't arrest him."

Charlie couldn't believe it. "You didn't arrest the guy? After what he did?"

"He wasn't the perp. It was the other guy. The John Doe."

"You're kidding." Charlie looked from one deputy to the other. "I've seen lots of muggings, but this?"

Rodriguez shrugged. "That's what it looked like to us at first, too."

"What happened?"

"Apparently John Doe pulled a knife on"—Rodriguez flipped through his notepad—"Brian Kurtz and tried to rob him. Doe fits the ID of a guy we've been looking for in a handful of similar robberies. Witnesses corroborated Kurtz's story, so we'll write it off as self-defense unless we find something that says otherwise. Of course, we want to talk to Doe as soon as we can. When do you think that might be?"

"No way to know just yet. Dr. Rigel will be his neurologist. He'll make that decision."

"Thanks. We'll finish our report and get back on the road. Another deputy will be here soon to guard him until he's well enough to go to the jail ward. If you have any problems, give us a call."

Charlie turned toward Trauma Room 2, but lingered for a moment. He attempted to construct a mental image of the patient who waited inside. What kind of person could have done this?

CHAPTER 13

I DROPPED T-TOMMY OFF DOWNTOWN SO HE COULD HOOK UP WITH Scotty Simpson and help orient the half dozen new HPD uniforms that had been assigned to the task force. I needed to swing by my lumber company, the one I inherited when my parents died, to sign some checks, Monday being payroll and bill-paying day. I told him I'd be back well before we had to sit down with Luther.

Only took ten minutes to drive over to Walker Lumber. When I pulled into the front lot, I saw Milk, talking with a customer beside a blue pickup loaded with two-by-fours. The beams stuck out the back a good four feet, so Milk was tying a strip of red cloth around the end of one so that anyone behind the driver wouldn't run up underneath them.

In the South, nicknames are as common as Baptist churches. Some nicknames even have their own nicknames. Bertie Jackson had one of those. To most he was Buttermilk, a moniker given him by family members because of his love for his mother's buttermilk biscuits. To close friends he was simply Milk.

He had been one hell of a baseball player. Even now, thirty years later, his exploits as a kid on the field of dreams were legendary. Now a bit exaggerated, but not by much. He played a few years of Double-A ball before calling it quits, realizing the pyramid to the big leagues was just too steep. That's when he came to work for my dad. When the company dropped into my lap, I gave him a piece of the profits and turned the day-to-day stuff over to him.

He slapped the tail of the pickup as the customer drove away.

"How's it going?" I asked as I climbed out of my car. The sun was hot and insistent.

"Mighty fine. Mostly." He scratched an ear. "Got another bad load of Sheetrock. Chipped, several cracked."

"Same outfit up in Tennessee?"

He nodded. "I had a few words with them. Hate to give up on them since they've always done right by us. I think the problem is that the company changed hands." He sucked his teeth. "I got a couple of feelers out just in case."

"Hopefully it won't come to that."

"If it does, it does. Come on." He nodded toward the office. "I got all the checks ready for you. They're on the desk. I got to go help the guys load up some roofing tiles. Catch you before you leave." He walked past the office and out among the stacks of lumber behind it.

The office was cool, the window-mounted AC churning against

the heat of the day. Took me only a few minutes to sign the checks and thumb through the books. A good week. I went out back and weaved my way among the stacks. The wood smelled fresh and warm. Nothing quite like that aroma. I saw Milk, instructing a pair of high school kids how to distribute the weight of the roofing materials on the company's ton-and-a-half flatbed truck. Football players. Getting in shape for the fall. We always hired three or four every summer.

I remembered the summers I did the same thing. All the sweating and lifting and hard work proved to be just the thing when August two-a-days began. I remembered one early August day, temp hovering in the high nineties, joined at the hip with the humidity. Maybe a week before fall football practice began. Milk and I took the tractor-trailer over to the rail yards to unload a boxcar of roofing tiles. The car had been parked off on a spur, and we pulled the truck right up next to the side cargo door and went to work. Forty pallets of tiles. Each pallet stacked with ten squares. Each square was three bundles. Each bundle weighed sixty-seven pounds. Had to be unloaded by hand. Inside the boxcar the temp was 130 if it was anything. I would toss a bundle through the door, where Milk would catch it and stack it. We swapped positions about every ten minutes, neither us able to stay in the sauna longer that that. Took all day. Damn near killed both of us. The silver lining? Made two-a-days a piece of cake that year. If I had ever entertained any idea of not going to college and med school, that day would have melted those doubts right away.

If that hot August day sealed my path to med school, Jill's abduction knocked me onto a different track. The one I was on now. Instead of taking care of sick folks, I had spent most of my adult life dealing with why. Why did this person rob a bank and that one kill his wife and that other one torch his business? Why did Billy Wayne Packwood choose Huntsville for his hunting grounds? Why had this killer chosen Mike? Why couldn't I save my sister? Why did I let her down? The only thing I hated more than whys were what ifs.

My life could have been different. Maybe better, maybe not. There is no way of knowing. Not that I would really change it. Not most of it, anyway. Losing my parents, I'd change. Losing Jill, I'd change. The rest of it was what it was. In high school, I'd been a good student and a pretty good athlete. Good enough to start at quarterback and make All City my junior and senior years. Didn't play ball but did well academically at Alabama. Chem major. Then medical school in Birmingham. Almost finished. Three months from the golden ring. Then Jill disappeared. Bang. Gone. Just like that.

Many people can divide their lives into two distinct parts, demarcated by some time-cleaving event. An event that profoundly changed their life journey. Spun it 180 degrees off-kilter. For me, that moment was 7:13 p.m. on October twelfth, a dozen years ago. I remembered it in slow motion. In great detail.

A cold, drizzly night. I was a senior in med school, doing my ER rotation; Jill a junior at UAB. She planned to study at the library until six, which was when I got off. I would then meet her at my car, and we would go to Mom and Dad's for dinner. The student lot was four blocks from the hospital and not all that well lit.

I was late. Over an hour late. Just before I was going off call, a gunshot to the chest came in. The internal bleeding was massive. The victim in profound shock. No time to take him to the OR. The surgical resident prepared to open his chest in the ER. Not a common occurrence. I stayed. To watch, to help, to do whatever he and my intern would let me do. It was an educational opportunity I couldn't pass up.

Later, as I stood in that lot, my life went wobbly. Jill's shoe. A Mephisto. Brown. Resting on one side. Laces still tied. Her purse. Strap ripped away at one end. Contents strewn across the asphalt. Wallet, cash, a gold bracelet. It wasn't a robbery.

Months of self-recrimination and isolation followed. Continuing med school was out of the question. Life was almost out of the question.

That Jill's disappearance was my fault wasn't debatable. Not to me. Probably not to my parents. They denied they blamed me. Gave me consoling words. But what went unsaid told a different story. The way my mother stared into space, sadness pulling her shoulders downward. The way my father retreated into himself, the light gone from his eyes. The uncomfortable silences that punctuated the next year lay there like a bloodstain on a white lab coat. Impossible to ignore or deny.

When my parents were taken in a car accident, it was almost

anticlimactic. Part of me was already dead. Part of me knew this was punishment. Deserved punishment.

It was during this period of depression that Claire and I married. Not the best start. To this day I love her for saving me. Not that I ever really considered suicide. Not really. It crossed my mind a few times, but I always pushed it away as cowardly. As too final. I knew there was light out there; I was just having trouble getting a fix on it. If Claire did nothing else, she helped me find it.

After we decided to give up on the marriage deal, I joined the Marines. Seemed like the right thing to do, and for me it was. Two years. MP duty. Not a bad gig. Considered staying on but in the end the military wasn't the right career for me. Too rigid. Too many rules.

I hung up my uniform and returned to Huntsville. T-Tommy tried to lure me to HPD, but I opted to work at the Alabama Department of Forensic Sciences. I told everyone that I took the job because I was interested in it and wanted something where I could use my medical training . . . as incomplete as it was. That was half the truth. The other half was that Jill's abduction pushed me in that direction. I wanted to find her. To learn how to find her. I apparently wasn't that good of a student. Maybe not very smart, either. After twelve years this is what I knew:

Jill was abducted.

Three other young women disappeared under similar circumstances.

None of them have ever been found.

That's it. That's all I had. No clues, no witnesses, no bodies, no bones, not a damn thing. And I wasn't smart enough to figure it out.

Jill was dead. That I knew. I never said so out loud, but in my soul of souls I knew that to be the case. I also knew the guy who did it, to Jill, to the other girls, had moved on. Another state. More victims. That's the way it works.

Now, twelve years later, a day doesn't go by that she isn't in my mind. Even working a case like this one, Jill is always there. The really painful part was that my entire family was lost to me. Not just physically gone, but completely gone. No real memories. I had smeared images of my dad, teaching me to hit a baseball or throw a football. Showing me how to load Sheetrock on a flatbed truck without cracking it. Right here. Right where I now stood.

Mom? Vague memories of her cooking Thanksgiving dinner or teaching me some of our family recipes. Of her tending her roses, always the pride of our street. Of her singing in church, a place I never went now.

What images I could extract from the past were gauzy and didn't seem real. Maybe I remembered them as I thought they should be and not as they were. The ones I knew to be true were of them sitting on the sofa not speaking, not moving, barely breathing. No laughter, no life. No color. All the images I could call up were black and white.

And Jill? I only saw her face in my dreams. Never while awake. Never when I wanted to.

CHAPTER 14

DR. CHARLIE BECK PUSHED OPEN THE DOOR TO TRAUMA ROOM 2, expecting to see . . . what? An angry, aggressive brute? A frothing maniac? A monster shackled in chains? To his surprise, the young man sitting on the stretcher was none of these. Though tall and muscular, he was not a maniacal hulk. He had intelligent blue eyes, and aside from his disheveled hair and torn, bloodstained shirt, he seemed calm and rational.

"I'm Dr. Beck."

"I'm Brian Kurtz." He offered a benevolent smile.

"Sorry you had to wait so long, but we've had our hands full today."

"No problem."

"Let's see what we have here." Charlie slipped on a pair of surgical gloves and removed the gauze from Brian's arm. "Not bad. I've seen worse."

"I bet you have, Doc."

Charlie probed the wound with a sterile cotton swab. "Let me know if this hurts."

"It's okay. Go ahead."

"Looks like a clean cut. Should be easy to repair. One of the nurses will clean up your wound and soak it in a bug-killing solution. Then I'll be back to sew it up."

The bright surgical light burned his eyes, but Brian sat quietly while the young nurse cleaned his arm with some red, medicinal-smelling liquid. She said it was called Betadine or something like that. Her name tag indicated she was Deborah Studen, RN. Her manipulations were painful, but only a minor distraction. Pain meant little, a temporary thing, easily controlled, easily forgotten. His anger was a different story. At least he had managed to shove it into that corner of his brain where he kept it captive.

That's how he pictured it, anyway. A dark cave, deep in one corner of his brain. Out of sight but always rumbling and growling like some caged dragon. The beast would occasionally flick out a tongue or snake out its long tail. Just enough to give him a pleasant surge of energy. It was definitely a love-hate thing. More love than hate.

But sometimes the beast would lurch from his cave, breathing a white-hot fire that was ferociously intense. Uncontrollable and unyielding, it completely consumed him, pumping the fear that it would never end through his veins. Yet afterward, the calmness that followed was nothing he had ever experienced. Like now. The rage he had vented on that piece of street trash had been explosive, but now he felt calm, even lethargic. The beast had returned to its cave. Not sleeping, but recharging. He could feel its bubbling, sonorous breathing. No problem. He could control it. Long enough to get out of here, anyway.

They would never know how much he wanted to kill that piece of shit. After he left, they would say: "He must have been very afraid to hurt that man so severely. He's too nice to have done that without good reason."

But he did. And he enjoyed it.

"Is this hurting much?" the nurse asked.

"Not at all."

Charlie injected Lidocaine into the area around the wound. "This'll sting for a second or two."

"Go ahead," Brian said.

Charlie couldn't reconcile the two images in his head. This polite, pleasant young man and the monster that beat John Doe half to death. It didn't fit. In his years of practice, he had seen all kinds— the stoic, the maniacal, the angry, the depressed, and the downright crazy. Illness and injury always brought out the best, and the worst, in people. Most were quietly heroic, others aggressive and nasty.

Brian Kurtz was an enigma. So calm and polite, when just an hour earlier he obviously had been a raving madman. There must be an explanation. Odd and wildly shifting behaviors always happened for a reason. But what? Brian was obviously not schizophrenic. Too rational. Not delusional in any way. He showed no sign of being on any drugs. Not the sleepy confusion of narcotic users, nor the wide-eyed paranoia of a coke abuser, nor the hyped-up mania of a meth tweaker.

"How'd this happen?" Charlie began placing stitches in the wound.

"Some dude tried to rob me. Came at me with a knife."

"So, you defended yourself?" Charlie tied another suture.

"Wouldn't you?"

"Sure." Charlie pulled the next blue nylon suture snug. "You did a number on him."

"Nothing he didn't deserve. I should've killed him."

"You came close."

Brian smirked. "Not close enough. I should have ripped his head off, cracked his skull open, and stomped his sick fucking brain into the ground."

Charlie felt the muscles in Brian's forearm contract as his hands curled into tight fists. *Back off. Don't confront him. Diffuse the situation.* Charlie changed the subject. "I see you work for a phone soliciting company."

"That's right."

"Bet you meet some interesting people that way."

"Mostly arrogant jerks with no time and less brains."

"I see." Another suture.

"Do you?"

Charlie felt increasingly uneasy. Again he searched for some safe ground. "Let me ask a few questions about your medical history while I finish up here."

"Is that necessary?"

"Afraid it is."

"I don't see how," Brian said. His eyes narrowed, his jaw flexed.

"Everybody's different. What's good for one person might be dangerous for another." He smiled at Brian, but got only a cold stare in return. "Are you allergic to anything?"

"No."

"Do you have any medical problems, such as heart or lung disease?"

"No."

"Any history of injuries, surgeries, or previous hospitalizations?"

"Got shot once."

Charlie looked up. "How'd that happen?"

"US Army. Iraq. A couple of years ago. AK-47 to the leg by one of those towel heads."

"Anything else?"

"Skull fracture. Playing football in high school. Left me with almost constant headaches."

"You see a doctor for that?"

"Dr. Hublein. Robert Hublein. You know him?"

"I know of him. Never met him. He heads the Neuropsychiatric Research Institute down the road here, doesn't he?"

"That's him. Supposed to be the best."

"He's very good, so I've heard. Does he have you on any meds?"

"Yeah. Don't know what it is, though."

Charlie removed his gloves. "We're done here. I want you to keep the wound clean and dry and come back in two days so I can check on how it's healing."

"Is that necessary?"

"Afraid so."

"Whatever you say, Doc."

The politeness had returned.

CHAPTER 15

ONCE I GOT BACK DOWNTOWN, I FOUND AN EMPTY OFFICE ACROSS from the task force room and called the BAU in Quantico, Virginia. The office of Mort Canfield, an old friend, and an FBI profiler. After getting past his assistant, I heard him come on the line. "Agent Canfield."

"Mort. Dub."

"Hey, Dub. It's been a long time."

"I see you're still hard at work."

"Not much longer. I'm getting out in three months."

"I never thought you'd retire."

"Me, either. How's tricks in the Heart of Dixie?"

"Been better. I need your help on a series of murders down here."

"What's the story?"

"You remember Mike Savage?"

"Sure. How is he?"

"He's one of the corpses."

"Jesus. What can I do?"

"Let me run what we have by you and see if I'm on the right track."

We talked for thirty minutes. Mort mostly agreed with my assessment and, as usual, had a few insights of his own. I thanked him and told him I'd keep him in the loop. I then scratched out a cursory list of what I liked to term *psychological elements*. These were simply aspects of a crime that spoke to the perpetrator's psyche. Basically, the reasons he did certain things or acted in a specific way. Some people would call this *criminal profiling*, and indeed it was. But the term *profiling* could also be a trap.

If a profile is generated for a particular suspect and if the investigation focuses too intensely on this particular view of the unsub, the real guy might be overlooked. If the profile says the bad guy is early twenties, unemployed, and a loner, other potential suspects who might be married, employed, and over thirty might not get the hard look they deserve. Blinders were the kiss of death in a murder investigation.

That's why I preferred to call them psychological elements. Semantics maybe, but useful semantics. Besides, I introduced the term in my second book so I'm more or less married to it. Here's what I scratched on a piece of paper:

1. Attacks at night: Lives alone or with relative—wife or family would not allow nighttime disappearances; unemployed or day work—maybe night delivery or patrol—cop?

2. Victims geographically widespread: Access to car—employed, has money, or has benefactor—nondescript vehicle—probably high mileage

3. Scenes mixed:

Organized: Careful planner—wears gloves—uses sound suppresser—knows entries/exits—skilled with locks—brings weapon (after Petersen)—possible trial runs

    Conclusion: Late twenties or thirties—smart—educated—mentally stable

Disorganized: Overkill—handy object for mutilations—bodies left at scene

    Conclusion: Early twenties—schizophrenic?—psychotic?

Unsub description:

Physical: Six foot to six foot two—200 pounds—right-handed—no noticeable physical defects

Motive: Anger or mission driven—goal is to release stress or make statement—or both?

Note: Knows victims—must for planning and trial runs—knows layout—knows victims' schedule/habits—knows he has time at scene—how?

CHAPTER 16

BRIAN PACED THE HOSPITAL WAITING ROOM FOR NEARLY HALF AN hour before the cab he had called arrived. The smell of cigarettes and sweat greeted him when he jumped in the backseat.

"What took so long? I've been waiting forever."

"Sorry. Got stuck out at the airport." The driver's voice was weak and coarse. He appeared ill, maybe fifty, with ratty hair and sallow skin. Nicotine-stained fingers punched the meter to life. A wet, rattling cough racked his body.

"Where to, buddy?"

"Gulf Coast Telemarketing."

"Where's that?" Again his body convulsed in an attempt to expel phlegm from his lungs.

Brian gave him directions.

"What happened? Looks like you got your arm all bandaged up there."

No shit, you ignorant bastard. "It's nothing."

"It ain't broken, is it? My wife broke her arm once . . ."

He driveled on and on, but Brian paid little attention. He worked his hand into a fist and then relaxed it several times. The bandage tugged at his skin as the muscles of his forearm flexed, but the pain was minimal. He settled back in the seat and closed his eyes, tuning out the driver's droning.

The cab finally rolled to a stop in front of Gulf Coast. Brian paid the fare and jumped out. He intended to get in his Jeep and head home. No reason to hang around this place. Unfortunately, the door swung open and Glenda Riordan in all her cockatoo glory stepped out.

Great.

She turned and yelled back through the door, "Wanda, everybody, Brian's back."

Several of his coworkers came out and walked down the walkway toward where he stood in the parking lot. Exactly where he had beaten the mugger. Brian could see dried bloodstains on the asphalt. His blood. And the mugger's. They gathered in a semicircle. Not close, each keeping a comfortable distance.

"Are you okay?" Wanda asked as she joined the group.

Like you give a shit, bitch. "Just a scratch." He held up his bandaged arm.

They stared blankly at him, their anxiety palpable. He knew they wanted to be somewhere else, but their curiosity held them. Frightened little curious rabbits.

"My God," Glenda said. "Weren't you scared?"

No, you cow, I wasn't scared. Not like you are now. "Of course I was scared," Brian said. "He had a huge knife."

"Who was he? Did you know him?" one of his pathetic coworkers managed to squeak out.

"Just some street person. The police said he had robbed some other people."

"Is he all right?" Wanda asked. Her brow furrowed with concern. "He looked like he was hurt pretty badly."

Not badly enough. "The doctor said he thought he'd be okay."

Wanda shook her head. "I can't believe this happened. Are you sure you're all right?"

There it was. Wanda's sweet, syrupy false concern. "I'm fine. I just need to get my car."

He turned and headed that way. Wanda followed. He reached the vehicle and pulled open the door.

"I'm sorry," Wanda said. "This hasn't been a good day for you."

He looked down at her. "I'm okay."

"I spoke with Dr. Hublein. He said you would be seeing him later this week."

"I see him every week."

"You get well and I'll have a job for you when he says you're better."

"I'm better now." He climbed in the car, closed the door, started the engine, and pulled away, leaving her standing there.

Brian raced out of the lot and navigated his way to Memorial

Parkway. He sped up the entry ramp, wedging his Jeep between a minivan and some Japanese tin can. The tin can swerved and flashed its lights. Brian flipped the driver off.

The day's events tumbled around in his head. That Kushner asshole; the mugger; the arrogant Dr. Beck; the smelly, babbling cab driver; and Wanda Fisher, Glenda Riordan, and the rest of the clowns he worked with—all conspired to ramp up his anger. He had struggled to keep it in check, but now his knuckles whitened on the steering wheel as he fought the urge to plow his Jeep into another minivan. Those damn things seemed to be everywhere. Take control, he told himself. Now is not the time.

Brian Kurtz knew anger. Had known it all his life. His father's intoxicated rages; his mother's schizo tirades; not to mention his own short fuse that had led to more fights than he could remember. Since childhood, he had wrestled with his internal turmoil, mostly winning, occasionally failing. Failures that would have ended his high school years early had he not been a star football player. Failures that had attracted the police and the courts on more than one occasion.

But now his anger was different. It had mutated into something else. More powerful, more demanding, more difficult to control. Definitely more explosive. Over the past two months, when stressed or angered, his rage would rise abruptly, and it took all his strength to control the impulse to lash out. Sometimes he won this internal war, and at other times some unlucky soul, like that dirty piece of street trash, or some nearby inanimate object, would lose. Then there were the other times. The times when it drove him to do things he couldn't understand. Petersen. Allison. Savage. Why?

This new rage both scared and enticed him. Its intensity and the ferocity of his own actions terrified him, yet . . . Savage had been . . . what? There wasn't a word for it. *Overwhelming? All-consuming?* Not strong enough. Not even close. *Intoxicating?* Yes, but more than that. Oddly, when he later relived the events, he found what he had done repulsive. But, at the time, when it erupted inside, it produced such feelings of power and fulfillment that he reveled in its heat.

That was the real problem. The thing that ate away at him. His addiction to this white-hot rage was growing. An addiction was exactly what it was. As surely as if he shot his veins full of heroin or inhaled the exhaust of a crack pipe. It seemed that planning his next "outing" consumed his every waking hour. The anticipation only made the final release more powerful. It seemed that each hit of the anger and rage he took sank him deeper into its embrace, an embrace as warm and as welcoming as that of a comforting mother.

CHAPTER 17

I LEANED AGAINST THE WALL NEAR THE WINDOW IN LUTHER'S office. T-Tommy and Scotty sank into the sofa along the opposite wall, Luther behind his desk. I hadn't noticed before, but Luther appeared to have aged a decade in the past year or so, the mantle of sheriff taking its toll. His short-cropped hair had receded considerably and was now peppered with gray. His election two years earlier had not been without controversy. Not so much that he was black, but that he had been with the department only five years. Made him somewhat of an outsider. An endorsement from the retiring Mike Savage helped, but it was his tough stance on crime that sealed the deal. The Madison County electorate could overlook his inexperience and the color of his skin if he would lock up the bad guys.

"So, T-Tommy was right," Luther said. He squared the stack of papers on his desk. "The ballistics connects two of the three scenes." He looked at me. "What about Petersen? Can we include him in the mix?"

"That'd be my bet. The savageness of the beatings. Used a handy

84

object, not something he brought with him. Attacks were at the victims' homes at night. Bodies left at the kill sites with no attempt to hide or dispose of them. The cotton fibers. There're some differences, but I think we can assume a connection."

"Unlike the others, he didn't shoot Petersen," Luther said. "That bother you?"

I shook my head. "Petersen was the first victim. An old man. Judging from the photos, not a very big guy. Probably didn't look like much of a threat. Of course, he did put up a hell of a fight. Probably frightened the killer. Decided that in the future a gun might be wise."

"Learned from his mistake," T-Tommy said.

"These guys often change their MO. Adapt. Get better at what they do."

"So, who is he?" Luther asked. "What kind of person are we looking for?"

"I called Mort Canfield. Profiler with the FBI Behavioral Analysis Unit. An old friend from when I was there. I ran all this by him to make sure I was putting things together right." I propped one hip on the windowsill. The warm breeze that came through the cracked window felt good against my back. "The scenes are primary, not secondary dump sites, and overall give a mixed presentation. On the one hand, this guy is careful, methodical. Doesn't just rush in. Plans and likely cases each victim. Maybe even a trial run or two. All this suggests an organized offender. Mature, clear thinking." I scratched an earlobe. "If you just go on these facts, the profile would be late twenties to early thirties, employed, might be married, might have a family. He would be sociable, have friends, and basically seem normal to anyone who knew him."

"But?" Luther said.

"There's always a *but*, isn't there? And this is a big one." I heard a truck rumble by on the street below. "The mutilations. The complete overkill. Particularly the postmortem stuff. Except for wearing gloves, he makes little attempt to hide his crime. Doesn't move or dump or try to conceal the bodies. A disorganized scene. Immature and impulsive. Here the profile would suggest that he was late teens to early twenties, unemployed or working in a low-paying, menial job. Probably lives alone or with a female relative. A mother or sister. A loner, with few if any friends. Maybe even truly schizophrenic."

T-Tommy looked up. "If this guy is schizo, how does he plan all this shit?"

I shrugged. "That's the problem. If he is schizophrenic, he's more or less high-functioning. Until he gets a corpse in front of him anyway."

"If he's already killed the victim, why do all this other stuff?" Scotty asked.

T-Tommy grunted. "Because he had to."

"Bingo," I said. "If this guy's as unstable as the crime scene suggests, the killing isn't the goal. It's what comes after. It's how he deals with his demons."

"He kept it together long enough to break into the Erskine,"

Luther said. "That was no walk in the park."

"Which reminds me." I looked at T-Tommy. "You have the security cam tapes from there?"

"Yeah."

"Can I get a copy?"

"Sure. Why?"

"Got a buddy over at NASA. Wendell Volek. Helped design the VISAR system."

"Think he can help?"

"Can't hurt."

"Do it," Luther said. He looked at me. "What else?"

I pushed away from the window and crossed my arms over my chest. "What bothers me the most is the quick kill."

"Why's that?" T-Tommy asked.

"Serials don't typically kill that way. Some do . . . like Berkowitz . . . the Son of Sam . . . but most are hands-on killers. They need to control, humiliate, and demean their victims before they kill. The preamble is the thrill. The actual murder is often an afterthought. Necessary to silence the witness. Many say they don't enjoy the actual killing. And Drummond said there was no sexual assault in any of these cases."

T-Tommy nodded.

"That's troublesome," I went on. "Most serials kill out of some bizarre fantasy. The victims are part of a complex sexually motivated script known only to the killer, probably imprinted early in life. That's why they don't typically cross ethnic lines or mix sexes. Whites kill whites. They choose either males or females, not both."

"All the victims are male," Luther said.

"Jeffrey Dahmer, Randy Kraft, and John Wayne Gacy liked men. Ted Bundy and the Buono/Bianchi duo preferred females. None of them crossed sexual lines."

"Why is that?" Scotty asked.

"Remember, these guys are fantasy driven. Fantasies that take years to tweak and perfect. That are very specific. Sex, size, hair color might all be important in victim selection. Bundy chose women with long dark hair, parted in the middle. Very specific. But our guy isn't in the sexually sadistic category. There was no sexual assault or genital mutilation. His victims are as different as can be. An old man, a young gay man, and . . . Mike. These are not likely the objects of a fantasy."

Luther laced his fingers and rested his chin on the tips of his index fingers. "I'm confused, Dub. Is this guy a serial killer or not?"

"I'm as confused as you are. Not really sure what he is. Our boy's wires are crossed, but not the same way most serials are. Some might classify him as the mission-oriented type. These guys have a goal. To right some wrong or rid society of 'undesirables.' Whatever he defines that as. Remember Gary Ridgway, the Green River Killer? His mission was to rid the world of prostitutes. A group he felt didn't deserve to exist."

"But, as you said, these victims are all different," T-Tommy said. "What is it about them that attracted this guy?"

"When we know that, we'll be on our way to identifying him." I uncrossed my arms and shoved my hands into my pockets. "You guys know me. Know I'm not big on psychobabble and labels. I think each killer is different. With different motivations. Sure, serial murderers have common elements, but prematurely shoving any one of them into some predefined pigeonhole can screw up an investigation in a heartbeat. This guy doesn't fit into any of the traditional pigeon-holes anyway. He's a hybrid . . . for lack of a better term. Part spree, part serial. Probably more spree. He's filled with rage, not fantasies, yet he seems to have a sort of cooling-off period between killings. Uses that time to plan the next one. If he just moved from place to place, killing strangers, he'd be a more typical spree type. Doesn't look like he's doing that. His attacks are planned."

"That's a pleasant thought," Scotty said.

"He's been angry a long time," I said. "He didn't just hatch a few weeks ago. Been existing in a sort of lunatic fringe. Probably for years. I don't know what put a weed up his ass, but based on what I've seen so far, it's not some wild sexual fantasy that he recruits unwilling players into."

Luther bounced the point of a pencil on his desk. It made sharp clicking sounds. "More rage than fantasy."

I shrugged. "Look at the scenes. Pure unadulterated rage. Stripped of all morals, all conscience. As if he were trying to dehu-manize or completely obliterate the victims."

Luther dropped the pencil. "I hate these psychos."

"Then you'll really hate this," I said. Luther looked up at me. "He's just getting started. He'll keep killing as long as he has a target for his anger."

Luther raised an eyebrow.

"He likes it," I continued. "Got a fever for it. The killings, the mutilations, they satisfy something inside. He won't . . . *can't* might be a better word . . . stop."

"Great," Luther said.

"It gets better," I said.

Luther sighed. "You're just full of good news."

"He knows the victims." No one said anything, but I had their full attention. "He knows the layout of each location. The habits of the victims. Knows he has all the time he needs at the scene to kill, mutilate . . . to eat cookies . . . to clean himself up. He knows he's not going to be interrupted." I paused for a minute and let that sink in, then said, "This means he's probably already selected his next victim and is planning the kill right now."

"You're giving me a headache," Luther said.

"Sorry. You did ask for my opinion."

"I thought you were going to say we had another plain-vanilla loony. But this?" He massaged his temples. "Where do we go from here?"

"Find out what sparks him," I said. "His trigger. How and why he selects his victims."

T-Tommy nodded. "We're digging into the victims already. Who they are, who they know, where they go, what bank they use, who mows their lawns, who calls them, and who they call. Everything. Maybe we'll find the connection."

"Look at violent crimes in the past year or so," I said. "These killings aren't our boy's first trip out of the box. He probably has a record."

Luther glanced at his watch. "What should I tell the press and public? That he's a spree killer? A serial killer? Something we don't have a name for?"

I thought about that for a minute. "We want to warn the public and recruit their eyes and ears. Right?" Luther nodded. "Then call him a serial killer. Remember the movie *Jaws*? The mayor told Sheriff Brody not to mention that a shark attack had occurred since that would scare the tourists away at the height of the season. He said if they used the word *barracuda*, everyone would say, 'What?' But, use the word *shark*, and a panic would ensue. Not that we want a panic here, but we do want to get the public's attention. A little fear can be a good thing. Saying *spree* is like saying *barracuda*. Serial killers are sharks."

"I hope you're right." Luther stood, indicating the meeting was over. "Press conference in fifteen minutes."

CHAPTER 18

BACK IN HIS APARTMENT, BRIAN CHANGED INTO SHORTS AND A T-shirt and snagged a Dr Pepper from the refrigerator. He turned on his computer, and while it finished the booting process, removed a binder from his pack. He pulled out the last three pages and spread them on the desktop.

He rested his fingertips on the first page and read the name at the top. *Carl Petersen.* He remembered climbing the stairs at the Russel Erskine and then standing in the quiet hallway in front of Petersen's door. Rage and fear warred inside him, one pushing him forward and the other causing him to glance toward the EXIT sign at the end of the hall. He wanted to run to it, down the stairs, back to his Jeep, a safe cocoon where he could subdue the impulses that drove him. He could still feel the apprehension that had prickled his skin.

He had hesitated with his hand on the doorknob. Even through the gloves he wore, it felt icy cold. Moment of decision. Run or go inside? He knew that once he crossed that threshold, violated

Petersen's home, there would be no turning back. The rage would win.

And it did.

When he stood above the sleeping man and felt the solid wooden bat in his hands, the rage took over. When he raised the bat and struck the first blow, an electric surge of power, suffocating in its weight, swelled within him. When the old man fought back and cried out, his fear rose, but fell silent as his frantic blows struck their mark. Later, after his anger had dissipated, after returning home, he crawled into bed, curled beneath his blanket, shaking with cold fear, and swore he would never give in to his rage again.

Yet, deep inside, in that dark corner where the dragon lived, he knew it was a promise he could never keep.

His gaze shifted to the next page. William Allison. Again, the unlocked door an invitation. He could see the young man asleep and vulnerable. He remembered thinking he seemed soft and delicate and not at all as he imagined he would be. On the phone his voice had been deep and masculine, his language vulgar and aggressive. The person before him appeared too passive. He thought so right up until he exploded his head with a 9 mm round.

Next page. *Savage.* That was the best. The rage had reached new heights, the release a new intensity. He closed his eyes and called up the images. His breath quickened. The dragon stirred. He pulled himself back. Not now.

A knock at the door. Hard and aggressive.

He slipped the pages back into the binder and stood. Through the gap along the edge of the window curtain, he saw Carl Millonzi. What did that jerk want? He pulled open the door. Carl was tall— maybe six-three—but thin. Very thin. His baggy jeans rode low on his hips and his pale blue T-shirt appeared a couple of sizes too large.

"Where was my wife last night?" Carl asked.

"Ask her."

"She lies." The veins along the side of his neck looked like ropes. "I called three times. Between midnight and two. She didn't answer."

"Not my problem."

"It could be. Was she over here?"

Brian felt the heat inside flare. His fist automatically balled at his sides. "Like I said, ask her." He started to close the door, but Carl stopped it with his shoe.

"I'm asking you."

Brian stepped toward Carl. He grabbed a handful of his hair and yanked him forward. He placed his lips near Carl's ear. "There are six billion people on this planet. I'm the last one you want to fuck with." He shouldered Carl in the chest. Hard. Carl stumbled back- ward and collided with the porch railing. "Now get the fuck out of here before I hurt you." He closed the door.

CHAPTER 19

I STEPPED OUT OF THE DOOR ON THE SOUTH SIDE OF THE COURT-house, shaded by the white-columned portico that wrapped around the building. Luther had set up a podium at the top of the stairs. Below, nearly two hundred citizens and reporters milled around the sidewalk. The hum of their collective voices sounded like a swarm of bees.

The Madison County Courthouse filled the downtown square. The modern building, which had replaced a more traditional Southern courthouse—one of those stately structures with massive columns, broad steps, and a four-faced clock cupola—had long been a source of controversy. Many residents thought the nine-story gray monolith was downright ugly. They weren't exactly wrong.

The history of Huntsville lived around the square. To my right, Alabama's first bank, now the Regions Bank, anchored the southwest corner and overlooked Big Spring, the 1905 birthplace of the city. The square's west side had been Cotton Row, where tons of the staple had changed hands every year. To my left, on the southeast corner stood the gray, three-story Schiffman Building, another slice of Huntsville history. The birthplace of Tallulah Bankhead, one of Huntsville's most famous daughters. Said so right on the metal marker that topped a pole near the entry.

I remembered standing by that marker with my father. I was maybe eight or nine at the time. He told me about Tallulah. I had never heard of her. An odd name and, as I later learned, a world-famous one. I remembered reading the plaque. Tallulah was born in 1902. Died in 1968. Daughter of former Speaker of the US House of Representatives William B. Bankhead. I remember it listed a few of her movies. My favorite was *Lifeboat*. I'd watched it half a dozen times.

I later learned that Dad had edited out all the good stuff. Tallulah was as well known for her antics as for her acting. Particularly the things that came out of her mouth. More than her habit of calling everyone "Dahling," she was a repeated embarrassment to her father, once saying of him, "My father warned me about men and booze . . . but he never said anything about women and cocaine." I wished she were still alive. I'd love to sit down over a bottle of bourbon with her. Bet Claire would, too.

I saw Claire, standing near the Channel 8 truck that sat against the curb across the street. She wore a navy blue Channel 8 jacket and was chatting with Jeffrey, her cameraman. She looked up, waved, and headed in my direction. I met her at the bottom of the steps.

"Reminds me of Packwood," she said.

The last time this many people had gathered on this spot to hear the sheriff speak was the first press conference we held in the Billy Wayne Packwood case. This had an eerily similar feel.

"Quite a collection." She waved a hand toward the gathering. "Met a guy down from Nashville, one from Atlanta. Even Blaine's here. Not much can pry him out of the office."

Blaine Markland was the *Huntsville Times* city editor. He didn't do much street reporting anymore, but this story brought out the big guns. "You got that right."

"Anything new?"

I shook my head. "What are you hearing out here?"

"The usual BS. That Sheriff Savage's murder was a Mob hit. Or payback from a parolee. One said that he heard a satanic cult did it."

The rumor mill. Nothing like it. "I think Luther plans to put a halt to all that."

"He going to say it's the work of a serial?"

"Yeah." The buzz began to die, and the crowd turned as one toward the podium as Luther approached. "You going to hang around after this?" I asked.

"Sure. For a few minutes anyway. Do some on-the-scene shots for my report tonight."

"I'll find you after this is done." I climbed the steps and took a position behind Luther, next to T-Tommy.

Luther adjusted the wad of microphones before him, bending them upward to accommodate his height. The reporters and citizens jockeyed for position. I saw Claire slide into a prime front-row spot.

Wouldn't have expected anything less.

"Ladies and gentlemen," Luther began. "Thank you for coming. I have a brief statement to make, and then I'll answer a few questions. Most of you already know that retired Sheriff Mike Savage was murdered last night in his home. We have no suspects yet, but our investigation is ongoing. We have established a joint task force that will be run out of my office. Heading the investigation for the sheriff's department will be Deputy Scotty Simpson. For HPD, the lead investigator will be Investigator Tommy Tortelli. Also, I've asked Dub Walker to consult on the investigation."

Several reporters fired questions, but Luther waved them away.

"I know you want to know why a task force is being put in place." He cleared his throat. "Some of you may have speculated that last night's murders are related to other recent murders in the county. I can tell you that we have evidence to suggest that that may be the case."

The crowd became an agitated beehive. Several reporters snatched cell phones from their pockets and purses and began punching in numbers.

"I don't want you to overstate or sensationalize the facts, and I beg that each of you be responsible in your reporting. I don't want a panic . . . but . . . the public has a right and a need to know the truth. It is possible . . . and I emphasize possible . . . not confirmed . . . that a serial killer may be responsible for these deaths." The buzzing increased. "In view of this, the public should take certain precautions. Keep your doors and windows locked. Leave lights on in and around your homes. Report any suspicious persons immediately. Do not, under any circumstances, confront a stranger yourselves. Now, I'll answer a few questions."

Hands shot skyward and waved for attention. Shouted questions came from every direction. Luther pointed toward Blaine Markland.

"What evidence do you have linking these murders, and how many victims were there in all?"

"We believe last night's homicide is related to at least one other case and possibly to a third. I can't disclose details of the evidence without compromising our investigation."

Markland jumped in again. "What time did last night's murder occur?"

"Between 10:00 p.m. and 1:00 a.m." Luther pointed to a stumpy, balding reporter from nearby Decatur. I recognized him but couldn't recall his name.

"Regarding the other two murders . . . who were the victims, and when and where did those take place?"

"Mr. Carl Petersen was killed on June twenty-fifth at the Russel Erskine and Mr. William Allison on July third at his apartment out near Madison."

Now Luther nodded to Claire.

"I have a question for Mr. Walker." Before Luther could say anything, she went on. "Is it your opinion that these murders are the work of a serial killer?"

Luther hesitated a beat and then waved me forward. "Most of you know Dub Walker. Probably read some of his books. Know that he's an expert in killings of this type. Know that he helped with the investigation that apprehended Billy Wayne Packwood a couple of years ago."

Luther stepped aside, and I moved up to the bank of microphones. "That's an excellent question, Ms. McBride." Mr. Walker? Ms. McBride? It was all I could do to keep from smiling. "The definition of a serial killer depends on who you're asking. Usually it is someone who kills three or more people at different places and at different times with a cooling-off period in between. We know the guy we're after has murdered two people. The evidence suggests he was also responsible for the death of Carl Petersen. If so, he would fit the definition."

Claire didn't hesitate. "Were you brought into the investigation because of your friendship with Sheriff Savage or because of your expertise with serial killers?"

"Probably a bit of both."

Luther moved forward, and I stepped back. He started to point to another reporter, but Claire was now in full bulldog mode.

"My sources tell me that the bodies of Mr. Petersen and Mr. Allison were badly mutilated," she said. "Was this also the case with Sheriff Savage?"

Luther glanced back toward me. Busted. "I have no comment on that at this time."

Questions came from all directions.

"Is it true, these were gang-related killings?"

"Do you think there will be more murders?"

Luther raised his hand. "That's all the questions we have time for. When we have more information, we'll let you know. Thank you." He headed back into the building. I motioned to Claire that I'd be right back and then followed him inside.

Luther chewed my ass for telling Claire about the mutilations, saying that I should have cleared it with him. He was right, but I countered that Claire could be an asset. So could the public if sufficiently aroused. I reminded him of what I had said earlier. Fear is a powerful motivator, and if the citizens knew the truth about the killings, they'd not only lock their homes a little more tightly, but also would pay attention to anything and everything. Could yield useful info. Or, as Luther pointed out, could crank up the wackos. The ones who confessed to everything. The ones who were sure the next-door neighbor was the killer because he never mowed his lawn. Too busy scouting future victims. Or kept his curtains drawn so no one would see him chopping up bodies. The public's imagination had no restraints.

T-Tommy did step in on my side, but drew only a grunt and a scowl from Luther. I apologized and promised not to step out of bounds again.

I went back outside and found Claire finishing her wrap-up shots. Positioned so the courthouse was in the background, she spoke directly into the camera. I waited until she was done and then asked Jeffrey about the tape from Mike's place this morning.

"I'll have it edited and burned on a disc in a couple of hours," he said. "I'll give it to Claire."

"Thanks." I looked at Claire. "How about a drink later? Sammy's?"

She glanced at her watch. "Got my report on the six o'clock broadcast. I could make seven thirty. How's that?"

"See you there."

CHAPTER 20

SAMMY'S BLUES 'N' Q WAS A HUNTSVILLE INSTITUTION AND A POPULAR local hangout. It had fed "Q" to just about everyone who visited the Rocket City. Scientists from all corners of the world, astronauts, senators, congressmen, even a president or two. Tom Hanks and Ron Howard dropped in while filming *Apollo 13*.

The weather-worn wooden structure with its tin roof and chipped, curled, and faded red paint could use some work, but patrons didn't care. Sammy's wasn't about aesthetics. It was about food and music. A rusted stovepipe chimney pumped the smoky aroma of ribs, brisket, and hot links—three of Sammy's specialties—several blocks in every direction, and the moaning sounds of the blues wafted through its open windows.

The spring-loaded front door snapped closed behind me when I entered. As usual, most of the thirty tables inside and the two dozen more on the screened-in addition Sammy had added a year ago were filled. On the small corner stage, Colin Dogget, a local blues man, scratched out his own brand of Delta blues on a National Dobro. Behind him a Gibson acoustic, a Les Paul, a road-worn Fender Stratocaster, and cigar-box Lowebow guitar, hand made up in Memphis by John Lowe himself, leaned on stands, awaiting their turn. The Lowebow was a gift to Colin from local blues legend Dave Gallaher. I often sat in with Colin, and when I did, I loved to play the Lowebow. Nothing quite like it.

Colin nodded to me and then to the empty chair onstage next to him. Wanted me to sit in. I nodded and mouthed, "Maybe later."

Besides being a temple to barbecue and the blues, Sammy's was also a cathedral to Crimson Tide football. The glasses, napkins, and tablecloths sported the school logo. Signed photos of former players covered the walls. Names like Namath, Stabler, Jordan, Neighbors, and Musso. A who's who of Alabama football. One wall was reserved for photos of the national championship teams. All thirteen of them. Behind the bar were dozens of photos of Bear Bryant. Houndstooth hat and all.

I grabbed a bar stool directly under the watchful eye of the Bear. Didn't have to order. Sammy Lange, the owner, poured my usual. Blanton's bourbon, neat.

Maybe seventy, no one really knew, Sammy was wiry tough, mostly bald, and without a doubt one of the finest people I'd ever known. Give you his last dime and never ask anything in return. He swiped a towel across the bar and then slung it over his shoulder, where he always kept it. Said it made looking for it a whole lot easier.

Sammy rested his forearms on the bar. "Can't believe this happened to Mike. It's been all over." He nodded toward the ceiling-mounted TV behind him. "I saw that press conference."

"Sorry you found out that way," I said. "I should've called."

"I suspect you've had your hands full today."

"Still, I should've."

"He killed those other folks, too?"

"Yeah."

"Was Mike . . . uh . . . damaged . . . like the others?"

I nodded.

"This is one messed-up rock we live on. Shit like this . . . someone like Mike . . . makes you wonder." He scratched his ear. "You going to get this guy?"

"Going to try to help."

Sammy's head cook, Willie Tucker, a huge black man wearing an undersized T-shirt beneath a sauce-stained apron, came out from the kitchen. He plopped a plate with a pair of hot links on it in front of me. "Something for you to gnaw on."

"Hmm," I said. "Smells great."

"Made 'em up special my ownself." Willie flashed his big grin. "These here got lots of pork, a smidge of crushed apple, and the tiniest little bit of cayenne. Should do you up just right." He turned and lumbered back toward the kitchen.

"Only needs one thing." I pulled my bottle of Tabasco from my jacket pocket and splattered the links. They were fork-tender and wonderfully rich. Willie was no doubt a genius.

Sammy propped an elbow on the bar, chin on his fist. "You up for a game today?" He always found a way to lighten the mood. Made me laugh when I didn't feel like it or at least feel better about things for a bit. The game? He and I had a trivia thing going. Always trying to stump each other. I was good. Sammy was better.

"Sure."

Sammy swiped the bar. "What state capitals begin with the same letter as the state name?"

"Honolulu, Hawaii. Indianapolis, Indiana. Oklahoma City, Oklahoma." I hesitated, letting Sammy think I didn't know the last one, and then said, "And Dover, Delaware."

He laughed. "Thought I had you."

"So we're doing state stuff today, huh? How about . . . name the three states that were independent nations before joining the union."

Sammy shook his head. His way of saying no-brainer. "Hawaii, California, and, of course, the Republic of Texas."

I glanced at my watch. 7:45.

"You got somewhere to be?" Sammy asked.

"Supposed to meet Claire McBride here. If she didn't get tied up."

"She didn't." Sammy nodded toward the door.

I swiveled toward the entrance. Claire blew through the door and marched toward us. She wore tan slacks, a black silk shirt, and a matching sweater tied loosely around her neck. Her red hair, tied in sort of a ponytail arrangement, wagged in her wake.

"Sorry I'm late." She slid onto the stool next to me.

"What can I get you?" Sammy asked.

"Dewar's. Rocks."

Sammy poured her drink and slid it across the bar. "How about I have Willie whip up some pulled-pork sandwiches for you guys?"

"That'd be great," Claire said. "I'm starving."

I pushed the links toward her. "Start on these. They're really good today."

"Did you put that pepper crap on them?"

"Don't bad-mouth the juice of life."

"I swear, you're going to pop a gut vessel and bleed to death someday."

"You have such a pleasant manner about you."

She tossed me a frown. "I'll wait for the pork. Save my stomach from the ravages of hell."

I took another bite of the link. "Don't know what you're missing."

"Heartburn? Had it. Didn't like it." She removed a disc from her purse and handed it to me. "Jeffrey edited out all the reporter stuff and burned a DVD for you. He said he got everyone there this morning. Also all the cars for two blocks in both directions, including the license plates."

"Thanks. I'll get this to the task force tomorrow." I slipped the disc into my jacket pocket.

"Hope it helps." She took a pull from her Scotch. "Anything new?"

"I can tell you that ViCAP turned up squat. Two violent

postmortem beatings in the past six months. A Florida man did his wife, and a mother drowned and beat a six-month-old in Massachusetts. Both in custody."

"That's not much." She turned her palm up and gave me a come-on motion with her fingers. "Gimme."

"Give you what?"

"The rest. The good stuff."

"That's it."

"Dub, don't sandbag me. You know. I know you know. And I know where you live."

"Do you sweet talk everyone this way?"

"I'll work on my people skills later." Again with the come-on move. "Let's have it."

"I already got my butt chewed for telling about the corpses."

"Good, you're not a virgin. Work with me here."

"You didn't hear it from me."

She gave me a don't-state-the-obvious look. Claire knew the game and knew how to protect a source. That's how she always got the scoop on other reporters. She'd hound you, maybe even harass you, but she'd never expose you.

"Two of the crime scenes are absolutely linked, and it's very likely that the third is, too."

"Ballistics?"

I nodded.

"Anyone else know this?"

"Not yet. As far as I know."

"Love scoops." She scribbled a few notes.

Willie appeared, carrying two plates. "Here you go. Pulled-pork sandwiches and coleslaw. My, my."

I splashed Tabasco on my sandwich. To her credit, Claire didn't say a word.

We ate in silence until she broke it. "I'd like to do a live interview with you tomorrow. On the six o'clock? Is that possible?"

"Why?"

"Credibility. It's one thing to report the news like some talking head. Quite another to get it from the horse's mouth."

"At least you didn't say horse's ass."

"You already know that."

I smiled. "You really do need to work on your people skills."

"I hear that a lot."

"Why not T-Tommy or Scotty Simpson? They're running the case."

"Because you're a local hero. After the Packwood case and all those books. You're a goddamn media darling."

Good grief. "I'll check with Sheriff Randall, but I'd suspect it'll work."

"Give me a call tomorrow as soon as you know, and I'll set it up."

CHAPTER 21

RESTLESSNESS DROVE BRIAN THROUGH A RIGOROUS TWO-HOUR workout. Didn't help. He drank four beers. Didn't help. He took a long hot shower. Didn't help, either. Now he sat on the sofa, naked except for the towel draped across his lap, and stared at the TV. He had it tuned to the news, sound muted. He didn't really give a shit what was happening out there in the world.

The phone rang. When he answered, the man said, "Unfortunate incident today."

"How did . . . ?" Brian didn't finish the question. He realized that whoever this was, he knew things. Seemed to know everything. Which meant he knew about the vagrant. "More so for him."

"Very true." A soft laugh. "Too bad about your job. Getting fired can't be fun."

"Dr. Hublein will get it back for me. It's part of my treatment, and he hates to fail."

"Maybe he will. Maybe he won't. It doesn't matter."

"To you, maybe. I have rent to pay."

"Don't worry, it'll work out."

"Glad you're so confident."

"Have you decided on Kushner yet?"

Brian couldn't hide his quick intake of breath.

The man laughed. "It's okay. I agree. He's an arrogant prick and deserves what he gets."

"How do you know?"

"What did he call you? An asshole?"

This was too much. How could he know of a conversation that was only hours old? Unless he had Brian's work phone tapped. He looked around. Maybe his apartment, too.

"Leave me alone," Brian said.

"I can't do that. You need me."

"No, I don't."

The voice hesitated for a moment. "You don't believe doors unlock themselves, do you? Or that a gun magically appears? Did you think you were just lucky?"

Brian hated this guy. Hated that he knew so much. That he planned everything down to the smallest detail. That he provided weapons and opened doors. That he acted so goddamn superior, as if Brian couldn't function on his own.

"Why are you doing this?"

"We've been through this."

"Humor me."

"I believe in what you're doing. It's a worthy cause. That's why."

"Glad you agree, but we both know I can do this without you."

He laughed. "I think not. You fucked up the first time. Almost let that old man get the best of you."

"He paid."

"Still, it could have gone badly, and that would have been it. There would've been no Allison, no Savage. None of those yet to come. You have so much left to do." Brian said nothing, so the man continued. "It won't be long. The feelings are rising again, aren't they?"

That was true. The rumblings in his gut had churned all day. It had started with all that crap with Wanda and then became white-hot when he was attacked by that piece of street trash. Then he had to endure that fancy ER doc and the cab driver with the death-rattle cough. Not to mention his puny-ass coworkers. The snakes in his belly were definitely aroused. "What if I don't give in? What if I ignore them?"

"They're too strong."

"So am I."

"Yes . . . you are. But this need is stronger."

"You don't know. You couldn't know."

"Really? It comes in fiery waves? Consumes all reason? Can't be controlled or bargained with? Can only be . . . what's the word? . . . *attenuated*? That about cover it?"

Fuck him. Yet, Brian couldn't avoid the truth of his words. The rage was all-consuming. He could wrestle with it, occasionally hold it at bay, but ultimately, it would win. It always won.

The voice continued. "I know what you're going through. I know what you need. I know how to help you."

Brian sighed. Fatigue pulled at him. He slipped off the chair, sat on the floor, and leaned against the desk. A shiver rippled through him, and he pulled his knees against his chest.

"I still want to know why. What's in it for you?"

"All in due time." The man said nothing for a few seconds, but Brian could hear his breathing, slow, steady, calm. Then he said, "Do you want Kushner?"

"Yes."

"The information you need is on the way. Read through it, and I'll get back to you." The line went dead.

Brian waited a couple of minutes and then checked his e-mail. As expected, a message from an anonymous sender. He opened it and read through the information on the screen before him.

At the top of the page: *Albert Kushner*. Below this, a detailed description of the route to his house. Attachments revealed a site plan of the neighborhood, Kushner's property, and the house's floor plan. Everything he needed.

CHAPTER 22

I SWUNG BY THE TASK FORCE ROOM, HANDED OFF THE DVD CLAIRE had given me to Scotty, and snagged T-Tommy. We grabbed a Starbucks off University Drive at Madison Square Mall before heading out to Redstone for our nine o'clock meeting with Dr. Wendell Volek.

The US Army's Redstone Arsenal had been established in 1941 and since then had been as much a part of Huntsville's history as the fertile soil that produced more cotton than anywhere in the United States. During World War II, a vast number of munitions rolled off the base's assembly lines. After the war, it became the headquarters of the US Army Missile Command, and in the 1950s, Werner von Braun and his German missile team moved in. NASA leased 30 percent of the base and set up shop as the Marshall Space Flight Center in 1960, and Huntsville quickly became the heart and soul of the space program. Under von Braun and his staff at the MSFC, the rocket engines that hurled satellites into orbit and lifted men above the earth and to the moon were designed, built, and tested in Redstone's 38,000 acres of rolling terrain.

We parked at the Visitors' Center near Gate 9, went inside, settled into the molded plastic chairs, and waited for our escort. I nursed my triple Americano, hoping to clear the cobwebs that seemed to have a stranglehold on my brain. Not much sleep last night. That's the way it always was when I got into a case.

Last night after Claire left Sammy's—at least she showed some common sense—I stayed and sat in with Colin, and we played until after midnight. It was nearly one by the time I wound my way up the Bankhead Parkway and crawled into bed. This was followed by an hour or so of flapjacking and pillow wrestling. No position felt comfortable, and sleep only came in brief spurts. The scene at Mike's, the crime scene photos, the autopsy room, Billy, Luther, T-Tommy, and Petersen's apartment at the Russel Erskine all marched through my head. Even Jill made a couple of appearances.

The dream, Jill's dream, a relic from the past, was always the same. It was the only time I could recall her face. Never when I actually wanted to. Jill, trapped in a deep, impossibly dark well. Just out of reach. I stretched and strained, occasionally brushing her fingertips, but was never able to grip her hand. Never able to pull her to safety. Instead she slowly sank deeper into the abyss until even her whimpers faded. The dream had once been a nightly visitor, but over the years it gradually faded. It had been a good four years since its last visit. And now it was back.

I rarely dreamed, or if I did, I rarely remembered them. A good thing, since the ones I could remember always seemed to come out ugly. I couldn't remember a time when they were pleasant. Maybe years ago when I was naïve, unexposed to the real world. Before I had consulted on so many senseless murders. Before I knew so much about the dark side of the human animal. Before Jill disappeared.

Our escort turned out to be a no-nonsense US Army MP. His name tag read P. Whitworth. I learned that the *P* stood for Paul. Shoulder stripes indicated his rank of sergeant. He was stiffly professional, creased, spit-shined, and punctuated everything he said with a crisp "sir." We climbed into the backseat of the white military van. Sergeant Whitworth drove through two guarded checkpoints, snapping a salute to the guard at each. Finally, he pulled to the curb in front of the MSFC headquarters.

The tall, rectangular, gray concrete, steel, and glass building loomed above me as I climbed from the van. Two rocket engines, balanced on their cone-shaped exhaust nozzles, sat on a grassy strip across the drive from the building. To my right a large red and white sign with black lettering indicated that this was Building 4200 of the George C. Marshall Space Flight Center. Just in case I didn't know. During the heyday of the space program, von Braun had occupied the ninth floor and penthouse.

Even though I had been here before, I never failed to sense the history of this place. Always gave me chills.

We thanked the good sergeant, receiving a stiff nod in return, climbed the front stairs, and pushed through the glass double doors.

A young NASA security officer named Tim Russett greeted us. Unlike Sergeant Whitworth, he actually smiled. We rode an elevator to the fifth floor, where he deposited us in a conference room, saying Dr. Volek would be in shortly. It was 8:45.

T-Tommy immediately sniffed out a corner table stocked with fresh coffee and muffins. He had one of each; I opted for coffee, no muffin.

"Well, well, fancy meeting you here."

I turned as Wendell Volek came into the room. Hadn't seen him in a couple of years. He hadn't aged a minute. Still tall, clean-cut, and showing only slight graying of his full head of brown hair. He wore a blue suit, white shirt, and red tie. He was one of those guys who oozed smarts. He was also the father of the VISAR system.

VISAR stands for Video Image Stabilization and Registration. The computer-assisted video enhancement program was first developed during the investigation of the 1996 Atlanta Olympic bombing, when a twelve-second video clip was brought to Volek by the FBI. The film, shot by a news crew, was dark and showed only a silhouette of an abandoned backpack leaning against a bench. Volek went to work, eventually cleaning and brightening the video so that the bomb inside and the wires snaking from the flap were easily identified. After that success, VISAR proved useful in many other famous cases: the Mike Bell murder, the abductions of Elizabeth Smart and Katie Poirier, and the Columbia shuttle accident, to name a few.

I introduced him and T-Tommy and then asked, "How are things?"

"Busy. With the solar investigation stuff we've been doing and with the Orion Project heating up, not much time for fun."

The Orion spacecraft, also called the Crew Exploration Vehicle, or CEV, along with the Ares rocket, was part of the Constellation Program, NASA's most ambitious project in years. It looked more like the old Apollo capsule than the planelike shuttle it would replace. Smaller, lighter, and more functional, the plan was that it would not only work in earth's orbit, but also in lunar and Mars missions of the future. The plans were to mate it with the Ares I rocket for a return to the moon by 2017, this time to set up permanent colonies. I keep up with this stuff. Have since I was a kid. Something about rockets always excited me.

In my youth, I had built a hundred of them in the backyard. Mostly powered by crushed match heads or gunpowder pilfered from Dad's shotgun shells. Some worked, some fizzled, and a couple blew up like the old Vanguard rocket. One nearly took out Jill and me. Dad wasn't happy. Mom less so. They nearly shut down our fledgling space program.

Volek poured a cup of coffee and sat at the table. "So, what have you gotten into this time?"

I settled in a chair across from him, told him about the series of murders, and then slid the tape toward him. "This is a copy of the original tape. It's from the security rig at the Russel Erskine, where the first murder took place."

He looked at me. "In the hotel?"

I shrugged. "Guy's got balls if nothing else. It shows a figure walking through the lobby and returning about thirty minutes later. Around the time of the murder. Doesn't look or walk like any of the residents, who are all over sixty."

Volek took the tape and moved to a stack of video equipment at one end of the room. He fed it into a VCR, and the images appeared on the large screen at the end of the conference table. I had left it cued up at the right spot, so after a few seconds of the quiet lobby, a man entered the scene from the lower left and climbed the marble staircase. On-screen only a few seconds, the view was mostly from behind. He appeared big, wore a Windbreaker and a cap. He walked like an athlete with long, purposeful strides, and he took the stairs two at a time. Definitely not a resident.

Volek ran it back and forth a couple of times. "Not a very good image. Can't see his face well." He ran it back again and this time watched it in slow motion. He stopped it. "Right here is a quick glimpse of a partial profile."

"Can you do anything with it?"

"Sure. Won't be easy and might not help much, but let me see what I can dig out." He stopped the video. "When do you need this?"

"Yesterday."

"I figured."

CHAPTER 23

Dr. Charlie Beck parked outside Memorial Medical Center's ER, walked up Madison Street, and then turned west on Saint Clair Avenue toward the North Alabama Neuropsychiatric Research Institute. As he approached, a sense of apprehension rose in his gut. He wasn't sure why, but his years of treating the injured, ill, and worried had taught him not to ignore gut feelings. They were usually accurate barometers.

Yesterday, after Brian Kurtz left the ER, Charlie had called Dr. Hublein's office, but found that Hublein was tied up all day. His administrative assistant, Catherine Frommer, a pleasant, efficient woman, suggested making an appointment. He did. Maybe it was the tension he sensed in her voice when he brought up Brian's name as the reason he needed to see Hublein that had him spooked. Maybe it was the institute's imposing five floors of gray marble and severely tinted black windows that now towered over him. Maybe he was simply being a ninny.

He rode the elevator to the fifth floor, where he exited into a world of opulence: a foyer with a gray marble floor and recessed lights that painted rose-colored walls and highlighted several works of modern art; a centrally placed pedestal table, which supported a watermelon-sized, expensive-looking oriental urn; two overstuffed chairs, flanking a table topped with a bulbous brass lamp and an arrangement of fresh flowers; and two very attractive, well-dressed young women, one blond, the other brunette, manning an expansive black marble reception desk.

They smiled in unison as Charlie approached. The brunette said, "Can I help you?"

"I'm Dr. Beck. Here to see Dr. Hublein."

"Yes, Dr. Beck. I'll notify Dr. Hublein's assistant that you're here. Would you care to take a seat?" She picked up the phone.

"Can I get you something? Coffee or a soft drink?" the blonde asked.

"No, thanks." Charlie sat in one of the chairs, sinking so deeply into the cushions he wondered if he would be able to get out. The perfume of the flowers settled around him.

The brunette hung up the phone and smiled at him. "Dr. Hublein's assistant, Catherine, will be with you shortly."

"Thank you." Charlie picked up a copy of *Architectural Digest* and thumbed through it but, finding nothing of interest, returned it to the table. He couldn't help wondering what his father, or better, his grandfather, both small-town physicians back in Iowa, would think of this place. He suspected they would be incensed by such opulence, which had nothing to do with treating "sick folks," and would consider it an insult to the profession. Charlie agreed.

"Dr. Beck?" Charlie looked up. "I'm Catherine Frommer. We spoke on the phone yesterday."

Charlie grasped the arms of the chair, and with great difficulty extracted himself from its depths. "Hello, Ms. Frommer." She was maybe midforties, trim, and well dressed in a gray pantsuit and white blouse. Her brown eyes came alive when she smiled.

"Please, call me Catherine. Let's go to my office. Dr. Hublein is expecting you, but he's on a conference call right now."

Charlie followed her down an art-infested hallway and through large oak double doors. Brass lettering indicated that Dr. Robert Hublein was medical director and Dr. Melvin Wexlar president of the North Alabama Neuropsychiatric Research Institute.

"Did you have any trouble finding us?"

"No. I've seen this building many times but never been inside. It's quite impressive."

"The doctors believe in doing everything top-drawer." Catherine offered him a seat and took her place behind her desk. "Looks like Dr. Hublein's still on the phone. He should only be a minute." Her mouth adopted a pleasant tilt when she smiled. "I understand you run the ER at Memorial."

"Guilty."

"I bet that keeps you busy?"

"Intermittently and sporadically. Do you ever visit the hospital?"

"No," she laughed. "Do I look sick?"

Charlie laughed with her. "Not even a little bit. I just thought you might have a reason to go there from time to time . . . for Dr. Hublein."

She shook her head. "Never been there."

"I haven't seen Dr. Hublein there, either. Does he treat hospital patients?"

"No. His practice . . . Dr. Wexlar's, too . . . is strictly outpatient. And their research, of course."

"They do a lot of that?"

"Lord, yes. I think we have twenty-six studies going now, and three more will start in the next month or two."

"Bet that keeps you busy?"

"Intermittently and sporadically." She flashed a crooked smile again. "They get offered studies all the time. Turn down more than they accept. Not enough time to do them all and do them right." She glanced at the phone. "Dr. Hublein's off now. I'll let him know you're here." She stood and walked through another carved oak door to Charlie's right.

When she returned, she ushered him into a cavernous office with dark wood paneling and bookshelves filled with thick text-books and encased journals. Two floor-to-ceiling windows, hidden behind heavy maroon drapes, occupied the far wall. A massive desk stacked with papers and lit by a brass lamp claimed a central position. Recessed ceiling lights cast more shadows than light and added to the gothic feel of the room.

Dr. Hublein skirted the desk with his hand extended. "Dr. Beck, welcome."

"Thank you for seeing me. Please, call me Charlie."

"Friends and colleagues call me Bob. Please, take a seat," he said, indicating a ladder-back chair opposite his desk.

The thinly cushioned chair was considerably less comfortable than the waiting room chairs. Apparently waiting was encouraged, meetings were not.

Hublein sat in the high-backed leather chair behind his desk. He was as big as the room, easily six-four and two hundred and fifty pounds. He wore an expensive blue suit, crisp white shirt, and a patterned red tie. A gold Rolex hugged his left wrist, and his right hand sported a pinkie ring with a large square diamond.

"I'm running late as usual, so let's get right to it. Catherine tells me you wanted to see me about Brian Kurtz."

"That's right. I treated him in the ER yesterday."

"What happened?"

"He was mugged."

"Mugged? Was he hurt?"

"Not seriously. Just a forearm laceration."

"Thank goodness." He appeared relieved. "So, how can I help you?"

"The problem is not with his injury, but what he did to the mugger."

Hublein's eyes darted around the room as if he were searching for what to say. Apparently he could think of nothing, and his gaze returned to Charlie.

"Broken ribs, punctured lung, fractured ulna, concussion. I see fight victims all the time, but this beating was over the top."

"That's unfortunately a problem with Brian. He came to us because of his violent behavior and problems with impulse control. I've been treating him for PTSD."

Charlie knew the Brian he had seen yesterday was a troubled young man. Hublein just confirmed his feeling. "We get PTSD patients in the ER, too. Mostly stress, headaches, sleeping problems, that sort of thing. A couple who were downright nasty. But Brian was . . . something else."

"He's had a rough life," Hublein continued. "Started with a difficult childhood. Alcoholic and less-than-enthusiastic parents. Not really abusive, but apparently never warmed to the idea of parenthood. He lived with his maternal grandmother for a while. Until she died from a fall down some stairs. Broke her neck. Brian found her body. It was a very traumatic event for him."

"I'm sure it was."

"After that he returned to his parents' house, unwanted, but he had no other options."

"He said you treat him for chronic headaches."

"That and his behavioral problems. Brian was a gifted athlete in high school. Expected to get a scholarship to play college football."

"But he was injured."

Hublein nodded. "Depressed skull fracture. Cerebral contusion.

In a coma for several days. Required surgery."

"So football was out."

"Absolutely." Hublein squared a stack of papers on his desk. "He somehow managed to get in the army, though. As a computer tech and communications officer."

"I understand he went to Iraq."

Hublein nodded. "No combat. Not directly. He did witness a few IED attacks. Saw a few friends get killed."

"And caught a bullet to the leg."

He sighed. "I wish that was all he picked up over there." He realigned the stack of papers. "After returning home, he had adjustment problems. His headaches worsened. He became increasingly difficult, fighting and the like, more violent and withdrawn. After his second arrest for assault, he was sent to me as part of a plan to keep him from doing jail time. We treat a number of individuals referred by the courts. Brian came to us over a year ago. I diagnosed his PTSD and have been treating him since. Believe it or not, he's made excellent progress."

"You think yesterday could be an isolated event?"

"I surely hope so."

"He said he was taking some new drug."

"He's in one of our studies. We do a great deal of research for various pharmaceutical companies, the NIH, others."

"What's the drug he's on?"

Again, Hublein's eyes darted around the room. "It's a new

benzodiazepine derivative. It appears to be very successful in PTSD. Brian's been on it about eight months now. It has dramatically reduced his headaches, and until this episode, his aggression seemed to be controlled."

"Maybe he stopped the drug on his own."

"That's not possible," Hublein said.

"Oh?"

"It's injectable. A slow-release depo-type preparation. He comes in once a week."

"Maybe his dose needs adjusting."

"Let's see." Hublein opened one of the charts on his desk. "We check blood levels on all our patients every three or four weeks." He leafed through the pages, stopping when he found what he was looking for. "Brian was last tested two weeks ago. It was fine then."

Charlie nodded.

"Regardless, I'll get him in for an evaluation and recheck his level." Hublein stood, indicating the meeting was over. "I want to thank you for bringing this to my attention."

Charlie stood. "I thought you should know."

"Brian really is a decent fellow." Hublein glanced at his watch. "I have a meeting to get to. Is there anything else I can do for you?"

"You've been extremely helpful."

He escorted Charlie to the door.

"Do you know if Brian is in trouble?" Hublein asked. "Was he arrested?"

"No. The police felt it was self-defense."

Hublein's relief was obvious. "That's good. Brian doesn't need any further legal problems. Is the mugger okay?"

"Actually, he's doing very well. Probably be transferred to the jail ward in a week or so."

"They arrested him, then?"

"Seems he'd robbed several other people. I guess he picked the wrong guy this time."

Hublein opened the door for him. "Again, thanks for your help." He closed the door behind Charlie.

"All done?" Catherine asked.

"Yeah."

The phone buzzed, and she picked it up. "Yes, Dr. Hublein." She frowned slightly. "I think Dr. Wexlar is over in research. I'll find him." She pressed one of the phone's intercom buttons. "Excuse me. Just a sec," she said to Charlie, and then into the phone said, "Dr. Wexlar, Dr. Hublein needs to see you in his office right away." She hung up and looked at Charlie. "I see you made him happy. What on earth did you tell him?"

"About a problem I had with Brian Kurtz."

"I see." Apprehension crept into her voice.

"How well do you know him?"

"I see him once a week when he comes here for treatment."

"And?"

"And what?"

"What do you think of him?"

"I can't talk about our patients."

"I'm his doctor, too. You can talk to me. What do you think of him?"

"He's spooky."

"Spooky? Now that's a medical term."

"It's the best word I can think of. I don't know what it is, but when he's here I feel . . . uneasy."

"Why?"

"I don't know. He's just spooky."

They both laughed.

"I agree," Charlie said.

"What happened?" she asked. "With Brian?"

Charlie told her the story. "The beating was total overkill."

"That's what I mean by spooky. Like a time bomb."

"Dr. Hublein says he is doing better since he started that new drug."

"He was . . . but . . . lately he seems worse. More tense."

"Really?"

"I'm probably wrong," Catherine said. "I only see him briefly when he comes in, and I'm no expert."

"You may be more of an expert than you think."

"Yeah, right."

"You see crazies all day, don't you?"

"We don't call our patients crazy," she said, and then smiled. "Even if some of them are."

"Then there you go. You have practical knowledge. And experience."

She laughed. "My first diagnosis."

CHAPTER 24

"GODDAMN IT, MELVIN." HUBLEIN LEANED ON HIS DESK AND LOOKED at Wexlar. "I knew this would get out of hand."

Wexlar waved his protests aside. "Bob, it's not out of hand."

"The hell it isn't. That goddamn Kurtz kid nearly beat someone to death. Don't you think that's a problem?"

"Not really."

"You wouldn't. This is your goddamn protocol. I was against it from the beginning. It's like all the other bullshit projects they've given us."

"Relax, Bob."

Hublein watched as Melvin Wexlar, his friend of thirty years, paced the floor. At only five-four, Wexlar was thin and wiry, with a stiff posture, as if someone had shoved a steel rod up his spine. Streaks of gray dulled his thinning red hair, as well as his thick mustache, which covered his mouth so that only his lower lip could be seen. As usual, his gold, wire-rimmed glasses dangled from his neck on a black cord. Always a fashionable dresser, today he wore an Armani brown three-piece suit, light blue shirt, and yellow tie, fixed with a diamond stickpin.

"Relax?" Hublein dropped into his chair. "When are we going to dump those clowns? Stick to the NIH stuff like I suggested?"

"Because those clowns, as you call them, pay very well."

That was true. Spellman Pharmaceuticals offered three times what any other company did. The NIH, the National Institutes of Health, was a joke by comparison. Of course, Spellman hadn't come up with a drug worth a damn in years. At least none in the neuro-psychiatric field. A couple of diabetic drugs and a new cephalosporin antibiotic, but the three psychiatric drugs they had sent Hublein's way were crap. Still, the pay had been very good. But this drug?

"I just have a bad feeling about this one." Hublein leaned back in his chair. "This drug has a bad pedigree."

"That was the old formulation. It's been tweaked. This one works. You've seen it work."

"Based on what Kurtz did? Sure seems to work well." He couldn't hide his sarcasm. Didn't really want to.

"We have twenty-five people in the study. Only Kurtz has exhibited this kind of behavior."

"I guess you're forgetting about Martin Hankins and Robert Swenson. What they did."

"Hankins had only been on the drug a month. He was violent by nature. The drug had nothing to do with it."

"You don't know that." Hublein swiveled his chair first one way and then the other. He couldn't decide whether to pace or sit.

"Weren't all his blood levels normal? Even low?"

That was true, too. That's why they never went to the police. Never told them that Hankins was on the drug. Should have. Too late now.

"And Swenson was simply crazy," Wexlar continued. "Maybe we made a mistake there. Maybe he should never have been in the study." Wexlar scratched his ear.

"What if the police trace Swenson or this Kurtz business back here?"

"They won't."

"How can you be sure?"

"Nobody even knows where Swenson is. After that incident with his girlfriend, he took off. Cops have been looking for him for a couple of months. He's way out of state by now."

"But he's not well. He could do it again. Get caught. Lead them right back here."

"So what? He and Kurtz both have violent histories. One more incident isn't going to make much difference. That's why they were chosen for the study. Why all of them were chosen."

Hublein walked to his concealed bar and opened the cabinet door. He poured an inch of Scotch into a glass and downed it in one gulp. He looked at his reflection in the mirror above the bar. Maybe Melvin was right. Maybe Spellman's new drug was a winner. It was designed for only the most aggressive sufferers of PTSD. Those with violent histories for whom none of the standard treatments seemed to help.

He had to admit that the drug had worked wonders for most of the people in the study. Except for Hankins, Swenson, and now Kurtz, the others had been model citizens. Something they had not been for many years.

Still, this drug had a checkered past. RU-1193, as it was called, was a derivative of RU-1186, a compound that had a very unsavory track record. But the new formulation, the RU-1193, had proven to be well tolerated and highly effective. Previous studies had shown that its only real side effect, an exacerbation of anger and aggressive behavior, only occurred if the blood concentrations rose to very high levels. Hankins, Swenson, Kurtz, and all the others had been closely monitored and their blood levels were all on the low side of the target ranges. Maybe he was overreacting.

Hublein poured another dose of Scotch. "Want some?"

"No."

"You're probably right," Hublein said. "The entire study cohort is a group of angry young men. It would be expected that the drug wouldn't work for some of them."

"Exactly." Wexlar continued to pace. "Besides, why would anyone blame us for their actions? Experimental drug or not. Just the opposite. We're their doctors, trying to help them."

"Some help we are." Hublein sank heavily into his chair and spread his hands on the desktop. "I just don't like the fact that three of our patients have had violent episodes."

"They were violent long before we got them. This was predictable. Expected. With or without our treatment, these guys were bound to have incidents. They did before, they will after. That's what the study is about. To see if this drug lessens the likelihood."

Hublein nodded.

"It isn't designed to cure," Wexlar continued. "Only to improve. That's exactly what it's done. These three aside."

Hublein sighed. "What do we do now?"

Wexlar sat on the sofa. "Let's have Pearce keep an eye on Kurtz for a while. If he gets into any more trouble, we'll pull him out of the study. Just to be overly cautious."

Hublein grabbed the phone. "Catherine. Find Harold Pearce and have him come to my office immediately."

Hublein had mixed feelings about Harold Pearce. He was a loner, said little, and never smiled. Half the time Hublein didn't know where he was or what he was doing. Which was mostly fine. Better that the man kept to himself. He came from Spellman as part of the three studies they were doing for them. Particularly the PTSD study, which could potentially be worth billions. The contract with Spellman required an on-site security officer to protect the project. Sniff out any competitive espionage. With so much money at stake, and with at least one other company developing drugs in the PTSD arena, this seemed reasonable, and Hublein agreed to the security arrangement. He just didn't care for Pearce personally.

"You wanted to see me?"

Harold Pearce stood in the doorway. Hublein hadn't heard him open the door. He was just suddenly there. He was not a big man, maybe five-ten, one-seventy, but he seemed fit. He had short-cropped, light brown hair, a square jaw, and today wore his typical khaki trousers, black pullover shirt, and black leather jacket.

"We have a problem," Hublein said.

"Not really a problem," Wexlar inserted. "A situation."

"Situation, problem, whatever. What is it?" Pearce said, stepping into the room, closing the door behind him.

"One of the subjects of the PTSD project might be out of control," Hublein said.

"What happened?" Pearce's steely gray eyes shifted back and forth between the two men.

Hublein returned his stare. "Brian Kurtz beat the hell out of some vagrant. The police were called. I want to pull him from the project. Dr. Wexlar feels otherwise."

"He was attacked," Wexlar said. "He merely defended himself."

Hublein stood and leaned on his desk. "Regardless, I don't like the attention he's attracted. The police and that ER doctor."

"What do you want from me?" Pearce asked.

"Keep an eye on him," Hublein said. "But don't let him know."

A smirk crept across Pearce's face. "Right." He shook his head. "Anything else?"

"No."

Pearce left as unconcerned as he had been when he arrived.

CHAPTER 25

HAROLD PEARCE WAS NOT A HAPPY MAN. NOT THAT HE WAS EVER cheerful, but this assignment had soured his stomach. After he left Hublein's office, he removed a bottle of Mylanta from his jacket pocket and took a swallow. How long had it been since his gut had bothered him this way? Five years? Maybe six. The last time he got stuck, idling in an office at the Pentagon. He had spent ten months wiping the noses of a bunch of West Point colonels. Nabobs. Biding their time until their pensions kicked in.

He rode the elevator to the basement, took another swig of the antacid, and walked down the windowless hallway toward his office.

What the hell was he doing here? Eight years in army intel, two in the Gulf, a decade with CIA Special Ops, and here he sat in No-Fucking-Where, Alabama, babysitting a couple of eggheads and a basket full of nutcases. He should still be in Special Ops where he belonged. Where his skills could be most effective. How many terminations had he done for them? There were a dozen he knew for sure. They had died before his eyes, some in his hands, exhaling their last breath in his face. Explosives, sniper rifles, blades, he had used them all. How many extractions had he done? The two pilots near Baghdad and the three spooks imprisoned in Iran that he could remember off the top of his head. Yet, here he sat. Maybe he shouldn't have punched out General McKesson. Fuck him. He was an arrogant son of a bitch, anyway.

Of course, he had accepted this job. What choice did he really have? McKesson blew up his military career. Special Ops, too. Dragged him through the mill at the Pentagon and then tossed him on the street. So, it was either this gig or doing the security guard thing. Somehow he couldn't see himself sitting in a warehouse all night, eating doughnuts, slugging coffee, and sleeping in front of a TV. Retirement wasn't an option. The twenty grand he had in the bank wasn't exactly a golden fucking parachute.

So, when Smithson dropped this proposition on him, he took it. Smithson better not fuck with him, and the bag of coin he'd been promised better be at the end of this.

He entered his office, pulling the door closed behind him. Spartan would be the proper description for the space. A simple desk, a plain black swivel chair, a phone, a well-worn gooseneck lamp, a heavy metal safe, and a computer. Beige walls. No windows, no pictures.

Pearce sat in the chair and swiveled toward the safe that squatted in the corner behind his desk. He spun in the combination, yanked open the heavy door, and removed his black surveillance bag. He checked its contents, tossed in an extra bottle of Mylanta, and pulled out the cell phone Smithson had given him.

Smithson answered on the second ring. They spoke for less than five minutes. He then booted up the computer and opened the e-mail Smithson had just sent. Encrypted and routed through multiple secure computers, there was no chance of the message being compromised. As he read, he almost smiled.

CHAPTER 26

WHEN T-TOMMY AND I ENTERED THE TASK FORCE ROOM, I IMMEDI-ately noticed the third cork panel now contained crime scene photos from Mike's place. I looked away, refusing to relive it.

Scotty Simpson sat at one of the tables, papers spread before him. He looked up. "Have you guys seen Luther?"

"No."

"He's looking for you, and he didn't look happy."

"What'd we do?" T-Tommy asked.

Scotty shrugged. "He didn't say, and I knew better than to ask."

I picked up today's *Huntsville Times* from the corner of the table. The front page displayed a photo from yesterday's press conference, and the caption beneath read: "Forensic Expert Dub Walker Joins Sheriff Luther Randall, Deputy Scotty Simpson, and Homicide Investigator Tommy Tortelli in Search for Brutal Killer."

I handed the paper to T-Tommy. He gave it a glance and then a soft grunt. His way of saying he wasn't impressed. T-Tommy had a knack for keeping your feet on the ground and your head out of . . . well.

"Anything new?" I asked.

Scotty shuffled through the papers on the table and handed me a page. "You already know the firearms and the autopsy results. Tox screen shows Mike had a BAC of point-oh-four."

"Scotch," I said. "Mike liked Scotch."

"All the blood tested so far belonged to Mike. Sidau found a few hairs at the scene. In the sink and on the towel. They don't belong to Mike and are likely the killer's."

"Any follicles?"

"Yeah. Sidau said he could make a DNA match if we find a suspect."

"I assume he'll do a profile and plug it into CODIS."

"In the works."

"That's more than we had yesterday." I glanced at T-Tommy. "Want to go see what Luther has to say?"

"Guess we have to."

Alice, Luther's administrative assistant, gave us a look as she pushed open the door to Luther's office and held it for us to enter. The look that said we were high schoolers, she was the teacher, and we were entering the principal's office. I fixed a smile on my face, but it evaporated when I saw Luther's scowl. He didn't ask us to sit. He stood behind his desk, arms locked across his chest. This was exactly like the principal's office.

"Well, well. I got a call this morning from Billy Holcomb. Said a couple of guys leaned on him. Said one of them threatened him. Said they forced their way into his apartment. Want to tell me what happened?"

"Nothing," I said. "Took a look at the crime scene. This Billy character gave us the tough guy routine."

"And?"

"And nothing. He invited us in."

"Don't fuck with me." He caught T-Tommy's grin and glared at him. "You think this is funny, Tortelli?"

T-Tommy shook his head. "He did invite us in."

Luther let out a small snort. "Just like that? Please, come on in and look around?"

"More or less," I said.

Luther sat down. "Tell me."

"T-Tommy simply explained his options, and Billy said he'd love to show us his place."

Luther massaged his forehead. "Let me guess. Warrant? Toss the place? Those kinds of options?"

I shrugged. "More or less."

Luther turned to T-Tommy. "Anything you want to add, Tortelli?"

"I didn't touch him. Didn't even threaten him. Not with physical harm." T-Tommy scratched one ear. "Boy seems to like his weed. Might've mentioned a visit from the narc guys. Something like that."

Luther balled and relaxed one fist and stretched his neck as if trying to relieve a cramp. "Let me make this clear. I can't have you two screwing up this investigation. Can't have some citizen filing a complaint or going to the media with some police intimidation story. Clear?" We nodded. "We're under the scope here. The public's wound up tight. The mayor is up my butt. They expect us to track down this guy. They expect us to protect them. They don't expect us to push them around."

I had no response. Neither did T-Tommy. We did nod our agreement. I think mine was more sincere than T-Tommy's.

"Get out of here," Luther said.

"There's one more thing," I said. "Claire McBride wants me on tonight's six o'clock news."

Luther leaned back in his chair, his brow wrinkled. "What kind of questions does she have in mind?"

"Don't know for sure. Probably about what type of person we're looking for. Things like that." I hesitated, but Luther offered no response. The crease in his brow did deepen a bit. "Another chance to get the public involved. Let them know who we're looking for." Luther pursed his lips, as if thinking it over. "Can't hurt," I added.

He gave me a sideways glance. "Right." He did sarcasm well. He shook his head and looked right through me. "Don't screw it up."

"Will do."

"Won't," T-Tommy said. "You won't screw it up."

"Yeah. That's what I meant."

Luther pointed toward the door.

CHAPTER 27

"QUIT CLOWNING AROUND," CLAIRE SAID. SHE PLAYFULLY THUMPED the back of my head.

She stood behind me. I looked up at her reflection in the mirror I faced. "It tickles."

"You're making faces, and if you don't quit, Maria will never finish. We go on in eight minutes."

"I don't need makeup."

"Trust me, Dub, you do." She shook her head and then to Maria said, "We go through this every time he's on the show."

Maria Sanchez, who wore too much makeup for my taste, swiped the soft brush across my nose, causing it to do an involuntary waggle.

"It's not really necessary. You just like to torture me."

"That's true," Claire said. "Maria's only adding a little color and taking off the shine. Otherwise you'll look like a wanted poster."

"I feel like a cover model for *Transvestite's Quarterly*."

"Not likely," Claire said through a laugh. "Somehow I can't picture

144

you in lace and pumps."

"Funny, I can picture you that way."

She thumped my head again. "Play nice."

"All done." Maria removed the makeup bib.

I inspected myself in the mirror. A layer of tan makeup covered my face, and my lips reflected a faint red cast. *Jesus.* I looked like one of those guys from KISS.

I followed Claire down a hall and into the studio just as the anchorman tossed the feed to a commercial. Some guy with headphones clamped over his ears led us past light stands and cameras and over a dozen or so electrical cords that spider-webbed across the floor. He sat us behind a desk to the left of the two anchor reporters and clipped small microphones on our lapels.

"You ready?" Claire asked.

"I look like a clown."

"Not to them." She nodded toward the camera.

The intense lights pulled beads of sweat onto my forehead. Maria suddenly popped up in front of me and dabbed my face with that tickly brush again. She stepped back, examined her work, flashed a smile and a thumbs-up, and disappeared beyond the curtain of glaring lights.

To our right, the anchorman said, "And now back to our top story, the series of murders that have occurred here in Huntsville. With her report and special guest is Claire McBride. Claire."

Claire spoke to the camera, seeming impervious to the lights. I felt like a chicken on a rotisserie.

"Tonight, we are fortunate to have with us a man many of you know from his books and from past appearances on this and other news programs. You might also remember that Dub Walker helped with the capture of Billy Wayne Packwood, a notorious local serial killer. Now he is working with the joint sheriff's department and HPD task force to help track the brutal murderer who has claimed the lives of three people. Dub, thank you for being here."

"Thanks for having me."

"Let me first ask . . . is the task force any closer to apprehending the killer?"

"The crime scenes have yielded some evidence that we believe will ultimately lead to his capture. Let's say we're cautiously optimistic."

Claire had on her professional face and had locked in her reporter's voice. At Sammy's or in any other social setting, she was tough, witty, and at times more than a bit crude. Her speech took on its natural drawl. Particularly after a couple of drinks. But here, at work, her face, voice, body language, everything changed. A pro in every respect. Of course, I pictured her with a bourbon in her hand. Or maybe in lace and pumps.

"We talked before we went on the air about the type of person who could commit such murders. This killer is different from most serial killers, isn't he?"

I nodded and looked into the camera. "In many respects. Most serials capture their victims by force or by employing some ruse, incapacitate them, and take them to a remote area where the murder takes place. They then hide or dump the bodies, usually in an area where they won't be easily found. Like Packwood did. The individual perpetrating these killings, however, sneaks into the victims' homes at night, kills them as they sleep, and makes no attempt to cover his crimes."

"What does this tell you about the killer?"

"That he's either socially incompetent or a coward. He doesn't have the skills to sweet talk his way into someone's home, and he can't confront his victims out of fear."

"You believe this guy is a coward? Afraid of his victims?"

"Two of the three victims were shot in the head. The first victim, Mr. Carl Petersen, a frail, seventy-year-old man, wasn't. The evidence indicates that Mr. Petersen put up a heck of a fight. I believe this scared the killer, since the other victims were shot before they had a chance to fight back. To me, that's cowardly."

Claire nodded and glanced at the notes she had before her. "From my research, I understand that most serial killers are driven by some deranged sexual fantasy. But you feel that this killer isn't. Why is that?"

"There have been no sexual assaults of any of the victims," I said. "I'd suspect that this guy is driven more by rage and anger than by some warped sexual fantasy. He has many of what we call spreelike features."

"What do you mean?"

"A spree killer is one who kills several people in different locations in a more or less frenzied fashion. Like Andrew Cunanan. The guy who killed Versace. The problem with classifying this guy as a spree killer is that he seems to have a cooling-off period between his murders. Unlike the classic spree killer, he doesn't rush from place to place and kill folks. He plots and plans. More like what we call an organized serial. I'd suspect the guy we're after is a mixture . . . part serial, part spree. At least that's my reading of the information we have so far."

"What else should the public know about the killer?"

"He's six feet to six feet two, around two hundred pounds, and right-handed. He is likely very strong and might work as a manual laborer or perhaps works out with weights."

"How do you know that?"

"I can't give any details. Let's just say the crime scene evidence suggests that this description is accurate." Claire started to ask another question, but I went on. "I would add that he's most likely sexually impotent and may be a latent or practicing homosexual. I say this because his target victims are men."

Claire hesitated for a beat, looked at me, and then said, "How could an impotent coward, as you say, kill so brutally?"

"Make no mistake, this guy is big, strong, and filled with rage. Probably has a short fuse and is easily angered. Probably lives alone or with a family member. His outbursts wouldn't be tolerated by most people. He probably has a history of violent acts."

"He sounds scary."

I nodded. "All that and more."

"Any advice for the public?"

"Until we catch this guy . . . and we will . . . keep your doors and windows locked. If you have an alarm system, use it. If you see any suspicious activity, notify law enforcement. Under no circumstances should you confront a stranger. This guy is as bad as it gets."

"Thank you, Dub. You've given us a lot to think about." She turned to the camera. "You can pick up Dub Walker's latest book, *Multiple Murderers: Nature or Nurture?* at your local bookstore."

The anchor jumped in and began to introduce the next segment. We made our way back through the cameras and cables. I followed her to her office. She tugged the door closed and turned toward me.

"What was that all about?"

"What?"

"Don't game me, Dub. I wrote the book. All that homosexual stuff. I thought you said this wasn't a sex-driven creature."

"He's not."

"Then what the hell was that?"

"Look, we've been on the defense here. I wanted to lob a grenade in his direction. Maybe knock him off balance."

"He is off balance. He's full-tilt nuts."

"And if we can stress him, maybe he'll screw up. That's our best chance of getting this guy."

She blew a wayward strand of hair from her face. "You should have told me. I wasn't expecting it, and I don't like on-air surprises."

I smiled. "You handled it well." She frowned. "Besides, he

might not even see it. Maybe he's not a fan." Her frown deepened. I was pushing my luck. Time to drop it. "Can I wash my face now?"

Claire couldn't stop the smile that crept across her face. She never could stay mad at me. I didn't think so, anyway. "Please do. Don't want you scaring the kiddies."

CHAPTER 28

BRIAN KURTZ LAY ON HIS BACK ON THE WORKOUT BENCH. Two fifty-pound metal plates gripped each end of the thick iron bar that rested against his chest. With a grunt, he shoved the 225-pound barbell upward and, resisting the weight, slowly lowered it. He quickly went through his third set of bench presses, mentally counting the reps, each punctuated with a grunting breath. Thirteen, fourteen, fifteen. He settled the bar in its cradle and sat up. His two-hour workout completed, he went through his stretching routine, then sat at his desk for several minutes cooling down, wiping sweat from his face with a dark blue towel.

Kushner's file sat on the desktop. He flipped it open and read each page for the fifth time. It contained more information than he needed. Much more. The caller had left out nothing. He closed the file, stretched out on the floor, laced his fingers behind his head, and stared at the ceiling.

Who was the caller? How the hell did he know so much? What

was the payoff? He had learned long ago that there was always a payoff. No one did anything just for the hell of it.

Brian knew he could have done this without this guy's help. No problem. Doesn't take a genius to break into a home and kill someone. Of course, Petersen was a bit of a trick. Getting in and out of the Russel Erskine had been dicey. No doubt the guy helped there. Knew the right time. Knew the best route. All laid out for him. Still, he could have managed. It only takes the will to do it. Focus and determination. That's what his basic-training DI always said. Keep focused. Keep moving forward. Never lose sight of the mission.

Maybe that was it. The caller didn't have the focus, the determination, the guts to do it. Sure he could plan, write up detailed scripts, draw little maps. Who couldn't do that? But . . . to go inside . . . into the kill zone . . . to do what was necessary? To stay focused while your heart thumped against your chest and your brain twisted and squirmed and screamed for you to get the hell out? That was the hard part. The scary-fun part. The part that fed the beast. The caller was simply using him to do what he couldn't.

Still, he had to admit, this guy, whoever he was, made things easier. Even if he was an arrogant prick. Like the Kushner situation. He had told . . . no, actually ordered . . . Brian to stay away until he said so. Said that Kushner was out of town until tomorrow and maybe tomorrow night would work. That he'd decide when and let Brian know. What did he think? That he was just his errand boy? Fuck him. If he wanted to check out Kushner himself, he'd do just that. If this dude didn't like it, well . . . let him come over and complain. Brian would like that. See how arrogant the bastard was face-to-face.

CHAPTER 29

I STOOD IN THE KITCHEN AND TORE LETTUCE INTO PIECES, PLACING them into a large wooden bowl while T-Tommy fussed over a pot of his famous bolognese sauce. I added sliced mushrooms, chopped olives, diced tomatoes, and a handful of caramelized pecans to the salad. Crumbed blue cheese, a homemade vinaigrette, and a good tossing followed.

I had invited Claire and T-Tommy for dinner. T-Tommy said he'd come only if he could cook. He had been at it for an hour. Claire sat at the table on the back patio, sipping wine and absorbing the fading sunlight, now only a reddish glow to the west. She tapped on her laptop, a new MacBook Air, probably putting together her next broadcast.

My small two-bedroom cottage-style house clung to the western crest of Monte Sano Mountain, one of the last bumps of the Appalachian chain. Heavily wooded, Monte Sano looked down on the city of Huntsville. As did my backyard and the deck where Claire sat.

The house sat where Old Church Road ended in a tight loop around a hundred-year-old live oak tree. The other end branched off Monte Sano Boulevard, a tree-shaded two-lane road that wiggled its way across the spine of the mountain, ending at busy Governors Drive to the south and serpentine Bankhead Parkway to the north, the only two connections to the city below. The stone remnants of the antebellum church that gave the short lane its name sat at the intersection of Old Church and Monte Sano. It had burned nearly a hundred years earlier, and now only a chimney remained, the stone still blackened from the fire.

As T-Tommy fed fresh fettuccine into a pot of boiling water, he said, "Your birds are attacking your ex."

My birds were Kramden and Norton. Two crows that I had rescued from a neighbor's pine tree after their mother disappeared. Probably killed by a hunter. Dropper feedings, then mushed-up worms and grains, and they grew into annoying young adults. That's when I opened the walk-in cage I had built for them and let them take to the sky. They now roamed all over the county with others of their kind but managed at least one visit a day here. Usually for food or to bring some shiny object they had picked up. Crows are natural thieves and love anything with a gloss to it. Norton was the best thief; Kramden was the fat one. And the noisy one.

I looked out the window. Kramden hung his head over Claire's computer screen as she worked the keyboard. Norton stood to one side, eyeing her.

"She can handle them."

She did. She scratched Kramden's head and gave Norton a cracker from the tray of cheeses and crackers I had prepared earlier. Norton snatched it and bounced across the table and out into the yard. Kramden followed and a squabble erupted. Once they devoured the cracker, they swirled into the sky, still going at each other, and headed west, their silhouettes starkly black against the red-orange sky, their cawing echoing off the trees. Time for them to find a roosting spot.

With the food ready, we settled on the deck table and began to eat. The pasta was great, as usual. T-Tommy knew his way around the kitchen. Learned it from his mother. Old family recipes. We washed it down with some Biale Black Chicken Zinfandel.

During dinner, we talked about the case. Nothing new, just a rehashing of what we had. Not much, but I found that talking through cases often changed the way you looked at them. Something that slid by your eye jumped out when spoken. Not this time. Not yet anyway. Maybe when we had more to go on.

Claire refilled her wineglass. She offered T-Tommy and me some. Me yes, him no. "After the show tonight I did a bit of research on spree killers," she said.

"Glad I could inspire you," I said.

"You always inspire me, Dub. Mostly toward homicidal rages, but inspired nonetheless."

"Funny."

"I work at it. As I was saying before being rudely interrupted, these spree killers tend to be impulsive. Rarely plan things. Just act and react. Often attack randomly. Targets of opportunity. Right?"

"That's right," I said. "They might target a particular person or group or organization, but on the way to and from they kill whoever they run into. Andrew Cunanan killed a couple of guys he knew and took off. In Minnesota, Jeffrey Trail and David Madson. Then he killed Lee Miglin in Chicago and William Reese in New Jersey. He needed their money and their vehicles. Then he headed south. Once he got to South Beach, he went after Versace. Maybe Versace was the focus of his anger all along. Maybe he simply represented something Cunanan couldn't have. A club he couldn't join. Could be either. We'll never know since Cunanan put a gun to his own head. Too bad he didn't do that first."

"That sounds like the guy you're after," she said.

"Mostly."

"I also read these guys often go out blazing. Shoot up a restaurant or get into it with the police."

I nodded. "Let's hope he screws up before that happens."

"If this guy's this crazy, wouldn't someone know? Wouldn't he have been arrested or seen a shrink or something like that?"

"Looking into that," T-Tommy said. "And Dub going on TV with you tonight might help. Let the public know who we're looking for."

"Maybe someone will call in with just the right tip," she said.

T-Tommy grunted. "Problem is that everyone will call in. Sure

CHAPTER 30

TUESDAY 9:47 P.M.

"GODDAMN IT. I'M TIRED OF THIS CRAP. WHAT TIME IS IT, ANYWAY?"
Deputy Larry Curtis was not having a good night. He had a headache, his stomach burned from too much pizza, and he felt trapped
in an ever-shrinking room.

He and deputies Marvin Kilborn and Mickey Fitch were rookies.
Meant they got the shit assignments. Like this one. For the past dozen
or so hours, they had shuffled through hundreds of department records
of violent crimes. Four-foot stacks of files filled two tables and half the
floor space in the cramped windowless room. The room smelled of
sweat, stale coffee, crumpled McDonald's bags, and empty pizza boxes.

"It's going on ten," Kilborn said.

Curtis continued his rant. "I didn't hump through the academy
to sit on my ass. I want to be on the street, doing police work."

"This is police work," Fitch said.

"Bullshit."

"Bullshit, what?"

Curtis looked up to see Jeanette Hopkins standing in the doorway, a stack of files clutched to her ample chest.

"Not you again," Curtis said.

She laughed. "I'm not feeling the love here, guys."

Jeanette was the head file clerk of the Madison County Sheriff's Department. Had been for three decades. Today, she had agreed to work overtime to sift through the files and separate out the violent crimes. No one knew the file room better, and few knew as much about crime. Every thirty minutes or so she would appear with yet another stack of files. A never-ending supply, it seemed. At least this time she had only a few rather than the cartful she usually wheeled in.

Curtis took the stack from her. "We love you, Jeanette. But these files? Maybe not so much."

"You'll be happy to know that that's the end of it. For today, anyway. These are from this weekend and a couple from yesterday."

"Hot off the press," Kilborn said.

"You boys have fun. I'm going home."

"Take us with you," Fitch said.

"Hmm. Wonder what my husband would say if I brought three handsome studs home?" She laughed again, turned, and headed down the hallway.

Curtis settled the files on the table in front of him. "This is a waste. We haven't found a damn thing except thieves, wife beaters, and gang scum. I'm not even sure what we're looking for anymore."

"Exceptionally violent crimes," said Kilborn.

"You mean like murders, assaults, and rapes? Then all of these qualify." Curtis waved his hand toward the stacks of files.

"But those are common violence. We are looking for the uncommon and excessive," Fitch said.

"Okay. Let's see what we have here." Curtis snatched the next folder from the stack before him. "A fresh one, just yesterday. We have one John Doe. Now that's an original name. Wait a minute. John has a name . . . Dan Hargrove. Looks like Danny Boy resides on our streets. He attempted to rob a Mr. Brian Kurtz with a knife, but Mr. Kurtz took exception and beat the shit out of Danny Boy. Now, is that common or uncommon violence?"

Neither Kilborn nor Fitch responded.

"They should give Mr. Kurtz a medal. If we had more victims like him, our job would be easy." He dropped the file on the stack of folders to be returned to the file room.

"Let me see that one," Kilborn said.

Curtis tossed it to him and then picked up another file and started thumbing through it.

Kilborn read through the pages and then said, "Let's hold on to this one."

"Why?" Curtis asked.

"It looks like Hargrove ended up in the ICU. I'd say that's excessive."

"Probably deserved it," Curtis said.

"Probably," Kilborn nodded. "Still excessive, don't you think?"

CHAPTER 31

TUES꒠AY 10:05 P.M.

BRIAN KEPT PACE WITH THE OTHER VEHICLES THAT SPED NORTH ON ME-morial Parkway. After crossing Sparkman Drive and blowing past the Alabama A&M football stadium, he swung east onto Winchester. Traffic grew lighter and the road darker. Civilization melted into farmland with only a smattering of county roads and rural homes.

He then zigzagged north into a new, sparsely developed area. Not far now. A few twists and turns and he was on Manfred Drive. Kushner's street. A half mile long and only six houses. Kushner's at the end, left side, just before the pavement gave way to a rutted dirt road that was blocked by a three-barred metal fence. A weather-worn white sign with red lettering hung slightly askew from the top bar and stated: *Private Property*.

Kushner's house, white clapboard over a red brick with brick chimneys at each end, had a large front yard that smelled of freshly mowed grass. Neatly trimmed shrubbery hugged the house, and a dim yellow bulb lit the front stoop.

Brian made a U-turn and headed back up Manfred. Every home was dark except for one where the flicker of a TV screen strobed against thin window curtains. People went down early out here. At the end of the street, he made another U-turn and then parked his dark blue Jeep two hundred yards from Kushner's place. He killed the engine and sat quietly.

Using a small penlight, he again examined the map and other information he had printed from the caller's e-mail. Albert and Roberta Kushner, forty-two and forty. Owned a strip center and a couple of service stations. Gave generously to several charities. Sat on the advisory board of a local museum. Elks Club. Lions Club. Blah, blah, blah.

Made Kushner seem like a model citizen, man of the year. Total bullshit. Brian knew the man's arrogance and hostility. Like the others, he felt he was superior and could be rude and demeaning to those he believed were beneath him.

The last line on the page read: "Kushner away on business. Back tomorrow."

A twenty-four-hour stay of execution, Mr. Kushner.

The caller had told him not to go near the house. That everything was set. That all the recon, as he had called it, was done. *Fuck him.* He stepped from the Jeep. He wore black sweatpants and a T-shirt and snugged a dark blue cap on his head. The weight of the gun and silencer inside the fanny pack he snapped around his waist felt solid and comforting. Too bad he wouldn't be using them tonight.

The night was warm, the sky black. A three-quarter moon hung low above Kushner's. Along the western horizon he saw lightning flicker. Too far away to hear the thunder.

Kushner's house seemed to pull him forward. He walked down the street, past a sleeping house to his right, and then directly across Kushner's front yard. As if he belonged there. He circled the house and found that the backyard was more compact but as well manicured as the front. A birdbath, wreathed by flowers, stood in the middle of the yard; a two-person swing hung between two poles to his right; and thick, unruly hedges lined the far side of the property, insulating it from the prying eyes of neighbors. Perfect.

He crept toward the back door, where an ornate lamp cast a weak light on a small patio. To the left of the door a flimsy screen covered an aluminum-framed window. Entry would be a snap. Cupping his hands around his eyes and pressing them against the screen, he peered into a large darkened room. A big-screen TV, faced by a sofa, filled the left wall. A table and four chairs were to his right and beyond a small kitchen. According to the caller's diagram, the hallway directly across from him led to the bedrooms.

But no Kushner. His wife was probably there, asleep, but Kushner, far away. He felt a stirring in his gut and the familiar warmth rise into his chest. *Not now.* He backed away, fearful he would smash the window. He moved to the swing and sat.

An odd feeling settled over him. A mixture of power and contentment. Here he sat and no one knew. The sleeping woman inside had no idea that the predator was so close. That the one who would end her life, her husband's life, in less than twenty-four hours was here, waiting and watching. In no hurry. A predator is exactly what he felt like. No different than a thickly maned lion on the Transvaal. Surveying the potential prey before him. Selecting the one that needed taking.

Involuntarily, he began to swing, the to-and-fro motion comforting. The rusted chain squeaked softly, reminding him of the backyard swing at his family's house. One of the few refuges he had had. A place where he would glide back and forth and fantasize about running away, living with another family. A normal family. One that didn't stay drunk or fight or scream or belittle.

He took a last look around before circling the house and heading back to his Jeep. As he reached for the door handle, he hesitated. Something wasn't right. He felt exposed. Naked. As if he was being watched. He looked up and down the street, but saw that nothing had changed. Except the TV watcher had given that up and now even his house was dark.

He felt foolish and angry with himself. For letting this feeling creep inside. No one was watching. Everyone for miles in any direction was fast asleep, safe and warm, totally unaware of his existence.

He climbed into his Jeep and sat for a minute. The anger continued to grow. Why now? What had ignited it? Was it his anger with himself? The fact that he was so close to Kushner? The heat and the rumbling expanded.

Drive, he told himself. *Get away from here.* He cranked the Jeep to life, spun a U-turn, and quickly made his way back to Memorial Parkway, where he headed south. Not for long. His chest tightened and his vision seemed to narrow into an endless tunnel. Sweat soaked his shirt. He had to get off the road.

He took the next exit, turned left, and then whipped a right into a quiet neighborhood. He slid to a stop, the Jeep's right front tire smacking against the curb. His hands shook as he rolled down the window. His mouth dry, pasty, metallic. He tried to control his breathing. In . . . out . . . in . . . out. Willing the anger to recede. It wouldn't.

He saw that he had parked in front of a small house. Light yellow with white window shutters and trim. A white two-rail fence embraced the yard. The sweet stench of roses and flowering shrubs thickened the night air. A wave of nausea swept through him.

Kushner might be out of town, but these people were home. Asleep and vulnerable inside their cute, little fairy-tale cottage. He wanted to burst into the house and kill everyone there, no plan, no thought, simply pure action. He could almost taste the shocked inhabitants' fear. That deep, visceral fear that knew no limits. The fear of knowing that death had arrived and escape wasn't possible.

Who would be there? Old? Young? Man? Woman? Child? What would they do? Cower and beg or run? Would they resist? Not likely. He would explode into their lives with such fury they would be overwhelmed, with no chance to resist. He gripped the steering wheel as another surge of heat rippled through him.

Why was this happening? How could these impulses rise so quickly, so uncontrollably? With little or no provocation? He had always had self-control, been able to put aside anger and fear and pain. Football and the military had taught him what his alcoholic parents hadn't. These feelings and emotions were temporary. Ride them out and they'll fade. It had always been that way. Even though he could still subdue pain and fear, his anger had changed into something else again. It could rapidly become so intense that containing it required all his strength.

Like now. His knuckles ached from gripping the steering wheel as he struggled to rein in his growing rage. He failed.

It took less than a minute for him to jump from the vehicle, hurdle the fence, race up the walk, and drive his shoulder into the front door. The door had no chance. The jamb cracked and splintered as he went through. One hinge maintained its grip so that the door hung cockeyed. He charged through the living room and into a hallway. Three open doors led to two deserted bedrooms and an empty bath. A fourth door, at the end of the hall, was closed. Surely whoever hid within the room was awake now. Shocked, confused, disoriented. *Here I come.* He drove his shoulder into this door, too, shattering it even easier than he had the front door.

He expected to hear screams and see eyes wide with terror, but the room was empty. The rage was on him then. He stormed through the house. Tables, chairs, plants, lamps, pictures, chests, a cabinet filled with china, everything fell to his attack. The rampage

CHAPTER 32

"What can I get you?" The middle-aged, rail-thin waitress wore a ketchup- and grease-stained apron. Her red lipstick strayed outside the line here and there, a couple of flecks on her teeth. A yellow pencil pinned her dull brown hair into a topknot. As she spoke, she peered over half-glasses, anchored around her neck by a cord that appeared to be two shoelaces tied together.

"Cheeseburger, fries, and coffee, black," Brian said.

She scribbled on a pad and disappeared into the kitchen.

After his rampage at the fairy-tale house, he had driven around, wrestling with his demon. He took Highway 20 past the space museum with its night-lit rockets blazing white against the night sky, and continued all the way to Decatur. He drove fast with the windows down, the night air rushing and swirling around him. He flew across the bridge at the Tennessee River, exited at Wilson Street, and looped back onto the highway toward Huntsville. Finally, the demon released its grip, and his high settled in his gut, transforming

169

into hunger.

For thirty years Mac's Diner had served customers twenty-four hours a day, every day, including Christmas, attested to by the window sign that boasted WE NEVER CLOSE. As usual for this late hour, it was quiet with only two of its red-vinyl booths filled and the counter empty. Except for Brian, who sat on one of the stools, his elbows resting on the once-yellow, now faded and worn, Formica countertop.

Ten minutes later, the waitress placed his food in front of him. "Ketchup and mustard?"

"Sure."

The burger tasted good, the fries even better. While he ate, he watched the wall-mounted TV behind the counter. A well-dressed man and a perky blonde parroted the night's big news stories: a midafternoon, three-car pileup on 431 near where it crested Monte Sano Mountain that snarled traffic for several hours; a drive-by shooting in West Huntsville; a child nearly drowning in a backyard pool in nearby Limestone County. Same shit as yesterday.

"And now, back to our top story," the anchorman said. "The murders of retired Sheriff Mike Savage, Carl Petersen, and William Allison. Earlier, on the six o'clock news, we had a live report from Claire McBride with her special guest, noted author and forensic expert Dub Walker. Here is a portion of that segment."

Brian focused on the TV as Claire McBride's face filled the screen. "Previously Recorded" appeared in the lower right corner. She sat straight, shoulders squared, and looked into the camera. She seemed to be looking right at him. Then this guy appeared. This Dub Walker. Brian had never heard of him. They went back and forth, talking about him. Saying all kinds of vile shit. He heard words like *sexual fantasy, impotent, latent homosexual,* and *coward.* The demon stirred. Brian's head began to pound, his chest constricted, and he felt heat collect in his ears and quickly spread to his face. He dropped his half-eaten burger on the plate.

The waitress refilled his coffee cup and eyed him over her glasses. "Everything okay?"

The roaring in his head made her voice sound distant and flat. "I'm fine."

She placed his bill in front of him and moved toward the kitchen, glancing back over her shoulder a couple of times before pushing through the swinging door. Brian dropped a twenty on the counter and headed toward the men's room.

He splashed water on his face, welcoming the coolness. He then relieved himself in the single urinal, once-white, now stained with brown streaks from the water that continuously drizzled from rusted pipes. He read the graffiti on the wall in front of him: crude drawings of naked women and ejaculating penises, phone numbers, poetry, and bits of philosophy.

Shithouse poets.

He zipped up and left the restaurant, a "thanks" from the waitress following him out the door.

During the twenty-minute drive home, the skies opened. Brian slowed down and rolled up the windows, leaving them cracked so he could smell the clean, ozone-laced air. Lightning skittered across the sky. The TV interview had soured his mood and rekindled his rage, and now the heavy raindrops that pounded the Jeep's roof only added to his fury. Who the hell did this Walker asshole think he was? Spewing all those lies.

Once home, he was too wound up to sleep. He did several sets of bicep curls and bench presses, but it didn't help. The phone rang.

When he answered, the caller said, "That wasn't smart. Snooping around Kushner's. Trashing that house."

"How'd you know that?"

"All that matters is that I know. The question is . . . are you going to follow directions or not?"

"Fuck you. I'm not your puppet."

"I'm simply here to help."

"You want to help? Give me that guy who said those things about me on the news."

"Yes, I saw."

"And that reporter bitch."

"I'll see what I can find on them."

Brian was surprised. He had expected resistance.

The caller continued. "I'll deliver them, but first we have to deal with Kushner. Unless you blew that, too."

"No one saw me."

"I did."

His intuition had been right. He had felt someone was watching. How? From where? "I don't believe you."

"Looking in a window? Sitting on a swing in plain view? Think that was very smart?"

Brian's stomach knotted.

There was silence on the line for a moment, and then the man said, "You've got to focus on Kushner. He's the one. The . . . how was it you put it? . . . The deserving prick."

Brian smiled. He liked that. The caller was now quoting him. *Deserving prick.* The perfect description. For Kushner, for all of them. "Okay, but then I want those two."

"At the right time, they're yours. Kushner is all set for tomorrow night. Family usually goes down early. Any time after ten."

CHAPTER 33

I WASN'T EXACTLY SURE HOW IT HAPPENED. AFTER DINNER AND AN hour or so of talking about the murders, T-Tommy had headed home. Claire stayed. We watched a movie. I did, anyway. Claire stretched out on the sofa and fell asleep. Until the storm rolled in.

A strobe of lightning and a clap of thunder pulled her upright. The rain drummed against the roof. She walked to the back door and pushed it open. Cool, clean air followed.

"I love a good storm," she said. A web of lightning danced across the sky, this time farther away, out over the city. The pulsing light sharpened her silhouette. Several seconds later a guttural rumble of thunder rolled up the hillside. "It's so energizing." She hugged herself.

I moved up behind her. The scent of her perfume mixed with the aroma of the night air.

She turned. "Want me to stay?"

I smiled. "I wouldn't mind. You?"

She put her arms around my waist and kissed me. Long, slow,

174

and intense. That's how it started.

Now, we stretched out next to each other on my bed, sweat slicking our bodies, and our breathing gradually returning to normal. I noticed that the storm had subsided and now only a gentle rain peppered the roof.

"That was fun," she said, snuggling against my chest. "Even if you did ply me with alcohol and seduce me."

"You started it."

"I suppose you were merely an innocent bystander?"

"Just being polite." I pulled a sheet over us, the air now a bit cool.

"Polite, my ass."

"That, too." I laughed, giving that part of her anatomy a squeeze.

"This was always good, wasn't it?"

"More or less."

She punched my ribs. "I never heard any complaints."

"You never will."

The room and our bodies cooled, the thin sheet no longer enough, so I pulled the comforter over us. Claire snuggled more tightly against my chest, and we fell into a comfortable silence, where only our soft, synchronous breathing could be heard. I soon felt her relax and her breathing slow as she drifted to sleep.

Not me. How many nights had I spent staring at the ceiling, going over and over details of some case? Asking myself questions. At times even leaving the warmth of the bed to walk around the backyard, barefoot, feeling the cool grass between my toes. Trying to put evidence into an understandable package. Particularly cases like this one. So much violence. So many unknowns. So personal. Why Mike?

We had nothing. No real clues that would lead to who was doing this. We had little that even narrowed the search. Shoe prints and DNA. Neither of much value until we had a suspect. I did know one thing for sure: he would do it again. Soon, and often. He wanted it, needed it. That was the scary part. Wants can be suppressed, delayed; needs can't be ignored.

I was exhausted, but fought sleep. I knew the key to this was out there. Somewhere. If I slept, I might miss the very clue I needed when it ran through my mind. Besides, the dream was also out there, waiting. Hoping I'd drift off so it could slide into my head again.

The return of my nightmare the other night was no accident. Mike Savage's murder was no accident. It was God or whoever extracting payment. A debt I owed for my failure.

The phone's shrill ring startled me. Claire stirred. As I reached for the phone, I flashed on Luther's call telling me Mike had been murdered. That call had been in the light of day, but now, middle of the night, it could only be bad news. Another murder?

CHAPTER 34

"DUB WALKER?"

"Yes."

"I'm glad you're home. It's such a pleasure to speak with you now that you're a celebrity and all."

I swung around, sat on the edge of the bed, and flicked on the bedside lamp. "Who's this?"

"You don't know me, but I'd bet you're thinking of me right now."

"Who the hell is this?"

Claire sat up. Concern etched her face. I touched her hand in an attempt to ease her anxiety even as my own rose.

"If I told you, you wouldn't have to work to find out." The voice was cool and dispassionate. "That wouldn't be much fun."

"Depends on your definition of fun."

"No need to get angry."

"I'm not." Yes, I was.

"I think you are. I like that."

"You wouldn't if you were here."

"Is that any way to talk to someone who's making you famous? Maybe I should say, more famous. You have quite a reputation. Front page? A real hotshot."

"What do you want?"

"To tell you I'm thrilled these local buffoons called you in. I'm flattered. They must think I'm a tough case."

"Some are, some aren't. What makes you think you are?"

"I'm smart. Maybe smarter than you. Definitely smarter than the other cops."

"I don't think so."

"Sure, you do. I'll bet you often think the cops you work with are plodding and pedestrian. Don't their simple minds drive you crazy?"

"You hold that thought. See where it gets you."

"It's gotten me on the front page, too."

"Might get you in the obits."

Claire slid across the bed and sat next to me. She pulled the comforter around her shoulders. She started to say something, but I raised a finger and shook my head.

"Not likely. You see, right now, you're deciding if this call can be traced. It can't. You'll have your phone tapped. It'll make no difference. I'm way ahead of you, Dub."

"For now."

He laughed. "You're a smart guy. Maybe even a tough guy. But here's a little secret for you. You're as vulnerable as your friend Sheriff

Savage was."

I felt anger flush my cheeks, but took a deep, calming breath. *Don't let him push your buttons.* "Why Mike Savage? What'd he do to you?"

"He's an asshole. Rather, he was an asshole."

"You knew him?"

"I know he was an arrogant jerk."

"Then you didn't really know him."

Again, he laughed softly. "What did you think of my work?"

"Not much."

"Your buddy Savage was my best. A true piece of art."

"Maybe in your diseased mind."

"Oh, yes, I forgot. You've proclaimed that I'm a psycho and . . . what was it you said? . . . An impotent coward."

"I think most psychiatrists would agree."

"Most psychiatrists are fucked up themselves. Hardly stable enough to offer opinions on another's sanity."

"Do you know any?"

"Not really."

"Somehow I think you do. I think you have some bad wiring and went to a shrink to fix it."

He laughed again. "Tell me, Dub, do you regret not getting to play doctor? So close and yet so far. Sort of a failure, wouldn't you agree?"

Don't play his game. Dig for information. "What about Allison and Petersen? Why them?"

"Fag boy and the old grouch? They were assholes, too."

"How'd you know? You killed them in their sleep."

"Maybe I'm clairvoyant."

"That's probably it." I paused, but he offered no response. "So, where do we go from here?"

"More of the same."

"When?"

"Soon. Maybe tonight. Maybe the next."

"Who?"

"You want me to give you the address? Maybe you could meet me there, have a beer afterward."

"Maybe before."

"I don't think so. I'll tell you this much . . . it's a couple. They're already dead and don't even know it."

"Why?"

"I have my reasons."

"I'd suggest you focus on me. I'm the enemy. I'll find you sooner or later. You'll fuck up, and I'll be right there."

"Maybe I'll add Dub Walker to my list. Maybe the TV bitch, too. After all, the good Claire McBride is telling lies about me."

"Leave her out of this."

"Rushing to her defense, I see. She is quite attractive. Probably a good fuck, too. Is she? Or was that why you two divorced?"

I ground my teeth, needing to lash out, but instead held it inside, not wanting to give him any advantage. "She's got nothing to do with this," I said. "She's simply a reporter."

Claire's eyes widened. I squeezed her hand.

"Really? You two do go back a ways. Sure you're not still slipping it to her?"

The thought that he could be right outside, looking at Claire's car in my drive, crossed my mind. "Concentrate on me. I'm sure you can find me." I waited for his response, but he offered none. "Maybe you're afraid. I'm not some old man or undersized gay kid."

"Maybe I will visit you. Maybe I won't." He laughed again. "It's all up to me, isn't it? You have no say in the matter."

"Listen . . ."

"Dub, I could talk all night, but I have a busy day . . . or rather night . . . ahead. We'll talk soon." The line went dead.

CHAPTER 35

"THAT WAS HIM, WASN'T IT?" CLAIRE ASKED.

"Yes."

She pulled the comforter tightly around her as if to protect herself. "What'd he want?"

"Trying to spook me."

"And me?"

"He's not pleased with you, either."

"I didn't do anything."

"Psychopaths see everyone as the enemy, including all the messengers."

I walked to the window and pulled back the curtain. Rain slanted across the streetlamp's light cone. Everything seemed quiet, normal.

"I don't like this crap," Claire said.

"It'll be okay." I turned from the window. "He's just trying to shake me up." I sat on the bed and grabbed the phone. "I need to call T-Tommy." When he answered, his voice was raspy with sleep.

182

"T-Tommy, wake up."

"Dub?"

"Got a call from our friend."

"What? Who?"

"Mike's killer."

"What'd he say?" T-Tommy's voice was now clear.

"Mainly taunting me. He did confirm that he did all three killings."

"Means that he read the newspaper or saw you on TV last night."

"And now he's stuck his head out of the foxhole," I said. "We can use that. Just need to keep him communicating."

"Until he screws up."

"It gets worse. His next victims are a couple."

"Which means you were right. He does know the victims."

"Yes, he does. I don't know how, but he does."

"We've checked every possible connection. Banks, churches, gardeners, meter readers, trash services . . . you name it."

"Check them again," I said. "There's a connection. We just need to unravel it."

"Can I have the boys put a tap on your phone? In case he calls back."

"My cell, too. I doubt it'll help. He guessed we'd do that."

T-Tommy sighed. "I'll see if we can locate the origin of tonight's call. Probably a pay phone, but it's worth a try."

"He may have had contact with a psychiatrist at some time. Get some of the guys on running that down."

"Will do," T-Tommy said.

"One more thing. I have to let Claire McBride know he called."
I glanced at her.

"Why?"

"He mentioned her. Even threatened her. She has to know."

"Luther might not agree."

"I'll handle any blowback. Just wanted to let you know."

"See you in the morning."

I hung up and sat for a minute staring at the floor. My number
was unlisted, yet he got it. He knew about my busted medical career.
He knew about Claire and me. I removed my S&W .357 from the
drawer of my bedside table, flipped open the cylinder, saw it was fully
loaded, and snapped it closed.

"What's that for?" Claire asked.

"Just in case."

"You think he might come here?"

"Not likely. He wouldn't have warned me if that was his plan."
I lay down, and we slid back beneath the covers. I rolled on my side
to face her. "He knows things. About me. About you. That we were
once married. And probably a lot more than that."

"You sure?"

"Sounded to me like he still had cards to play. Like he was
holding back."

"Should I be worried?"

"Cautious."

"What does that mean?"

"Stay around other people. Don't be alone anywhere."

"I live alone, Dub."

"Want to stay here until this blows over?"

"So I can protect you?"

"Funny. I'd sleep better if you did."

"No, you wouldn't."

"That's right. You hog the covers."

She hesitated and then said, "Okay, but I don't do dishes, floors, windows, or cook breakfast."

"You never have done any of that."

"Just reminding you."

"I remember."

"Can I bring my own gun?"

"I've got one."

"I mean a real one. Not that puny-ass little peashooter you carry around."

I knew Claire kept a .44 Magnum at her bedside. And she knew how to use it. "Are we still talking about firearms?"

She laughed. "That one's okay. It's that little revolver that doesn't cut it. If this psycho shows up here, I want to make sure he gets more than a flesh wound."

"Okay, you can bring your own gun."

"Great. It'll be just like a high school spend-the-night party."

Jesus.

CHAPTER 36

EARLIER, CLAIRE AND I WENT ANOTHER ROUND IN THE SHOWER. I guess we needed it. Before last night, we hadn't hooked up, as they say, in more than six months. In the years since our divorce, we had run hot and cold. We'd go on a streak and then cool off. Seemed to work fairly well for both of us.

This morning was her fault. I was under the spray, and she slipped in while I was washing my hair. After we caught our breath, showered, and got dressed, Kramden and Norton showed up. They cawed at the kitchen window and bobbed around the patio table. Must have woken up hungry. Claire took them a bowl of corn. While they fought over it, I locked up, and we headed to our cars.

I told her I'd follow her home. Don't know why I felt the need to do that. Maybe just my innate paranoia. Maybe the killer's call last night got under my skin more than I wanted to admit. She gave me a ration about it, but after I told her I was doing it anyway, she laughed and called me a *knight-errant*. Wasn't sure if that was a good thing or not, but I believe that she felt better that I volunteered. She'd never admit that, of course.

On the way, we stopped at The Bagel. Felt weird without Mike. This was his favorite breakfast spot. A young girl with purple-streaked hair and a gold ring through one nostril waited on us. Pleasant but looked about fourteen. We had bagels and coffee. While we ate, I reminded Claire to stay around people and to come straight to my place after her evening broadcast. She had a must-show event to go to. The mayor was giving her a certificate of appreciation for a series of stories she had done on the HPD a few months back. The presentation and the following reception would be at the mayor's house over on Adam's Avenue.

"Want to join me? Be my date?" She laughed.

"I don't play dress up well."

"I know, but that wasn't the question."

"I'll pass and see you when you get to my place. What time?"

"These deals can drone on. Probably eleven, give or take."

"Just be careful."

She shook her head. "Dub, I'll be with the mayor, the chief of police, and a few dozen cops. That safe enough?"

She had a point.

After watching Claire get safely through her doorway, I headed downtown. The task force room was empty, so I grabbed a cup of coffee and sat at the table near the window. For the next hour, I went over what we had on the killings. Photos, files, my own notes. Didn't add up to much. Then T-Tommy and Scotty showed up. Scotty carried a short stack of files. He tossed them on the table.

"You guys look terrible," I said. Both were disheveled, unshaven, and dark crescents hung beneath their eyes.

"Not much sleep, but we got a lot done," T-Tommy said. "We put the tap and trace on your phone and cell and tracked down the source of last night's call." He nodded to Scotty, who continued the story.

"Prepaid phone."

"That's just great," I said. "This guy's no dummy."

Most criminals are stupid, which is a good thing. They seem to think that since cell phone calls travel through the air, they're immune to tracking. Not like home or other landlines. So, the husband who hires a killer to do in his wife makes a handful of calls to the trigger-man right before and right after the murder. Then denies knowing the killer. His cell records show the time, duration, and the number called for every call he made. Or received. Oops. Easy money for a prosecutor.

Cell tracking can also show the general area where the call was made. Which tower routed the call. If the caller is moving, he'll switch towers along his route and that, too, can be tracked. I'd seen many cases cracked on just such evidence. A killer's protest that he was nowhere near the crime scene goes up in smoke when it's discovered his cell phone pinged a nearby tower around the time of the murder.

None of this gives you the name of who actually made the calls, and that little bit of information is critical to solving the case. The phone is, of course, registered, and the first person the police will visit is the guy who pays the bill. He'll have some explaining to do. Was it you? Who had access to the phone at the time of the calls? That kind of thing.

Prepaid cell phones are a different story. Tracing the owner is a bitch. Actually impossible. Anyone can simply walk in, pay cash, and walk out with a phone. Activation's a snap. A single call to the company with a false name and address will do. Leaves no way to trace it back to the user. The phone will work until the purchased minutes run out. The owner can then buy more time or simply toss the phone and get a new one. Drug dealers use them all the time.

"We have the cell carrier in the loop, so we'll know immediately when and where the phone is used again," Scotty said.

"Where did last night's call come from?" I asked.

"A tower out near the Cummings Research Park. Caller was stationary, or at least didn't jump towers."

"Any other calls on it?"

Scotty shook his head. "First one."

"So it's a new phone."

"Not exactly," T-Tommy said. "We traced the codes. This was one of forty or so phones clipped from a warehouse a few months ago."

"Which means, unless we find who stole them, there's no way to trace them," I said.

"We might have a line on that," T-Tommy said.

"How?"

"Not how, who. Shaniqua Waters. Head of Satan's Sisters. The Sisters have been in the phone and credit card racket for years. Anything on the street she probably had a hand in, and if not, she'll know who did."

"Anything new on the victims?" I asked.

Scotty shook his head. "Nothing. It's as if they lived on different planets."

"They didn't." I finished my coffee and tossed the empty cup into the trash. "The killer knew them, and according to what he said last night, knows his future victims. The question is . . . why did these victims attract his attention?"

Luther walked into the room. No pleasantries, he just jumped right in. "Yesterday, when I heard your interview with Claire McBride, I thought you might've pushed too hard, pressed the wrong buttons. Maybe set him off. But after I heard he'd called . . . maybe . . . just maybe . . . pushing him is the right thing to do."

"That's what I hoped," I said. "I didn't expect he'd call me, but I felt that this guy has something to say. A message to deliver. By challenging him, I hoped he would have to respond. Couldn't just let it lie there."

Luther nodded. "You think we can smoke him out?"

"He's watching the news and he's communicating. That's something."

"Downside?"

"Could be big," I said. "He could decompensate. Go off on a real spree."

"Is that likely?"

"It's possible."

"You're not making me happy here."

"This guy's pissed. At somebody. Some organization. Something. That's how these spree types work. The natural course is to accelerate. The killings become more frequent and more violent."

"Don't see how they could be worse," Scotty said.

"They can," I said. "And they will."

Concern crept across Luther's face. "Won't challenging him make him even more dangerous?"

"It might also distract him."

"What do you mean?"

"He knows his victims. On some level. Something about them angers him." Luther started to say something, but I pressed on. "A murder has two participants . . . the killer and the victim. There is a dance between the two. A *danse macabre*, but a dance nonetheless. Maybe they had a relationship of some type. Maybe they simply communicated. Maybe it was a certain look, or a location, or an availability. But something about the killer and something about the victim put them in the same place at the same time and set the stage for what followed. Our problem is uncovering what brought each of them to the dance." I shoved my hands in my pockets. "Or change the dance."

"How so?"

"He's picked out his partners. Maybe we can offer him new ones. If I . . . or we . . . can draw his attention away from them and toward the police . . . or me . . . he might make a mistake."

"You think having him go after cops is a good thing?" Luther asked.

"Many of these guys kill themselves when cornered or commit suicide by cop. That seems better than murdering sleeping citizens."

Silence settled over the room as everyone absorbed this.

Luther sighed and massaged his neck. "I hear what you're saying, but there's a lot there I don't like. Unpredictable comes to mind."

"I wish I could reassure you, but unpredictable is exactly what this guy is. Can't say I've ever run across anyone like him. Last night I tried to piss him off. Nothing. Kept his cool. It's as if he lets out his demons only in very controlled circumstances. I don't think a meltdown is likely."

"But you can't be sure?"

"Mostly."

"I don't like mostly."

I leaned against the window frame. "The call last night proves he's following the news. If we can work him, he might say the wrong thing, give himself away." I captured Luther's gaze. "I think I should do another TV spot. Push harder. Up the ante a bit."

Deep furrows wrinkled his brow. I knew he was considering the angles, the fallout if things went south. "I can't say I'm entirely convinced, but it's the best thing we've got. Let's run with it." He started toward the door but stopped and looked back at me. "If this goes to shit, we'll have a ton of explaining to do." Then he was gone.

"And guess which way shit flows," T-Tommy said.

Scotty pointed to the files he had tossed on the table earlier. "The boys went through over twelve hundred files yesterday. Covered the last four years. Pulled out the extremely violent ones. Ones where the perpetrator wasn't in jail or dead at the time of these murders. Thirty-four in all. I've been through them, and I think only half a dozen are possibles. I have guys following up on all of them, but wanted your thoughts on these."

"Will do," I said. "First I want to call Claire. See if I can get on her six o'clock report."

"I've got to head back over to the Wheeler office and hook up with some of the patrol guys," Scotty said. "Catch you guys later."

"I'm off to harass the Sisters," T-Tommy said.

"Mind if I go with you?" I asked.

"Sure. Make your call. I need to chat with Luther for a minute. Back in a few."

I called Claire. "How's it going?"

"What can I do for you?" So much for sweet talk. Claire was back in work mode.

"Another interview. Tonight. Think you can swing it?"

"Will tomorrow work?"

"Not tonight?"

"Maybe. What is it? Something big?"

"Just need a vehicle to talk to the killer."

"So you want to use me?"

"Pretty much."

I heard her cover the phone and say something to someone. Then she was back. "Sorry. You think this guy'll be watching?"

"He did last night. Guys like him always do. It's a pride-in-workmanship deal."

"Let me see what I can work out."

"I owe you."

"Yes, you do." She laughed and hung up.

I shuffled through the six files Scotty had left. Robert Swenson. Beat his girlfriend to death with a tire iron. Two months ago. Long record of assaults. Out on parole at the time of this attack. Warrant out on him. Whereabouts not known. Possible. I put that one on the table to my right.

The next two were spousal abusers. Repeaters, but no arrests for anything else. Looks like money sparked one of them and an affair the other. Neither was our guy. The focus of their anger was right there, in the house. Someone should abuse them, though. I moved them to my left.

Next was Brian Kurtz. Put a mugger in the ICU. Two days ago. History of arrests. Mostly for assaults and fighting. Sees a shrink. Another possible.

Next guy, Frankie Alvarez, fired a gun through a neighbor's house and then attacked him with bricks when he came outside. Two other arrests for assault. One at work and one involving a road rage incident. Possible.

Last guy attacked his mailman. Two years ago. With a chain saw. Mailman used his bag for defense. Chain shredded it, but the carrier got away unscathed. Dude avoided a Federal beef for mail destruction by pleading guilty, doing sixty days in County, two hundred hours of community service, and completing an anger management course. Nothing since then. His file went on the left-hand stack.

Our guy wasn't likely a first timer. Or a wife beater. He had a more dangerous-looking record. Like Swenson, Kurtz, and Alvarez.

CHAPTER 37

THE ER WAS QUIET. EARLIER, A STEADY STREAM OF PATIENTS HAD kept Dr. Charlie Beck and the crew busy, but now only a fretful, colicky infant, cradled in his mother's arms, remained.

Marcy Clark plopped a new chart in front of Charlie. "Our favorite patient is back."

He looked at the name: *Brian Kurtz.*

"Didn't you go meet with his doc the other day?" Marcy asked. "At that research institute?"

"Yeah."

"What's that place like?"

"Plush to the extreme."

"That's what I've heard." She tapped the chart. "What'd he say about our bad boy?"

"Has PTSD, according to Dr. Hublein. Got him on some new drug."

"Doesn't seem to be working."

Charlie collected the chart and stood. "Let's get this over with."

196

Brian sat on an exam table, his arm resting on a metal surgical stand. He seemed calmer than Charlie remembered. Could he have been wrong about Brian? Maybe over-read the situation? After all, he came in right after a fight with an armed attacker. That could explain his agitation. He surely appeared relaxed now.

"Let's see how that wound's doing," Charlie said.

Marcy removed the dressing. "Looks good."

Brian opened and closed his fist. "It's not sore or anything. Can't even tell it's there most the time."

Marcy cleaned the area with Betadine-soaked gauze, patted it dry, and redressed the wound.

"Keep it clean and covered," Charlie said. "Come back in five days and we'll get those sutures out."

"Okay."

"How's everything else going?"

"Like what?" Brian's eyes darted back and forth between the two of them.

"You went through a traumatic ordeal the other day. It would be natural to experience some residual anxiety."

"Not really. It's over."

"Good."

Brian cocked his head and looked at Charlie. "I got a call from Dr. Hublein. He wants to see me tomorrow. Any idea why?"

"I spoke with him after you were here."

"Actually, you went to see him." Agitation crept into his

voice. "Why?"

"He's your doctor. I wanted to keep him in the loop. That's just good medicine. We do that routinely."

Brian gripped the table, blanching his knuckles. "Do you personally visit the doctors of every person you treat?"

Charlie glanced at Marcy, noticing the door behind her had drifted closed. "No."

Brian gave a smirking grunt. "Just me, I guess."

Charlie offered what he hoped was a benevolent smile. "You've got to admit that what happened the other day was a little unusual."

"Really? In what way?"

"You beat that man severely."

"I could have done worse."

Charlie involuntarily took a half step back. Hoping to defuse the situation, he said, "The mugger's recovering very well."

"Too bad." Brian's eyes were as cold and blue as packed ice.

"Why don't you talk this over with Dr. Hublein?"

"Thanks to you, I have to." He raised his arm, balled and released his fist a couple of times, and then twisted his forearm one way and then the other. His gaze came back to Charlie. "You do-gooders stick your nose where it doesn't belong, stir up trouble, and then walk away. Why don't you just do your job and leave me alone?"

"That wasn't my intention. Dr. Hublein seemed grateful I spoke with him and assured me you're okay."

"*Okay*? What the hell does that mean?" His jaw muscles hardened and his neck veins became thick ropes.

"He said you had some problems, but were doing very well with treatment."

"My problems, real or imagined, are not your concern."

Marcy opened the door slightly.

"Go ahead," Brian said. "Open it all the way if that makes you feel safer."

"It's not that," Marcy said. "We have other patients I need to tend to."

"Doesn't look very busy around here to me." Brian slid off the table and walked through the door, bumping Marcy with his shoulder in the process. She caught the wall to maintain balance. At the end of the corridor, the automatic doors hissed open and Brian disappeared into the parking lot.

"Jesus," Marcy said. "That kid's a time bomb." She elbowed Charlie. "You're walking me to my car after my shift."

CHAPTER 38

T-TOMMY AND I PILED INTO MY PORSCHE. TIME TO SEE THE Sisters. On the way, T-Tommy gave me a thumbnail of the Sisters' history.

Satan's Sisters was a black girl gang that held sway over a twelve-block section of West Huntsville. Only female gang in town. Didn't make them any less dangerous. Shaniqua Waters took over a year earlier when their previous leader, Lynette Baldwin, gunned down Ron Dog Jefferson, head of the Black Pythons, in a drive-by. Rumor was that Shaniqua had been behind the wheel. The Pythons had moved in on the Sisters' crystal meth trade. Lynette took exception. Ron Dog and two of his pals went down. Lynette did, too. Two days later, in a motel parking lot. She managed to wound one officer, but three others pumped eighteen rounds into her. End of story.

The Sisters not only dealt meth but also GHB, marijuana, and sometimes weapons. This meant they were always armed and high. Dangerous combination. The reason we were dropping by was that they also had a big stake in the stolen property trade, particularly

200

credit cards and electronics. The stolen phones, if not actually lifted by the Sisters, would have passed through Shaniqua's hands.

T-Tommy laid out Shaniqua's story, too. Unwed fifteen-year-old mother brought her into the world. Her father bailed long before Shaniqua took her first breath. Molested at eight by a neighbor who was still doing time down at Holman. Hooked up with the Sisters at ten. Did a juve stretch for armed robbery at thirteen. Out at eighteen. Couple of tags for assault since then but no major stuff. None that would stick anyway. Besides being the wheelman in the Ron Dog job, she was suspected in three other murders.

"How're you going to play this?" I asked.

T-Tommy shrugged. "Straight up. The Sisters don't take shit from anyone, including someone with a badge. But an implied threat might work. They like to stay off the radar."

"Would a little cash help?"

"Couldn't hurt."

"Maybe a couple of Benjamins?" I asked.

"Sounds good."

I turned off Governor's Drive onto Seminole and then, at the now derelict and abandoned, red-brick Dallas Mill, swung onto Ninth Avenue, a four-lane street famous for halfway houses, shelters, and hookers. It was also the home of Satan's Sisters. The white clapboard structure, sort of a criminal sorority house, appeared empty. I parked in the driveway. T-Tommy led the way around back, where we found the Sisters.

They had turned the backyard garage into a gym of sorts. Barbells, benches, stacks of weights. The garage door stood open. One Sister doing bench presses. Another spotting her. Three others looked up as we approached. The lifter settled the bar back on the cradle. One of the girls tapped her shoulder and nodded toward us. The girl rolled up to a sitting position, stood, and walked out into the sunlight. The others followed, spreading out behind her. Not a smile among them.

T-Tommy introduced me to Shaniqua. Six feet and in the neighborhood of two hundred pounds. Buff. Arms and shoulders most men would envy. She wore shorts and a wife-beater T-shirt, cropped enough to reveal washboard abs. Her deeply black skin glistened with sweat and reflected the sunlight. She propped her fists against her hips and cocked her head to one side.

"What the fuck you want?" she asked.

"Good to see you again, too," T-Tommy said.

She looked at me. "I know this white-meat motherfucker. You the book guy. The one on the news."

I smiled, hoping to look nonthreatening. Who was I kidding? Shaniqua didn't look as if anything threatened her.

She aimed her chin at me. "Why don't you get the fuck away from here before something bad happens?"

"Why don't you hear what the man's got to say?" I said. "Might be good for you."

She cut her gaze to T-Tommy. "That right?"

"You still peddling jacked phones?" he asked.

Her blank expression didn't waver. "Who wants to know?"

"I do."

"Why should I tell the man anything?"

T-Tommy said nothing. Just stood there, staring at her.

"'Bout that ex-sheriff getting popped?" she asked.

"Maybe."

One of the girls tossed her a towel, and she wiped sweat from her face. "What you got for me?"

"Two bills," I said. I pulled a fold of money from my pocket and peeled off a pair of hundreds. Didn't offer them, just held them.

"Wouldn't walk across the street for that."

"We're not here to negotiate," T-Tommy said. "You got something, we'll pay for it. If not, we walk. Try to jack me . . . let's just say I can shine a light on your little sorority here. Neither of us wants that."

She said nothing for a beat, two, and then, "What you want to know?"

"Batch of prepaid phones. Stolen a couple of months back. Know anything about them?"

She smiled. Her way of saying she did.

"Any of your girls laid off phones to someone unusual?" I asked. "Not your typical customer profile? White dude, most likely."

Shaniqua glanced over at a thick girl with a knife scar down one cheek, hair razored on the sides, top dyed a mixture of blond and burgundy. The girl jerked her head toward the garage and moved back inside.

"Hang a second," Shaniqua said. She followed the girl into the garage. They huddled near the back and talked, glancing our way a couple of times. Then, Shaniqua walked back into the sunshine. "Yeah. White dude. Maybe three weeks ago. Bought two."

"Only two?"

"It's what I said."

I nodded toward the thick girl. "She remember him? What he looked like?"

Shaniqua tilted her head toward the girl, giving her permission to talk.

"Smaller than you," the girl said. "Maybe five-eleven. Buzz cut. Hard. Looked like a fucking marine."

Smaller than me? Didn't fit the blood spatter pattern. Maybe a dead end. "No name, I take it."

Shaniqua laughed. "Sure. And a Social Security number, a thumbprint, mother's maiden name, and a letter of recommendation."

I handed her the pair of Benjamins.

T-Tommy's cell rang. He answered, listened for a few seconds, snapped it closed, and muttered, "Shit" under his breath. Then he said, "Let's go."

CHAPTER 39

THE PARKWAY PLACE MALL SAT AT THE INTERSECTION OF DRAKE Avenue and Memorial Parkway. The main entrance, obscured by a newly constructed parking deck, faced the parkway. I hung a left into the ground level of the deck. Red and blue lights strobed off its low ceiling and the scattering of L-shaped support walls. Two dozen patrol cars, three ambulances, and twenty or so HPD and sheriff's department officers congregated two hundred feet from the mall's entrance. Other uniforms herded a hundred or so shoppers toward the far reaches of the deck to keep them from the line of fire.

Near the periphery of the gathering and shielded by a support wall, the *Channel 8 News* truck sat between two cruisers. Claire stood nearby, talking on her iPhone. As we climbed from the Porsche, she snapped her phone closed and walked toward us.

"Did you beat the police here?" I asked.

She smiled. "Most of them."

"What's the story?"

She jerked her head toward the mall. "Some dude's shooting things up in there. I heard it began about a half hour ago. People coming out say it's a bloodbath. At least a dozen down. I've heard he's hunkered down with some hostages."

"One guy?"

"Looks that way."

"Any contact?"

"HPD's been trying, but so far nothing. Last I heard, anyway."

I nodded. "I'll be back."

T-Tommy and I zigzagged through the haphazard arrangement of police cars until we reached a quasi-police barricade—two HPD squad cars jammed nose-to-nose—only a hundred feet from the mall entrance. Scotty and a half dozen HPD and sheriff's department uniforms knelt behind the cars.

"I hear it's a single shooter?" T-Tommy said.

"Looks that way," Scotty said. "Apparently he's got a handful of hostages in the bookstore. Just through the entrance there. On the left."

"Got anybody in there?"

"Not yet. Perimeter's sealed. Guys at each entrance."

"Any communication?"

"Tried a bullhorn. Called the bookstore. Nothing."

I looked over the prowler's hood. The glass rear entry doors were shattered, pieces scattered over the ground, jagged scraps clinging to the frames. A body lay just inside. No movement. "How many hit?"

"Six confirmed dead. Eight more down that we know of. Two off to the hospital. Neither looked very good. Witnesses say there could be a dozen or so more dead or hit in the second-floor food court."

The thought crossed my mind that this could be our guy. Taking his final bow in an explosion of violence. The thought also crept in that this could all be my fault. I baited the guy. I wanted to draw him out, and this could be the result. T-Tommy apparently saw the concern in my face.

"What is it?" he asked.

"This could be our boy."

"Guess it's possible."

I looked at Scotty. "Got a description of the shooter?"

"Male in his thirties. After that it varies from witness to witness. Tactical unit's on the way."

Two department stores, Belk at the south end and Dillard's at the north, anchored the top of the T-shaped mall. The foot of the T was the entrance before us.

T-Tommy nodded toward the north end. "I'm going inside. I need to see what the deal is."

"I'm going with you," I said.

"No. You're staying here."

I shook my head. "Maybe we can get close enough to talk to the guy. If he's our guy, he knows me. We chatted last night. Old friends now. Maybe he'll listen to me. Worth a try, don't you think?" I could see T-Tommy was mulling that over. "Besides, this could all be my fault."

He looked at me, eyes narrowed. "Stay behind me."

"You can bet on that."

We made our way around the north end. At the entrance, we collected four uniformed officers and hurried through Dillard's. The main hallway stretched away from us. We worked our way toward the T-junction. A middle-aged couple lay near a cell phone kiosk. Both had been shot: the woman in the chest, the man in the head. I checked for pulses. She had one; he didn't. Nothing I could do. She needed to get to an ER STAT. T-Tommy sent an officer back to get the medics, and instructed another to stay with the woman.

We continued, passing three more bodies. All dead. At the T, we moved to the far wall and hugged it as we approached the bookstore. Two more bodies lay near its entrance; a pool of blood fanned out around them. Above them, the store's glass door and front window radiated spiderwebs from several bullet holes.

I heard a baby crying and then a man's voice. "Shut that fucking kid up."

A woman's voice. High-pitched, hysterical. "Please. He's just scared."

I peeked through the corner of the cracked window. Near the rear, left corner of the store, a man stood before a group of people huddled in front of a display of children's books. Eight that I could see—plus the baby. Fear pulled their faces tight, and I could see tear streaks on several. The man was maybe five-ten. He wore jeans and a loose, dark green T-shirt. The Glock in his left hand waved back and forth over the terrified group as if searching for its next target. Must have looked like a cannon to them.

This guy was a nut job, but he wasn't our nut job. Our guy was much bigger and right-handed. The relief that brought—that I wasn't the trigger for this guy's demons—was momentary. The carnage I'd already seen; his voice; the tightness with which he gripped his weapon; his erratic, angry pacing back and forth—his entire body language told me he wasn't someone to be reasoned with. Listening wasn't what he was about. He was dead and he knew it. He simply wanted to take out as many other people as he could beforehand. He had to be taken down—fast. I whispered as much over my shoulder to T-Tommy.

I could feel T-Tommy's breath on my neck. "Got no shot from here. Hostages are downrange."

The baby wailed again. The Glock snapped toward the woman. "Shut him up, or I'll kill you both."

One of the men said, "Let her go. You have the rest of us."

The man turned the gun toward him. "You want some of this? You want to stick your nose into my business?"

"Please," the man said, looking up toward the gun's muzzle. "Just let her and her baby go."

The gun boomed three times. The man jerked back, his chest blossoming with blood. He settled against the display case, dislodging several books. They tumbled over him as his head lolled forward. A chorus of screams rose from the others. Several scooted away from the dead man. The baby screamed even louder.

"Shut the fuck up," the gunman screamed. He ejected the clip from the gun and slammed another one home. He moved to the woman, grabbed her by her arm, and yanked her to her feet. "This is your lucky day. Get your snot-nosed brat out of here."

The woman clutched the child to her chest, but didn't move. Probably afraid to do anything.

"Leave right now, or I'll empty this fucking gun into you."

She staggered toward the door, glancing back over her shoulder a couple of times as if she expected to be shot at any moment. The glass on the floor crunched beneath her shoes. When she neared the door, she saw me. I immediately raised a finger to my lips. To her credit, she didn't react but rather clutched her child more tightly to her chest. T-Tommy used his drawn weapon to wave her toward the rear exit door. She hurried in that direction.

T-Tommy settled on his haunches beside me. "What do you think?"

Through the window, I watched the man pace back and forth before the hostages. He rubbed his chin with the gun barrel. His other fist opened and closed at his side. In profile, his face appeared flushed, his features fixed, his eyes wide, his neck veins protruding. His agitation level was definitely high and rising.

I dropped back beneath the window. "His world is flat, and his ship is about to go off the edge. We've got to do something to distract him."

"I could pop a couple of rounds into the ceiling above his head.

Maybe get him to move this way. Get a clean shot."

I thought about that for a second. "Or he could simply duck behind that bookshelf and unload his weapon on them." I looked back through the window. Two women whimpered. A man seemed to be praying, his eyes tightly shut and his lips moving silently. "Any other way into the store?"

"Probably a back entrance. Off the service corridor."

"Have a couple of your guys hold down the door. You and I can try to get inside."

T-Tommy turned to the two uniforms who crouched behind us. "Got that?" he asked.

They nodded.

T-Tommy and I retreated back up the hallway. Next to the bookstore was a cookie shop and beyond that a metal door stenciled with SERVICE AREA. EMPLOYEES ONLY. It was unlocked. We entered an unpainted, plywood-lined, fluorescent-lit corridor and moved past one gray metal door to the second one, near the end of the hall. T-Tommy pressed the handle down. The latch released with a soft click. "You ready?" he asked.

"Let's do it."

I hoped the hinges were well oiled. A squeak or creak right now could flush this whole deal. I held my breath. T-Tommy inched open the door. Smooth and quiet. So far, so good. Across the room, over the rows of bookshelves, the shooter's head moved back and forth, facing away from us. We slipped through the door, and I eased it closed.

Using the stacks for cover, T-Tommy moved toward the front, while I weaved my way toward the middle of the store. I came to the corpse of a teenage girl. On her back. Three books near her left hand. Two black eyes and a central forehead bullet hole looked up at me. *Jesus.*

I stepped over her and continued to the end of the row. Now only twenty feet from where the hostages huddled, I heard someone crying softly. The killer's shoes squeaked against the tile floor as he continued his pacing. The store suddenly felt hot and the air thicker. I felt naked and stupid. Here I was, almost face-to-face with a guy who had absolutely no compunction about shooting me or anyone else full of holes, and my .357 sat under the lamp on my bedside table. I could picture it lying there. Exactly where I'd placed it last night. Wouldn't do me much good there. I had a carry permit but rarely took it out of the drawer. Last night was the first time in . . . I couldn't remember.

Now what to do? I hadn't thought this through beyond getting close to the killer. Now that I was here, I didn't see very many options. I figured I could just step out and say, "Hello." Maybe stand up and shout, "Hands up." Worked all the time in the movies. Of course, I didn't have the script, so I didn't know how this one would end.

"You. Stand up."

I jumped. My heart did a tap dance before I realized he wasn't talking to me.

"You. Blue shirt. I'm talking to you. Get the fuck up."

"Please." A man's voice.

"Get up and stand over here."

I heard the shuffling of feet. Toward where I crouched. Then I saw him. The man was middle-aged and wore tan slacks and a blue shirt. He backed into my field of view, hands in front of him as if to ward off what might come.

"Please," he said. "I have a wife. And two kids."

The shooter laughed. "Like I give a shit about you and your fucking kids."

The gun exploded. The man clutched his chest and staggered backward. Blood oozed through his fingers, and a maroon blossom spread over the front of his shirt. He looked down at his chest, disbelief on his face. His knees folded. He wavered for a second and then collapsed on one side. His eyes locked on mine. He opened his mouth to speak, but before he could make a sound, his body fell limp and his pupils dilated into two black pools.

Then the shooter came into view. He stood looking down at the man. I froze. *Sitting duck* came to mind. His gaze shifted up, toward me. His eyes widened. The world dropped into slow motion. The gun at his side started a slow rise. I snatched two books from the shelf beside me, knocking several others to the floor in the process. The muzzle continued its rise: my knees, my abdomen, my chest. I hurled the books at him. He recoiled, using his gun hand to deflect them. I stood and began to move toward him. Had to get there before he recovered. Now his hand seemed to move quickly. I wasn't going to make it. I found myself praying that the first one would miss. My only chance.

The first bullet struck his shoulder, the second his throat, the third his chest as he spun. He staggered sideways. His gun dropped to the floor. He followed.

T-Tommy appeared. He kicked the shooter's gun across the floor.

CHAPTER 40

BRIAN WAS DOZING ON THE SOFA WHEN THE CALL CAME. "YOU ready for tonight?" the caller asked.

"Of course."

"No more showboating. Follow the script."

"Yes, boss." This arrogant bastard was pissing him off. "You got anything new for me, or is this a social call?"

"Turn on the news. Channel Eight. You don't want to miss it."

"Miss what?"

"Just watch." He hung up.

I found myself back in makeup, under the roasting lights, sitting between Claire and T-Tommy. Claire had decided to include T-Tommy, so she could talk with both of us about the mall shooting and then move on to the interview we had originally set up.

Claire faced the camera. "To update our top story, the shooting spree of Gregory Thomas Hay, I've just received word that another victim has died at Memorial Medical Center. That brings the death toll for the tragic incident to seventeen with twelve others injured, six critically. To understand more about what happened today and why, I have two special guests. HPD Homicide Investigator Tommy Tortelli and author and forensic expert Dub Walker. Welcome."

"Thanks for having us," I said. T-Tommy gave a nod.

She directed her first few questions to T-Tommy. "As was reported at the beginning of this newscast, you went into the mall in the face of so much carnage and took down the shooter. How did you pull it off?"

"Back door," T-Tommy said. "He was occupied with the hostages, so we were able to sneak in without him knowing."

"I understand the SWAT team was on the way but that you decided not to wait. Why is that?"

"This guy was very unstable. Shooting people at random. I felt the hostages were in immediate danger. Since minutes counted, we went in."

"Because you were convinced he would kill more of the hostages?"

"He had shown that he had no problem with killing. In fact, he shot one victim right in front of us. Without provocation."

Claire turned to me. "Investigator Tortelli is accustomed to being in such situations, but I suspect that you're not. At least not since you were a Marine MP. When was that? Ten years ago?"

I tried not to smile. Failed. She knew exactly when it was. Our divorce was finalized while I was in the service. I nodded. "That's right."

"As I understand it, the killer actually had his gun trained on you when Investigator Tortelli shot him. Scary?"

"Afterward. At the time, there's too much adrenaline pumping to be scared." That was a lie. My heart had been jammed into my throat.

"How did you find yourself in the middle of this?"

"I went in with Investigator Tortelli in case we got a chance to talk to the shooter."

"Talk to him?"

"One of the things we considered was that this guy could be the killer we've been looking for. The one who killed Sheriff Savage and the others. If so, I might have been able to talk him down."

"Was he? Was Gregory Thomas Hay the guy who has been terrorizing the county?"

I shook my head. "Too small. Only five-nine. The guy we're looking for is over six feet. Hay's left-handed. The killer's a righty. And there are other things that rule him out."

"Such as?"

"That information isn't being released yet."

"So, you went in thinking you might be able to talk him down?"

I nodded.

"Isn't that because the killer called you? At your home?"

That I hadn't expected, but then it was just Claire being Claire. "I can't discuss that."

"My sources tell me that the killer called you and actually warned that other killings were coming. True?"

Her sources? A wicked thought popped in my head. What would she do if I said that of course she knew about the call? That she had been lying right there. Naked. That would be fun. Instead, I said, "I can't say."

"Isn't that why you thought you might be able to talk to him? You two had a connection of sorts?"

"That would make sense. If your sources are accurate."

"Aren't they?"

I fought it, but again the smile won. "No comment."

"The Mall Killer . . . as some have named him . . . What do you know about him? Any idea why he did this?"

"We don't know much about Hay yet. Still looking into that." I felt sweat collect on the back of my neck. Wished they'd turn the lights down a notch or two. "He would be classified as a mass murderer as opposed to a spree or serial killer. Mass murderers kill several people in one place at one time."

"What would make someone do this?"

"Some deep-seated anger. At someone or something. A business or the government. Sometimes a person or group of people. The rage builds over time until they finally act out. Shoot up an office, a restaurant, or . . . a shopping mall."

"Is there any way to identify them before they do something like this?"

"Difficult," I said. "Most keep what's bugging them wrapped up inside. Might be sullen or isolate themselves. Might have a short fuse. Maybe not. Friends and coworkers often see nothing out of the ordinary." I took a sip of the water they had provided. "There are various threat assessment groups that analyze workplaces to see if any of the employees are at risk for this type of behavior. So they can intervene beforehand."

"Investigator Tortelli, did Hay work at the mall? Have any connection there?"

T-Tommy shook his head. "Not that we know of."

She turned to the camera. "We'll take a brief commercial break and then return with our guests."

She held her gaze on the camera until someone beyond the wall of light said, "We're out."

I looked at Claire. "No more about the calls. That's our best link to this guy, and I don't want a bunch of goofballs gumming it up."

She nodded. "Okay . . . for now."

I frowned. "Until I say otherwise. Okay?"

"For now."

"Play nice."

"I'm always nice." She smiled. "Until I'm not." She turned back to the camera.

The offstage voice said, "We're back live in three . . . two . . . one."

Claire instantly returned to work mode. "We're talking with Investigator Tommy Tortelli of the HPD and author and forensic expert Dub Walker." Claire looked past me toward T-Tommy. "Let's turn to the other case you two are working on. Anything new on the investigation into the murders of Sheriff Mike Savage, Carl Petersen, and William Allison?"

"We have several clues that are being worked right now. I can't discuss them, but we're hopeful."

"No suspects, I take it."

"Not yet."

She turned to me. "Last night you gave us your views on the type of person who is committing these vicious murders. What else can you tell us?"

I had decided that I would take the gloves off. Jump in this guy's chili. Put the heat on and see if he would wiggle out into the light. Not that I didn't have doubts about this strategy. He had been cool last night. Not even a tremor. But he had made the contact. Had prepped for it. Now, I was choosing the time and place to push him. In public, where it would be more humiliating. The possibility of another meltdown, another mall performance, chewed around the edges of my confidence, but taking a shot at him seemed better than sitting back and letting him set the rhythm of things.

I looked into the camera. "It's likely that he was psychologically and sexually abused as a child. By a male relative or neighbor. He may be a latent or practicing homosexual. He's a loner with few friends. Probably has violent mood swings and a history of altercations. He could have a current or past problem with fire-starting, animal cruelty, or bed-wetting, as these are fairly common among these types of killers."

There you go, asshole. Gnaw on that.

Claire took a quick glance at her notes. "Is it true that the killings have become more violent? Is the killer escalating his activities?"

"During the interview we did last night, I said that I believed this killer is driven by anger and rage. I also believe he's struggling with his rage, having a difficult time controlling it. His personality is deteriorating, which makes him increasingly dangerous."

"So, there might be other victims soon?"

"Unless we find him first, I'm afraid so. Of course, it's possible he might be unable to handle his own demons any longer and could take his own life. Or he might pick the wrong victim and get himself killed."

"The wrong victim?"

"A police officer, for example. Someone who knows how to handle such situations. An equal match."

"But without such a mistake, he's likely to go on killing. Isn't that correct?"

"He's got a real taste for it. He not only likes it, he needs it. Probably has an extremely poor self-image. Lack of confidence. Maybe downright crazy." I leaned toward the camera. Wanted the killer to sense I was talking to him. "The person committing these atrocious crimes has neither the strength of character to suppress his anger nor the mental stability to seek the help he needs. His demons are in control. He's weak, cowardly, and may be suffering from homosexual rage."

"You make him sound like an animal."

"Worse. Animals don't know better. He does."

"You've surely given us a lot to think about," Claire said.

I could sense she was getting ready to wrap this up, so I jumped in. "I'd like to say one more thing." The camera swung toward me, and I could tell the cameraman was working the zoom. "Someone out there knows this guy. Maybe knows everything. Maybe just suspects. Maybe simply has a feeling that something isn't right. If that's you, call the sheriff's department or the HPD. If not, you could become a victim. This is the type of killer that will turn on anyone. Don't think because he's a relative, a friend, a lover, whatever, that you're safe. No one's safe."

CHAPTER 41

BRIAN STARED AT THE TV. *YOU'RE GODDAMN RIGHT NO ONE IS safe.* His anger churned as Dub Walker's words lingered in his head. *You want a fight, asshole? I'll give you a whole fucking war.*

He raged around his apartment, threw a chair against the wall, put a fist through the drywall. Looking for anything to vent his anger on, finding nothing. He knelt on the floor and squeezed his head between his hands. *Now is not the time. Later, but not now. Kushner. Concentrate on Kushner.*

He made his way into the shower and stood under the cold spray, letting it cascade over his head and shoulders. It took fifteen minutes, but finally the rumbling rage receded to a low simmer. Out of the shower, he began to dry himself and heard a knock at the door. When he opened it, Laranne stood there. Just great. He didn't have the time or patience for her right now.

"You scared the shit out of my husband the other day," she said.

"He's lucky that's all that happened."

She moved past him and into his apartment. "He's gone." She smiled, head cocked to one side. "A two-day trip."

"I'm busy. Got somewhere to be."

"Later? Will that work?"

"Maybe."

She pulled the towel from his hands and let it drop to the floor. "Maybe just an appetizer." She sank to her knees.

After we left the studio, T-Tommy pulled out his cell and moved down the hallway, searching for a quiet place. I followed Claire to her office. She pushed open the door and moved behind her desk. She remained standing and looked at me.

"What was that about? You said you wanted this interview to talk to the killer. But Jesus, Dub. You trying to piss this guy off or something?"

"Exactly."

She stared at me, momentarily speechless. Not common for Claire.

"Look," I continued, "we don't have time to screw around here. This guy's headed over the falls. He's accelerating. Losing it."

"You want him to lose it on you?"

"I'd rather he didn't, but if I can distract him from the sleeping public . . . get him off his agenda . . . then he'll screw up. Right now that's what it'll take to catch him."

"I'm not sure making yourself the Judas goat is very bright."

"Bright is overrated." That got a smile from her. "I'm not trying to point him at me necessarily, but to the police. They can deal with him. They're armed and expecting him. The others . . . didn't have a chance."

Claire dropped into the chair behind her desk. "Pardon my French, but you're fucking nuts."

"I've heard that before." I sat down in the chair that faced her. "You were there last night. You know his next victims are a couple. An unsuspecting pair of normal people."

"So you're trying to draw him away from them and toward you or the police?"

"Seems like the best option right now."

"I knew you had balls, Dub. But this?"

CHAPTER 42

BRIAN FOLLOWED THE SAME ROUTE HE HAD THE PREVIOUS NIGHT and again turned north off Winchester Road. Rather than heading back toward Manfred Drive, he now followed the directions the caller had sent and soon found himself on a two-lane blacktop in the middle of nowhere. Thick stands of trees hugged both sides of the dark road until he came to a grassy turnout. Exactly where the caller's map indicated it would be. He eased off the road, snuggled the Jeep beneath a canopy of twisted tree limbs, and killed the headlights.

His Glock and a tubular sound suppressor lay on the passenger's seat. Until a few weeks ago, he hadn't owned a gun, hadn't held one since leaving the military. Then this one appeared. In a paper bag, lying in the floorboard of his Jeep. That was two days after his visit to Petersen. At the time, he had no idea who had put it there. Or how. The doors were locked, with no evidence that someone jimmied them.

That night the call came. The weapon, a gift from the caller.

He told Brian to practice and get comfortable with it if he wanted to avoid another Petersen situation. He resisted, saying that he would never kill again. The caller laughed and told him what he already knew. He had enjoyed killing Petersen. Had reveled in the fear and anger. Knew he would do it again.

He had driven well out of the city to practice. The Glock's weighty feel, hard recoil, and the way it exploded every can or pinecone or tree limb he targeted proved thrilling. So did what it had done to Allison, and Savage.

He picked up the gun, screwed the suppressor in place, and tugged on the gloves. Stepping from his Jeep, he stuffed the weapon beneath the waistband of his black sweatpants and adjusted the hem of his T-shirt to cover it. According to the map, Kushner's place was a half mile due south, through the trees. He pushed a limb aside and stepped into the forest. Clouds muted the moon and obscured the stars, making the night much darker than it had been last night. And quieter. The damp forest floor and moist air, remnants of last night's storm, muffled the crunch of pine needles beneath his shoes and deadened the snapping of twigs that caught on his pants. It even muted the sound of his breathing.

He soon reached an open strip, maybe two hundred yards wide. Dry, brown grass stubble covered the ground. Overhead, TVA power lines swagged from three massive support towers and released a barely audible hum. He crossed beneath them and slipped back into the trees, here much denser and darker. He needed both hands to push aside the limbs he felt more than he saw. At one point his foot snagged a fallen sapling, and he nearly went down. *Damn it.*

Now in the deepest part of the woods, the world seemed completely black, the heavy scent of pine suffocating. He stopped. Shouldn't he have reached Kushner's by now? He turned a three-sixty. Darkness in every direction. Had he gotten off course? Maybe he was going in a circle. He had walked a straight line from his Jeep toward Kushner's. No way he could have gotten off track. The house had to be just ahead. Confident, he moved forward.

The darkness exploded.

A wild thrashing, whirring, cracking sound. It seemed to come from every direction. He recoiled, stumbled, and fell to his knees. He reached for his gun, but it snagged on his waistband. He yanked, but it wouldn't come free. *Come on. Come on.*

The thrashing noise swirled around him, moved forward and to his right, and then faded into the darkness. The silence that followed was broken by a scratching sound. Like something scurrying across the pine needles. Ahead and to his left.

His panic and confusion settled into realization. Quail. The explosive sound had been the wings of those that took to the air, beating against the brush and tree limbs. The low scurrying and scratching came from those that sought safety in the brush. He had simply spooked a resting covey. *Jesus.*

He took a deep breath and waited for his heart to find a slower rhythm. He swiped sweat from his face with the front of his shirt before standing and continuing forward. At the edge of the trees, he ducked beneath a final branch and saw the back of Kushner's house. He squatted near the trunk of a hickory tree. Everything appeared peaceful and ordinary. The occupants were obviously asleep, completely unaware that tomorrow their home would be the focus of terror. It would crawl with cops, newspeople, and curiosity seekers.

The heat stirred. What the newscast had earlier ignited, and the cold shower and Larrane's talents had dampened, was now on the rise. He moved toward the house. Unlike last night, the rear door light was out, and as he drew nearer, he saw that three of the screen's anchor points had been loosened. The window behind was cracked open slightly. His path had been prepared. This guy, whoever the hell he was, was good.

He tugged the screen free, lowered it to the patio, and slowly raised the window. He slithered through and then stood quietly, listening, calming himself for the task at hand. He crept down the hallway. It was dark except for the faint light cast by a seashell-shaped night-light in a bathroom on the right. Just beyond was Kushner's bedroom. He pressed his ear against the closed door. The wood felt cool and comforting.

I'm here, Mr. Kushner.

The doorknob turned easily; the door whispered open. He could see little, but heard the soft breathing of the sleeping couple. He moved closer and saw Kushner sprawled on his back, mouth slack. His wife curled on her side, facing away.

Remember me, Mr. Kushner? Remember how rude, how abusive you were? Of course you don't. I was nothing, an aggravation. Brian rotated his head against the tightness building in his neck. His pulse raced. Pressure swelled in his chest. *Want to file a complaint now?*

He leveled the gun six inches from the sleeping man's face and squeezed the trigger. The silenced gun spit. Kushner's right eye exploded, his head recoiling as the round shattered the back of his skull. Blood fanned out across the pillow. It appeared black in the darkness.

The woman moved, but did not awaken. He placed the muzzle near the back of her skull. The 9 mm lurched. She convulsed with a sharp intake of air, held the spasm for several seconds, and then relaxed with a slow exhalation.

He grasped the man's ankles and tugged him off the bed. His body thudded against the floor. The pull chain of the bedside lamp tinkled against the base. The red numerals on the clock radio said it was 10:33. He dragged Kushner's corpse down the hall to the family room. He moved back up the hallway, but as he neared the bedroom, a dark form startled him. In the doorway, shuffling toward him. He stopped. It was the woman. She tried to say something but managed only a wet, rasping sound, punctuated by gurgles and wheezes. The bullet had disintegrated the right side of her face. Her left arm hung limply at her side, and her left leg lagged behind her as if it were unwanted baggage.

He stepped back. On she came, right arm outstretched, fist opening and closing rapidly like some crazed robotic appendage.

Her remaining eye, glazed, unfocused, reflected the glow from the night-light, giving it an unearthly appearance. Another step back, another, and another. His heel snagged the carpet. He fell on his back. Hard. The woman now over him. Panic crushed his chest and prevented coordinated movement. He flailed at the wall as he tried to retreat, but his feet tangled with hers and she fell on top of him, her fingers grasping at his throat. Blood foamed from her mangled mouth and cascaded over his chest and neck. He slammed his fist against her face, knocking her against the wall. She let out a last sibilant breath, trembled slightly, and went limp.

Brian sat against the opposite wall, sucking air into his lungs, waiting for his jackhammering heart to slow. It took several minutes for him to calm enough to stand. He dragged her body to the family room. As he stood over them, Kushner stared at him with a lifeless eye.

"See what you've done," he said aloud. "See what your arrogance has gotten you. Look at your wife." He paced around them, clenching and unclenching his fists, his rage boiling. "You arrogant fuck. You treat people like dirt . . . and . . . this is what you get."

He knocked one of the dining room chairs on its side and slammed his foot down. The joints creaked, but did not give way. "Goddamn it." He shook with rage and again crashed his foot against the chair. The joints groaned, cracked, and collapsed. He grasped the fractured chair and ripped it apart. Clutching one of the legs, he returned to the bodies, flailing at random, not caring who or what he struck, seeking only to quench the firestorm. His rampage continued until he could no longer raise his arms. He collapsed to his knees, exhausted, gasping for air. Sweat poured from him, slicking the blood that stained his torso and arms.

"See what you made me do?" His voice sounded soft, almost a whisper.

He struggled to his feet and on quivering legs moved to the open window. The cool night air tasted sweet, but he felt lifeless, inert. He turned from the window. The bodies before him produced no emotion. No anger or pity or revulsion. Only relief. And an unfathomable emptiness.

Yet, deep within, he sensed a vague twinge. Weak, tentative, amorphous, but there nonetheless. Usually it was many hours, even a day or two, before it reawakened. Why was it reemerging now so soon after its release? For a moment, he feared it would swell within him and again take control. If it did, he was too weary to fight the monster. Thankfully the feeling lingered only briefly before beginning a slow retreat.

He walked down the hallway to the bathroom, stepped into the shower stall, and twisted the cold-water handle. The shock caused him to flinch, but as the water cascaded over his head and shoulders, he soon felt invigorated. He stood beneath the spray for ten minutes, letting the water leech the blood from his clothes. He watched it spread across the white tile floor and swirl down the drain.

He turned off the spray. Stark silence followed, broken only by a soft dripping noise from the drain. He stripped off his pants and shirt, leaving his gloves and shoes in place, and squeezed water from them. Using a towel from the rack, he blotted his skin and hair dry, and then redressed. The wet clothing proved difficult to pull on, and felt cool against his skin. His shoes made squishing noises as he walked toward the den. He avoided the corpses and the blood that surrounded them, picked up his gun from the dining table, took a last look around, and slipped back through the window.

CHAPTER 43

AN HOUR EARLIER, HAROLD PEARCE HAD PARKED NEAR THE END of a dirt road a quarter of a mile away. His path through the trees to Kushner's was on a ninety-degree angle from the path he knew Brian would take. He had found a place to squat among the low branches of a cedar tree, a location that gave him a clear view of the rear of Kushner's house. Soon Brian showed up. He watched him slip through the window and disappear inside. He trained his night vision scope on the house and waited. For nearly half an hour. His legs ached from the awkward position. How long was this loony going to stay in there?

Finally, Brian slid through the window, lowered himself to the patio, crossed the yard, and disappeared into the trees only thirty yards from Pearce's position. Pearce waited until the soft rustling of Brian's clothes against the foliage faded in the distance. He crossed the yard, slipped on a pair of latex gloves, and pulled his small Maglite from his pocket. He aimed the light through the open window. The harsh beam scythed through the interior darkness. At first he saw nothing unusual, and then the beam reflected off the bloody pile of flesh in the middle of the floor.

Jesus.

He climbed through the window and circled the bodies, careful to avoid the dark splotches on the carpet. The air was rich with the coppery smell of blood and raw flesh. Using his small digital Nikon, he snapped several pictures before returning the camera to his pocket. As he moved back toward the window, he felt something firm beneath his shoe. He picked the object up and examined it. This, too, he slipped into his pocket.

After he returned to his car, he sat for several minutes, rerunning the scene. He had participated in how many killings during the past twenty-five years? Too many to remember. Most often with a single clean shot, but occasionally with a knife, garrote, poison, arrows, or explosive devices. Whatever the job required. Killing never bothered him. It was part of the job and often the best part. The contracts he had fulfilled were professional. Clean, efficient, in and out. Quick and simple. But this Kurtz kid was none of that. Beyond anything he had ever seen.

He rummaged through his black canvas bag until he found his cell phone. Hublein answered on the third ring.

"This is Pearce."

"Yes."

"Get Wexlar and meet me at the institute. Now."

"I beg your pardon?"

"Don't fuck with me. I said now."

"You listen—"

Pearce disconnected the call.

CHAPTER 44

MURDERERS INTRIGUE ME. ALWAYS HAVE. NOT JUST ANY MURDERER, though. Not those who kill a spouse or a coworker in an isolated fit of passion or anger. Not those who kill for greed or revenge. Not even those who kill to make a statement or conceal another crime. These are far too common. Vanilla. Barely make the evening news unless the victim, or the killer, is someone of importance. The truth is that anyone could commit such a murder. If the perfect storm hit at just the right time, I believe that all of us are capable of killing another human being.

But those who kill again and again and again are a different story. The ones like Billy Wayne Packwood. Like the guy who killed Mike.

The real question about multiple murderers was, why do they do what they do? What goes on deep inside all those areas of the brain I had studied in sophomore neuroanatomy? The lumps and bumps and striated pieces of gray matter I had held in my hand in anatomy class. These clumps of brain tissue look the same in all of us, yet, for some reason, there are those whose neurons don't work right. Misfire. Generate too much static. Cross-connect in some odd fashion. Create a life script that the rest of us simply can't get our minds around.

Why do some people, born under the same umbrella of humanity, step out into the sunlight, while others slide toward darkness?

Earlier, after I returned from the TV station, I had gone for a run and then a grueling ninety-minute workout in the gym I had set up in the small shed that sat along the back edge of my property. Weights, sit-ups, push-ups, and three rounds with the heavy bag. I grabbed a hot shower and downed a meat-loaf sandwich and a couple of bourbons. I then spent two hours shuffling through the stack of notes I had put together on the case. I went over each piece of evidence twice, but found nothing new.

Now I stood barefoot, bourbon in hand, looking out over the lights of the city. The killer was out there somewhere. A family in his crosshairs, and I couldn't do a damn thing about it. Except wait. Wait for the bodies to be discovered. Far below, lines of head- and taillights moved up and down the parkway. Was one of them the killer? Was he going to or coming from the couple's home?

I glanced at my watch. 11:15. Time for the replay of the interview T-Tommy and I had done with Claire. I went inside, flipped on Channel 8, and sat on the sofa. The segment lasted eight minutes, including the commercial break. Interesting seeing it from this side. I thought I did well. I hoped the killer did, too. Hoped it shoved a weed up his butt.

I walked out on the deck. 11:25. Why hadn't Claire called? She said she would when she got ready to leave the reception. Maybe she forgot and was on her way. I stretched and took a deep breath. A thin layer of clouds smeared the moon. A soft breeze came up from the valley. I went back inside and sat on the sofa again. It was 11:29. Where was Claire? Why was I worried about her all of a sudden? Because there was a madman running around whacking people. That was part of it, anyway. The rest? Last night had rekindled feelings I wasn't sure I wanted to deal with. Not now. Maybe not ever. We had worked everything out between us. Came to a comfortable place. I saw absolutely no need to mess with that. Still?

I leaned back, rested my head on the cushions, and closed my eyes. My thoughts ran back to the case. I tried to visualize each murder. How did the killer approach unseen? Where did he park his car? Did he simply walk down the street, or did he approach more furtively? One by one I ran through the scenes.

At Petersen's, he made his way to the fifth floor of the Erskine, bashed the old man to death, and no one heard a thing. At Allison's he climbed the apartment steps, and at Mike's he jumped a fence, both clearly visible from the street, yet no one saw anything. It was as if he were a ghost or something. Maybe he was one of those invisible people, right there in plain sight but whom no one notices. I rejected that idea. At six feet or so and two hundred pounds, he would not be overlooked. Especially jumping fences or sneaking through yards at night. Maybe like Robert Johnson he had "gone down to the crossroads" and exchanged his soul for the devil's power. Here, cat-like stealth rather than Robert's musical talent.

The ringing phone yanked me from my reverie. "Hello."

"Hello, yourself." It was Claire. Finally. "What are you up to?"

"Waiting." I could hear voices in the background.

She laughed. "I'll be leaving this deal in about ten minutes."

"See you when you get here." I hung up the phone smiling, feeling foolish for worrying. The phone rang again. "What'd you forget?"

"I never forget anything." It was him. "You were expecting someone else, I see."

"Maybe."

"No matter. I'm glad you're home." His voice was calm and controlled.

"Why don't you come over for a chat?"

"Let's see. Old Church Road. At the end. Gray with white trim. Is that the one?"

The hair on my neck bristled. The bastard had been here. When? Was he nearby now? "That's the one. Come on by, I'll be waiting for you." I stood and carried the portable phone to the front window and looked out. The street was empty and quiet.

"I might take you up on the offer, someday . . . or some night."

"I'll be here."

"I assume you have the trap-and-trace set up on your phone by now." He laughed softly. "It won't help."

"Maybe it already has."

"Okay, I'll play. Where am I now? What have I been doing?"

"Why don't you tell me?" I said.

"I'm disappointed. Can't you even venture a guess?"

"Wouldn't want to spoil your fun. You enjoy telling it so much."

"You're right. Particularly since you can't do anything about it." He paused. "What's the word? *Impotent*?" He hesitated, but when I offered no response he continued. "I've been busy."

I stiffened. Here it comes. "I see."

"The couple I told you about. You should see them. Then, I guess you will, won't you?"

I tried to swallow, but my throat was suddenly dry. *Relax. Don't show your anger. Rein it in.*

"Such a lovely couple," he went on. "Of course, the husband was an arrogant asshole."

"You knew him?"

"Only briefly. He didn't get a chance to say much. Not like before."

"Before? When?"

"When he pissed me off."

"So you've met him?"

"Dub, I know what you're up to. Digging for facts, hoping I'll say something that'll lead you to my door. I don't see that happening."

"Sooner or later."

"Not likely."

"If you were angry at the man, why kill the wife?"

"I couldn't leave a witness, now, could I?"

Wrestling my anger under control was proving more difficult each minute. *Don't lose it.* "Where are they?" I said, forcing myself to sound calm, unaffected.

"All in good time." He chuckled softly. "I saw your mouthpiece McBride on TV earlier, telling more lies about me."

Time to press him. "Are they lies? Our profiles are usually accurate."

"Not this time."

What does it take to get to this guy? "No, I think I'm right. In fact, I'm sure I am."

No response for several seconds, but I could hear breathing. Then he said, "You should be careful what you say. You've seen what happens to people who piss me off. Remember, I know who and where you are, but you have no idea who I am."

"My invitation still stands."

"Maybe I'll do your TV bitch. Show you what I'm capable of."

"She's got nothing to do with this. It's you and me. That's all that matters."

"What really matters is that you'll be sorry for angering me."

He didn't sound angry at all. "I don't think so. You're an impotent little coward who kills old men and women."

Again, no response.

"You still with me?" I said.

"Just going over my options."

"What options?"

"Whether to do McBride or this other couple. A nice young

couple. Both are tempting."

"What couple?"

"Picture-perfect. Young man. Young wife." Cold, dispassionate. *Reptilian* came to mind.

"Do you know him, too?"

"Oh, yes. He's a rude, self-centered jerk. Just like the others."

"He knows you?"

"Not yet, but he will."

Time to try a different ploy. "So you believe they all deserved it. Is that it?"

No response.

I went on. "I know some people do and some don't. Why did these?"

"The usual. They were arrogant and demeaning. Dripping with false superiority."

"I know a few people like that."

After a moment of silence, he laughed softly. "Excellent. I see you studied your interrogation tactics well. Try to establish a bond with the suspect. Feign understanding and sympathy. Gain confidence. Ferret out information. It won't work. I know what you're up to."

"Maybe I mean it."

"I don't think so." Another soft laugh. "I could talk all night, but I've had a long day. And an even longer one ahead." The line went dead.

I hung up and called T-Tommy. "He just called."

"And?"

"He did the couple. Like he said he would."

I heard T-Tommy's heavy sigh. "Say anything else?"

"He's now looking at another couple."

"We've got to get this guy." In the background, I heard his cell phone go off. "Just a sec." I could hear him talking but couldn't make out what he was saying. Then he was back. "Cell phone company. They got someone on this around the clock. Know to call me if he uses the phone. This one came from up north. Came in through a tower near A&M. He was moving, though. South. Jumped towers twice. Probably on the parkway."

"Send some patrols up north. Bet that's where the victims lived."

"Pretty big area."

"We might get lucky."

"We could use that about now. I'll give you a call if anything turns up."

I then called Claire's cell. She answered on the second ring. I could tell she was in her car.

"Where are you?"

"On my way. Is something wrong?"

"He just called. Where are you?"

"Bankhead Parkway. Headed up the hill."

"Don't stop for anything or anybody and step on it. Is anybody following you?"

"No. It's pitch-black."

CHAPTER 45

"WHAT'S THIS ALL ABOUT?" WEXLAR ASKED AS HE ENTERED HUBLEin's office.

"I don't know. Pearce just said to get down here."

"Must be something from his surveillance."

"I assume." Hublein moved to the bar. "I don't like this, and I don't trust Pearce. He's a loose cannon."

"Let's wait and see what he has to say."

"It won't be good news."

"Maybe, maybe not."

"You're entirely too optimistic." He poured two inches of Scotch and gulped it in one swallow, then poured another. "Want some?"

"Maybe I'd better."

He sloshed a healthy amount into another glass and handed it to Wexlar. He then downed his second shot and refilled it before retreating to his desk. He sat with a heavy sigh. "I've got a bad feeling about this."

"Don't jump to conclusions. Maybe it's good news."

"Good news could wait until tomorrow. Good news could be given over the telephone. Only bad news is given in person . . . in the middle of the night."

"Maybe."

Hublein hooked a finger beneath his shirt cuff and lifted it to glance at his watch. "Where the hell is he?"

"I don't know."

"And who the fuck does he think he is? Calling and ordering us here with no explanation. He's a goddamn Nazi."

"Thank you."

Both men jumped. Pearce stood in the doorway. Hublein hadn't heard him enter the outer office or open the door. He simply appeared. Dressed in all black, he carried a black canvas bag over his shoulder.

"I'll take that as a compliment," Pearce continued.

"What's this all about?" Hublein asked.

"Brian Kurtz." Pearce dropped his bag on the floor, its contents protesting with a metallic clank.

"What's in there?" Hublein asked, indicating the bag.

"Things that don't concern you."

"Listen, you arrogant asshole," Hublein said. He pulled his huge frame up and leaned on his desk. "I don't know who you think you are, but this is our institute, not yours."

Pearce didn't flinch, didn't show a speck of emotion. "And my job is to protect it and this project."

"And us?" Hublein didn't even try to hide his sarcasm.

"Protect you, protect the project. Same thing."

"So, what is it?" Wexlar asked.

"Kurtz, your problem child. Broke into a house."

"Broke in?" Hublein said. "Was he caught?"

"By whom? The two corpses he left behind?"

Hublein felt the blood drain from his face and settle in his legs. They felt heavy and unsteady. He sank back into his chair. It creaked under his weight. Wexlar retreated to the sofa, sat down, and buried his face in his hands.

"My God." Hublein clasped his hands together to stop their shaking. "I knew this was out of control."

"It gets worse."

"How could it?"

"He mutilated the bodies."

All of Hublein's nightmares collided with each other. From the first time he read the project protocol, he had reservations. The drug hadn't been thoroughly tested and wasn't yet ready for phase three trials. Why didn't he reject it? Let someone else do it. He knew the answer. Money. Big-time money. More than the last five studies they had done combined.

"Very similar to the other killings in the news," Pearce said. "Sheriff Savage, the other two."

"How do you know that?" Hublein asked.

"I know, how is unimportant."

Hublein hated Pearce's arrogant, cold-blooded manner. Telling this tale of horror as if it was a bedtime story. No emotion. Like a goddamn reptile.

Wexlar looked up at Pearce. "You don't really believe Brian Kurtz is this crazed killer the police are looking for, do you?"

"Looks that way."

"Jesus." Hublein felt faint, and cold sweat erupted on his forehead. "What are we going to do?"

Pearce shrugged. "Deal with him."

"How?"

"By whatever means are necessary."

Hublein took another slug of Scotch. "What does that mean?"

A thin smile lifted the corners of Pearce's mouth. "We can't allow him to be apprehended, now can we?"

Hublein stared at Pearce. His mind raced. If Brian was the killer and if the police did arrest him, there would be a shitload of uncomfortable questions to answer. Why didn't he, Brian's physician, recognize the potential and prevent this? Why did he allow such an unstable person to continue taking an experimental drug? The lawsuits would be staggering.

"What can we do about it?" Wexlar asked.

"Make him disappear," Pearce said.

"Kill him?" Hublein couldn't believe he was actually having this conversation.

"Termination's an option."

"You can't do that," Hublein said.

"We might not have a choice."

"But . . . killing him? I won't be a party to murder."

Pearce stared right at him. "You already are."

Realization settled on Hublein, compressing him deeper into the chair. Pearce was right. "Still, there must be some other way."

"Like what?" Pearce said.

"He's coming to the office tomorrow. Let me take him out of the program, stop the drug. See if all this aggression subsides . . . in a few days . . . a week at the outside."

"And if he's arrested while you're waiting?"

"He won't be. Not if he calms down and doesn't . . ."

"Doesn't kill anyone else?" Pearce spat the words at him.

This was a nightmare. Hublein rubbed his chest, the pressure inside mounting. "You can't just kill him. It's not even his fault. It's . . . it's my fault." There it was. The truth. Hublein felt old, tired, dirty. It *was* his fault. He let this happen. "I knew this was wrong from day one."

"But you took the money anyway, didn't you?" Pearce's smirking grin mocked him.

"Yes, I did."

"You got what you wanted. Now it's time to do a little house-cleaning. That way no one will know about you, the money, or that Kurtz was a part of the project."

Hublein walked to the bar and poured more Scotch. A thousand thoughts vied for his attention, swirling and fluttering in his head like a flock of caged birds, looking for an escape route. "Tomorrow, I'll stop the drug." He was talking to himself more than to anyone else. He slumped into his chair again. "I'll stop it, and then he'll be all right. That will resolve this mess."

"If it's the drug," Wexlar said. "It might just be the way he is."

"Mel, he's taking an experimental psychotropic drug. A drug we're giving to him."

"All his levels have been normal. It's not like he's toxic or anything."

Hublein frowned. "It's experimental. We don't know all the problems it can cause. That's why we're doing the study." He sighed. "You know this drug has a less than stellar history."

"So?"

"Want to explain that to a jury?"

Pearce offered a slight grunt. "You two can do as you wish, but let's be clear on this . . . I'll take care of the problem as I see fit."

"Listen—" Hublein began.

Pearce cut him off. "You listen. Push some paper around. Get drunk. Take a vacation. Do whatever the hell you want, but I'm going to solve this." He collected his bag from the floor. "Truth is, I'm the only one that can pull your dicks out of the fire." He turned and left the room.

The two physicians sat in stunned silence. Hublein finally spoke. "Mel, what are we going to do?"

"Nothing. Pearce is right. Brian should disappear."

"You aren't serious? You don't agree with that animal, do you?"

"I don't like it, but I see no other way out. With no Brian, there's no trail back here. At least not one we can't cover with a few changes in his records. He's a violent kid, and if he vanishes no one will suspect our involvement, except as his caring physicians. If he talks, we're dead."

"Maybe not. Kurtz doesn't even know he's part of the project or even that it exists."

"But he knows he's on a new drug. How long do you think it will take a toxicology lab to figure out what it is? And where it must have come from?" Wexlar sighed and rubbed one temple. "They might then snoop into the others. Test Gregory Hay. Dig up Martin Hankins and test him, too. What if Swenson turns up? That would be four violent killers with our drug in them. A drug they could not have gotten anywhere else. We'd be royally fucked."

Hublein leaned back and stared at the ceiling.

"Like it or not," Wexlar went on, "Pearce might be our only hope."

"I can't believe this." Hublein searched his brain for some other solution. "Tomorrow, I'll stop the drug. Maybe if he improves, Pearce will back off."

CHAPTER 46

THURSDAY   12:32 A.M.

A RARE SMILE CROSSED HAROLD PEARCE'S FACE AS HE ENTERED HIS basement office. Hublein. What a moron. How did he ever get this far in life?

Pearce knew he had played Hublein and Wexlar masterfully. They were convinced he was on their side. That he was their protector, their salvation, their fucking knight in shining armor. What a joke. Right now they were too scared not to trust him. Fear and confusion are powerful allies.

Tomorrow, Hublein would pull Kurtz from the project. Kurtz would panic and grab any hand that could give him what he needed. Funny thing about anger and rage. They're as addictive as crack cocaine. And Kurtz was addicted. Big-time. Whom could he turn to? Who could supply the drug he so needed? He had to admit, Smithson had covered all the bases.

He unzipped his black bag and removed the two cell phones. He laid aside the prepaid one, the one he had used to call and taunt Dub

Walker. He flipped on the other phone, the secure one, and dialed Smithson. He knew this phone was completely untraceable. "Hell, the president himself couldn't track it," Smithson had said. Routed through a dozen computers in nearly as many countries, following its communication path would be no small feat. When Smithson answered, Pearce gave him a quick rundown of the evening's events and then laid out his plan for "engaging Dub Walker more fully in the situation."

"Excellent," Smithson said. "You're going to be a very rich man."

Pearce disconnected the call. Rich sounded good to him.

He pulled open his desk drawer and slid out a photo. He leaned back in his chair and imagined he was the guy in the picture. The guy lounging on a Tahitian beach with a potent drink and a slim young blonde.

Life was good.

CHAPTER 47

THURSDAY 6:21 A.M.

CLAIRE HOVERED IN THAT ZONE OF NEAR-WAKEFULNESS, HER BRAIN absorbing sensations: the softness of the thick comforter; Dub's rhythmic breathing; the warmth of his body against her leg; the unfamiliar, yet familiar, smell of his bedroom.

She opened her eyes to darkness. Perhaps dawn had begun to push against the curtains, but she couldn't be sure. She raised her head and glanced at the clock on the nightstand. 6:21. She settled more deeply into the bed and pulled the comforter up under her chin. Dub stirred but didn't awaken. She looked over at him. His chest rose and fell in a slow, steady rhythm. She couldn't believe she was lying here. This was two nights in a row that they had been together. That hadn't happened in years. Usually it was a hit-and-miss sort of thing. Maybe she needed it, maybe it was him. Either way it was a comfortable arrangement. But now what?

She was practically living here again. That overstated it a bit. She didn't really have any clothes here. Just some jeans and shirts.

And her gun. She had decided that dragging half her closet over wasn't practical. She could always go by home and dress for work. Still, since she couldn't sleep in her own bed, it felt like she was living here. She knew Dub wouldn't allow her to stay home alone. And for some reason she didn't seem to mind. Not really. Why not? Because she was comfortable here? Because she was afraid of the mad dog that was out there roaming the streets? Neither of those reasons were like her. She prided herself in being tough and independent. Not needing the comfort of a relationship.

Get a grip, Claire. This was a temporary situation. This killer would be caught, she would return home, and life would go on. She and Dub would continue as they always had.

Again she glanced at the clock. 6:38. She considered waking him and having her way with him, but decided it was time to kick the day in gear. She slipped from the bed, grabbed her purse from the floor, and tiptoed to the bathroom, closing the door quietly. She splashed water on her face, tousled her hair, and examined herself in the mirror. Not a pretty sight.

She took a quick shower and put on her makeup. She used very little, so it only took a couple of minutes. Now, what to wear? Jeans or the cocktail dress she had on last night, now draped over the back of a chair?

"Good morning."

She jumped and turned toward the bed. "You scared me."

"Sorry." Dub lay in bed, the covers up to his waist, his chest bare. "Aren't you a bit underdressed this morning?"

"Very funny."

"Why are you leaving so early?"

"I've got a newscast to put together. The one I should have researched last night."

"I see. Now that you've used me, you're going to leave me here all alone?"

She laughed. "That's right. Now that I'm satisfied, I can leave."

"I feel so cheap." He half-pouted, half-smiled.

"Poor baby." She sat next to him on the bed. "Want me to get your teddy bear for you?"

He pulled her on top of him. "I've got a better idea." His hand slid down her back and over her bare buttocks. "I take back what I said. You're perfectly dressed."

"Quite the comedian, aren't you?" She pushed his hand away and kissed him on the cheek. "Got to go." She rolled off of him. After wiggling into her dress, she said, "Mind if I grab one of the OJs in your fridge?"

"Sure. There are some granola bars in the basket on the counter, if you want."

"You sure know how to wine and dine a girl."

"I work at it."

"I'm out of here. Call you later."

Harold Pearce ducked as Claire's white Mercedes E550 went by. Parked beneath a broad magnolia tree just two doors down from Dub Walker's house, he watched her turn south on Monte Sano Boulevard.

He had arrived fifteen minutes earlier, intending to deliver his special gift right to Dub's door. Claire's car in the drive changed that. Meant she had been there all night. Meant they were back together. On some intimate level, anyway. A better plan emerged. His gift would hit her much harder than it would Dub. Dub would be angry, but she would be terrified, and if she was terrified, Dub would be furious.

His new plan was to place the gift inside her car, but when she appeared, wearing a sleek black dress, purse over her shoulder, shoes in one hand, obviously heading home after a night of whoring around, an even better plan evolved. The impact would be much greater if she opened the present when alone, with no Dub to lean on and no one to dampen her fear or soothe her revulsion. This was getting better by the minute.

Some might consider this a stroke of luck. Harold Pearce knew better. Luck favored the prepared, and if he was anything, he was prepared. Always. If not, he would have been dead long ago. Stuffed in some sand hole in Iraq or a woodland grave in Bosnia.

He followed the Mercedes across Monte Sano, down Governor's Drive, and onto Whitesburg Drive. He settled in behind her, keeping a two- or three-car buffer between them. When she hung a left on 4 Mile Post Road, his traffic cover evaporated. No problem. He knew where she was going. Bailey Cove and her cute little house. By the time he eased to the curb between two cars half a block away, she had pulled into her garage, and the door was closing.

Now, how to get the package into her hands without attracting a neighbor's attention? At this hour he didn't have the luxury of darkness, and the neighborhood was beginning to awaken. He could simply walk up and lean it against her door. Clean and easy. Act casual and no one would notice. Maybe stuff it in her mailbox. Maybe drive by and toss it alongside the rolled edition of the *Huntsville Times* he saw in her driveway. That would be even cleaner. He could then simply call her and tell her she had a surprise package. As he was mulling his options, another one presented itself.

A boy on a skateboard waggled by him, reached the corner, and jumped off the curb into the street, where he did a rear-wheel one-eighty. He then gracefully hopped up on the sidewalk and headed back toward him, cutting a serpentine pattern.

Pearce settled a blue cap on his head and slipped on a pair of sunglasses. He then tugged a white cotton glove on one hand, opened his black bag, and extracted a sealed envelope. He stepped from his car.

"Hey, kid," he said.

The boy slid to a stop and looked up at him, but said nothing.

"Want to make ten bucks?"

CHAPTER 48

I HAD GOTTEN UP JUST AFTER CLAIRE LEFT AND SHOWERED. I PUT out a bowl of corn for Kramden and Norton and then polished off some oatmeal. I now sat at the kitchen table, enjoying a second cup of coffee. John Lee Hooker and Bonnie Raitt droned "I'm in the Mood" from the stereo. I was halfway through the *Huntsville Times* when the phone rang. It was T-Tommy. Bad news always arrived early.

"It's ugly," he said. "Woman's sister found them. Came by to pick up some photos. She's a wreck, as you'd imagine."

"Give me the address. I'll be there in half an hour."

I hung up and called Claire.

"Well, I see Mr. Sleepyhead's up and about," she said.

"They found last night's victims." I heard her take in a sharp breath.

"Was he telling the truth?"

"Yeah. Kushner family. On Manfred Drive. North of Winchester."

"I'll get a crew together and meet you there."

Claire stood naked in front of her closet, trying to decide what to wear. She still needed to fix her makeup. What she had done at Dub's wasn't close to camera-ready, and a live report would be a must. She had already tracked down Jeffrey and told him to snag the van and meet her at the scene. She stared at the clothes, but her brain wouldn't function.

Last night, the idea that the killer had murdered a couple was merely speculation, leaving a measure of hope. Perhaps the killer had been lying, playing a sick head game, tormenting Dub with his gruesome tales. Now, it was fact.

Think, Claire. Any of the outfits would do. Why was this so difficult?

A knock at the door. She slipped on her bathrobe, moved through the living room, and opened it. A kid stood there, skateboard in one hand, blue cap cocked to one side. He handed her an envelope. "This is for you."

"What is—"

The phone rang. "Just a minute." She walked over and picked up the portable phone. "Hello."

"Good morning, Claire."

"Who is this?"

"You don't know me." The voice was cold, hard. "But I know you."

"Who is this?" She tried to sound forceful, but her voice sounded weak even to her.

"You were there last night. After I called your boyfriend." He chuckled softly. "I'm sorry . . . your ex-husband."

Her breath caught.

"Not much to say, I see. What's the matter? Cat got your tongue?"

"What do you want?"

"All in due time. You and Dub Walker are quite a pair. How cozy. All shacked up in that mountain-top house of his."

He was there. At Dub's. He must have followed me here.

"That's none of your business."

"Oh, but it is." His voice was cold and mocking. "Did you talk about me last night? Cook up more lies?"

"No." *Come on, Claire, get it together.*

"Don't lie to me. I know what the two of you are up to."

She examined the envelope. No address. No stamp. Not something delivered to the wrong address and the kid was just being neighborly. The killer must have handed it directly to him. Which meant he must be close. The kid? She looked toward the still-open door. He was gone.

"Where are you?"

"Very close."

She hurried to the door and pushed it shut. Too hard.

"Go ahead. Lock it. It won't help."

She pulled back the curtain and looked out. Everything appeared normal.

"It didn't help the Kushners," he went on. "You should go by. Take a look. A true work of art."

"Is that what you call it?"

"You know what they say . . . one man's art is another man's massacre."

Her gun? *Fuck.* It was at Dub's. The bottom of her overnight bag. Beneath her jeans. Her chest tightened. Her legs felt cold and dead. She moved to the dining table and sat. *Relax. Do what Dub did. Try to get information.* "What do you want?"

"I brought you a present. So we can be friends. Maybe you can convince your boyfriend to stop saying all those awful things about me." He laughed again. "The envelope. Open it."

"What is it?"

"I wouldn't want to spoil the surprise." The line went dead.

She tore the envelope open. Something tumbled out, clicked off the tabletop, her leg, and fell to the carpet. She scanned the floor. Where was it? She scooted her chair back, further widening her area of search. Nothing. She dropped to her knees and swept the carpet with her hands. She crawled forward and again swept the carpet, beneath the table. Her hand brushed against something. She focused on the object, small and beige in color. No immediate recognition. Picking it up, she sat back down in her chair and examined it.

"Oh, God!" She dropped the tooth on the tabletop and recoiled. Then, she saw the photos, peeking from the envelope. She spread them out. At first, she couldn't make sense of them and turned them one way and then the other. Then the images jumped at her.

Her stomach knotted. She staggered to the bathroom and collapsed over the commode. Her stomach lurched and ejected the OJ and granola. Again and again she retched until nothing else came up. As her spasms subsided, she rested her head on the edge of the porcelain bowl, its coolness comforting, solid, something to anchor to.

Dub. Call Dub. She grabbed a hand towel, wiped her mouth, and hurried into her bedroom. She pulled her iPhone from her purse. Four, five, six rings. "Come on, Dub, answer," she said aloud. His phone switched over to voice mail. "Damn it." She decided not to leave a message. She snagged the first outfit she saw, slipped it on, brushed her teeth and hair—makeup could wait—and headed toward the garage.

CHAPTER 49

"WHAT'VE YOU GOT SO FAR?" I ASKED T-TOMMY. WE STOOD IN KUSH-ner's front yard.

"Same song, different verse." T-Tommy jerked his head toward the house. "Come on."

I followed him through the living room and into a hallway that extended toward the rear of the house. Several bloodstains were easily visible on the tan carpet. Dark rails stretched away from me, and about halfway down a large circular stain spread out from wall to wall. We stepped over the stains and into what was obviously the master bedroom. A king-sized bed sat against the far wall. Blood soaked the sheets and comforter, which was bunched on the floor at the foot of the bed. Two distinct sprays of high-velocity impact spatter painted the headboard and wall. Two gunshots.

"Where're the bodies?"

"Down there." T-Tommy nodded back toward the hallway. "Appears he whacked them here, and then dragged them down to the family room." He led me back into the hallway and stopped near the large circular stain. "Sidau did some preliminary typing. Says this blood's from the woman." He pointed into the bathroom. "You ready for this? This psycho took a shower sometime during all this madness."

I glanced inside. I could see pinkish bloodstains around the shower drain and settled into the grout lines between the white tile.

"We also found a bloodstained towel, lying on the floor. Sidau has it outside drying." He moved on down the hallway. "He then dragged the bodies to the den."

I followed the bloody drag marks to a large room at the opposite end of the hall, where I was greeted by the Kushners. What was left of them. They seemed to be knotted together in a bloody heap. Like some macabre game of Twister. An arm here, a leg there, a raw oval that had once been a face. Distinguishing which part belonged to which victim was difficult. *Jesus.* A splintered chair leg protruded from the mass. The remains of the shattered chair lay against the wall.

"This the entry point?" I pointed to an open window.

"Definitely. Come on."

We went through the rear door to the backyard. Sidau Yamaguchi knelt beside several clearly visible shoe prints on the patio.

Sidau looked up at me. "Got some good prints here. Others back by the property line. In the mud. Good thing it rained night before last."

"Looks like the same pattern."

Sidau nodded. "But here's the strange part. There're two sets of prints."

"You sure?"

"No doubt."

"Maybe they were here before?" I said.

"Afraid not. This one"—Sidau pointed out one of the prints— "was laid down over the others, crossing and smearing this partial here and here. The second print has no tread pattern. Plain sole."

"Two killers?" T-Tommy asked.

"Possible," Sidau replied. "So far we haven't found any of these prints inside the house. Of course, the carpet isn't a good substrate. Just these here and another back there near the woods." He pointed toward the rear of the property.

"Perhaps an accomplice? A lookout?" T-Tommy asked.

This made no sense. Everything said this was a solo killer. Too crazy to have a partner.

"Dub?"

I stood and turned as an HPD officer approached. "Ms. McBride is asking for you. I told her the media wasn't allowed inside the tape. She said it was important and to tell you that she needs to talk to you right now."

"Bring her around the side of the house," I said.

"Will do."

I met Claire as she came around the back corner. She had left the officer in her wake. She appeared pale and drawn. I took her hands. They felt icy. "Are you okay?"

Scotty Simpson looked out the window above us. "Dub. T-Tommy. Abe Lasser just called. He used the cell phone again. Half hour ago."

"Who?" I asked.

"Me," Claire said.

"You?"

She removed an envelope from her purse and handed it to me.

I grasped it by one corner, looked inside, and then removed the three photos, touching only their edges. They were of the scene inside. Three different angles.

"Where'd you get these?"

"He had some kid bring them to my door. Then he called. Said they were a gift for me. Dub, he must have been right there, waiting. He called as soon as I got the envelope."

"Did you see him? A car? Anything?"

She shook her head.

"Sidau, you'd better handle these." I held the photos toward him.

Sidau stripped off his rubber gloves, tugged on a fresh pair, and took the photos. He looked through them and then looked up at me. "This is one sick puppy."

"There's more." Claire nodded toward the envelope.

I looked inside again. "Jesus. Sidau, grab a bag."

Sidau retrieved a plastic evidence bag and held it open. I inverted the envelope, and the tooth tumbled inside. He snapped open another one and slid in the photos and envelope.

"My prints are all over those," Claire said. "Sorry. I wasn't thinking."

"Don't worry," Sidau said. "We'll work around it." He flashed a sympathetic smile. "We'll need your prints, though."

"The kid," I asked. "What'd he look like?"

"I didn't pay much attention, and he didn't hang around. Maybe ten, twelve. Thin, with blondish hair."

"Seen him around the neighborhood before?"

"Maybe. I'm not sure. There're quite a few boys his age around there. He had a skateboard."

"How was he dressed?"

"Baggy yellow shorts, white T-shirt. And a blue baseball cap." She looked at me. "Can we talk? Alone?"

"Sure." I led her to the side of the house. When I looked at her, her eyes glistened with moisture.

"Dub, I'm scared. He was there. At my home. Your place, too."

"How do you know that?"

"He knew I was there. Must have followed me."

"Claire, I didn't—"

"You didn't what? Didn't think? Goddamn it, Dub, you're so consumed with getting this guy that nothing else matters. Not me. Not you. You used yourself for bait, and he's taken it. And now he's following me." She locked a hard gaze on me. "The bastard knows where I live."

"I'm sorry. Not for using myself as bait, but for not thinking that might put you at risk. It was stupid and reckless."

"Yes, it was." I reached for her hand, but she pulled away. "You do this every time."

"Do what?"

"Get so goddamn involved in a case that you don't see anything else." I had no argument for that. She looked at me, her eyes now full-on green. "It won't bring her back."

"I know."

"Do you? Sometimes I think you believe that every bad guy just might be the one who took her. That if you get him, she'll suddenly be found."

I knew that was illogical, yet there was a splinter of truth in there somewhere. "I lost my family. If I can prevent someone else from losing . . ."

Now she took my hand. "I know."

I let out a long, slow breath. "Look, he's doing this to get to me. Mess with my head."

"That's comforting. He just might think that killing me would get your attention. Then what?"

How did things get so sideways? Was I wrong to bait this maniac? Did I underestimate this guy's cleverness? Too late now. No way to unring this bell. "If that's his plan, then we have to flush him out. Soon."

"He was at my home." Her jaw tightened.

"That's not necessarily a bad thing."

"Are you crazy?"

"It means I got to him. More than that, he showed his face. To a kid, but that's something. If we can find that kid, we might get a description."

"I'm glad you're enjoying this."

"I'm not. Just trying to use what's handed to us. I'm sorry this happened, but it may be the break we need."

She shook her head. "You are so goddamn rational I could strangle you." She looked past me, toward Kushner's backyard. Probably deciding whether to use an open hand or her fist when she hit me.

"Look, it happened," I said. "We can't pretend it didn't or ignore it. Let's use it."

"Do I really have a choice?"

"You can walk away. Stay away from me."

She shook her head and offered a smirk. One of those that meant she thought I was an idiot. Seen that one before. "Maybe I wasn't clear. He knows where I live. He knows I was at your place last night. He knows he can get to you through me."

The logic of that was hard to argue with. "Then we have to smoke him out."

Using her fist, she hit me in the shoulder. "If you get me killed, I'll haunt you."

"Fair enough."

A faint smile lifted one corner of her mouth, and she let out a long sigh. "Okay. You're right. I hate it that you are, but . . . shit. What do we do?"

"I'll have one of deputies follow you home, check out the area, see if they can find the kid."

"And if the kid leads nowhere?"

"We continue to bait him until he screws up. And he will."

She looked skyward and exhaled through pursed lips. "I hope you're right." She glanced back toward the front of the house. "Give me twenty minutes. I need to put a face on and get some on-scene footage."

She was back in work mode.

CHAPTER 50

"ANYTHING ELSE?" THE WAITRESS AT MAC'S DINER ASKED AS SHE swiped the crumbs from the bagel he had eaten off the counter.

"No," Brian said.

He worked on his second cup of coffee as he relived last night's adventure. The odd part: it had dimmed his rage, but hadn't quenched it. Even the marathon session with Laranne after he got home helped little. Sleep didn't come until well after she had slipped away, and when it did, it was fitful and erratic. Twice, he awoke, heart racing, skin frosted with cold sweat, and with the remnants of vivid dreams still flashing in his head. This had become an almost nightly occurrence over the past week, but last night's dreams had been particularly vivid. And violent.

He drained his coffee cup, paid the bill, and walked up the street to his Jeep. He glanced at his watch. Plenty of time to make his appointment with Hublein.

He drove. Around Big Spring Park. Through downtown, making

272

several laps of the square. Up over Echols Hill and past the antebellum mansions on Franklin. The tension inside finally uncoiled. For a few minutes. Until he neared the medical center and parked at the institute. He rode the elevator to the fifth floor, where Hublein's two receptionists greeted him with fake smiles, flashed in unison. He had long ago tagged them Tweedledee and Tweedledum.

"Good morning, Mr. Kurtz," Tweedledee said. "Are you here to see Dr. Hublein?"

"No. I'm here because I like this place so fucking much."

The two women recoiled, eyes wide.

Good. You bitches should be afraid.

"I . . . uh . . . ," Tweedledum said. "I'll . . . uh . . . show you to his office."

"I know the way." He walked down the hallway, pushed open the heavy door, and entered. Hublein's assistant, Catherine, looked up from her desk. Her smile evaporated instantly.

"Mr. Kurtz, you're right on time."

"Is he running behind as usual?"

"I don't believe so." Her face flushed. "I'll let the doctor know you're here." He noticed her hand trembled when she picked up the phone and punched the intercom button. "Dr. Hublein, Mr. Kurtz is here."

Hublein hung up the phone.

"He's here, Mel. You want to sit in on this?"

Wexlar shook his head. "Better not. He might feel we're ganging up on him."

Wexlar exited through the side door as Catherine opened the outer door and held it for Brian.

"Brian, please have a seat." Hublein stood and extended his hand over his desk. Brian ignored the offered hand and sat facing him. Hublein settled into his chair. "How are you doing?"

"You tell me."

Brian's hard gaze never left Hublein's eyes as if challenging him. His muscular forearms tensed, knuckles blanching on the arms of the chair. For once, Hublein wished Pearce was around.

"I understand you were mugged?" Hublein began.

"Someone tried to."

"That must have been a frightening ordeal?"

"More so for him."

"So I've been told."

"Told what?" Brian's eyes narrowed.

"That you were attacked with a knife and that you became quite angry."

"Wouldn't you?" The veins in Brian's neck expanded.

"I was told you beat the mugger severely."

"Told by whom? That pretty-boy doctor from the hospital?"

"Well . . . I . . ." This was not going well.

"I know he came to see you. He told me."

"When?"

"Yesterday. He checked my wound."

"Is it healing okay?"

"We aren't here to talk about my arm."

"No, we're not." Hublein leaned forward, resting his elbows on the desk. "Look, Brian, we have a problem here."

"What problem might that be?"

"These things . . . what happened the other day." Hublein cleared his throat. "Your being fired from your job. I'm concerned that your behavior might be regressing. I don't want you to get in trouble again. Like before you came to see me."

"My behavior? You mean like defending myself? You mean like some hot-shit ER doctor thinking I overreacted? He wasn't there, doesn't know what it was like to be scared, afraid that you might be killed." Brian's words came through clenched teeth. His pupils dilated, compressing the blue irises into thin halos. He looked like a cornered animal. "Wanda can take her job and go fuck herself for all I care."

Hublein leaned back in his chair. His ears felt as though they were stuffed with cotton. The room closed in. He wanted to run. "Let's not make a big deal out of this." He hoped he sounded casual. "Of course you were right to defend yourself. No one believes otherwise. It's the fact that the police were involved that's troubling."

"They didn't arrest me. Just that scumbag."

"I'm glad to hear that. My only concern is your well-being, and

I think it might be a good idea to change your medications."

"In what way?"

"Take you off the new drug."

"It's better than any of the others."

"Remember, it's experimental. Its side effects are still unknown. I think prudence would dictate a degree of caution. Perhaps going back to the tried-and-true would be best. For a while anyway."

"I like this one. It makes me feel good. The others made me sleepy or gave me headaches."

"Let's try them for a couple of months. Then if everything is okay, we can go back on the new drug."

"No." Brian brought his fist down on the arm of the chair. His eyes flashed black.

"Look, Brian." *Be careful.* "You know that your probation is contingent on your staying under my care. On your being employed. Wanda Fisher has assured me that she'll take you back once we straighten things out."

"Maybe I'm not the one who needs to be straightened out."

"Brian, if you refuse to follow my advice, your probation could be revoked."

"Are you threatening me?"

"Of course not. I'm trying to help you."

"So, my choices are to do what you say or go to jail?"

"I wouldn't put it that way."

Brian stood and took a step toward the desk. "Exactly how

would you put it?"

The air thickened. Hublein hooked a finger beneath his tie and loosened it. "Your next injection isn't due until tomorrow. Why don't you think about what I've said, and we'll talk then. Maybe I can come up with another solution in the meantime."

Brian seemed to relax. A little. "You can't take me off the medication."

"Maybe I won't have to. Let me give this some study."

"Study it all you want. Just don't stop the medication. I won't stand for that." He turned and pushed through the door, leaving it open behind him.

CHAPTER 51

SIDAU POINTED OUT SEVERAL SHOE PRINTS, EACH STAKED WITH A red plastic flag. He was taking T-Tommy, Scotty, and me on a tour through the wooded area behind the Kushner house. We continued backtracking from Kushner's house, across an open area beneath TVA power lines, to a rural blacktop road. Two crime scene techs were making casts of a pair of deep tire impressions in the soft dirt just off the pavement.

I shielded my eyes from the sun and gazed up the road. The morning sun silvered the TVA lines that swagged above the treetops. They looked like new guitar strings, waiting to be tightened to the proper key. Higher up in the cloudless blue sky, a pair of buzzards gripped the air with broad wings and made wide, lazy circles, searching for carrion.

I tried to imagine the nighttime darkness. The killer pulled off the road here, and then made his way through the woods. He knew exactly where he was going. No randomness here.

278

We made our way back to Kushner's house. Nothing about the structure was distinctive. Nothing extraordinary that would attract attention. Except the couple inside. That was the attraction. Why these people? For that matter, why Mike? Why Allison or Petersen?

"Looked to me like all the prints back there were the Nikes," I said. "None of the others."

"That's right," Sidau said.

"Maybe he came another way," I said. I massaged my neck. "Which means he didn't come with him or follow him. He knew where he was going."

"An accomplice?" Scotty asked.

Could that be true? Could the killer have an accomplice? A lookout? Could a pair of deranged psychos, working in tandem, be responsible for these murders? Everything I had seen or knew about this killer said no. Then who left the other prints? A nosy neighbor? A neighbor who saw this and didn't call the police? No way. Someone following the killer? Stalking the killer? Who? Why? It didn't make sense.

"You think there's two of them?" T-Tommy asked.

"The profile favors this guy being a loner. Too unstable to have a sidekick." I kicked a clump of crabgrass. "I guess we could have another Hickock and Smith duo."

"Who?" Scotty said.

"Remember Truman Capote's *In Cold Blood*?"

Scotty shrugged. "Vaguely."

"Great book. Detailed the case. Late fifties or thereabouts. Dick Hickock and Perry Smith were two losers who killed the Clutter family in Kansas because they thought Mr. Clutter had a safe full of money in his home. He didn't, but they executed the entire family anyway. Their profile indicated that neither would have done it alone. But in tandem, they made a murderous pair. Hickock was the planner and Smith the hammer. Hickock got them there, and Smith went berserk."

"You really think our boy could have a partner like that?" T-Tommy asked. "Someone who sets him up and turns him loose?"

I shrugged. "Might explain a couple of things."

"Such as?" T-Tommy asked.

"The geographic profile, for one. If we add this scene into the mix, we have murders here way north of the city, Mike's down south, Allison out west toward Madison, and Petersen right downtown. Unlike the disorganized nature of the scenes themselves, this widespread pattern suggests a more organized offender. One who isn't afraid to travel. Feels comfortable just about anywhere. Disorganized ones tend to have a much smaller comfort zone. They feel stressed if they wander too far, so their crimes cluster closer to home."

T-Tommy puffed out one cheek and then the other, moving a pocket of air back and forth, before letting out a long breath. "You're saying we could have a hunter working with a killer?"

"I don't know." I looked up. The buzzards were now even higher in the sky. Broadening their area of search. Just like we were.

Difference was, they were looking for the dead; we were hunting for a living, breathing, and very clever killer. "It would also explain the phone calls."

"How so?" Scotty asked.

"Something I can't quite get my mind around yet. The killer is definitely disorganized. Rage-driven. The savageness of the attacks, leaving of the bodies at the kill site, no effort to conceal the crime. Yet the guy on the phone? Calm and rational. Even when I tried to provoke him, I got nothing. A killer this violent"—I nodded toward the house—"would have a very short fuse. He would likely lash out at anyone, particularly someone making personal attacks."

"Great," T-Tommy said. "A pair of psychos. That's all we need."

"That might not be the case, but we have to consider it."

T-Tommy shoved his hands in his pockets. "Dub, I hope you're wrong this time."

You got that right. "I'm going to take another look inside," I said.

I returned to the master bedroom, where I attempted to envision the killer's movements. He crept into the room and stood just to the left of the bed. The spatter pattern and the wound to Mr. Kushner's head indicated he was shot at close range while his head rested on the pillow. Asleep. Never saw it coming. Same for Mrs. Kushner. Her head was so badly beaten no entry wound could be identified, but the blood spatters above the bed indicated she, too, was shot where she slept. Meant that he definitely used a sound suppressor.

I moved back down the hall to the circular stain and knelt. The blood belonged to the woman, according to Sidau. The wall above the stain held more blood smears. Splotches, streaks, and a single bloody handprint. Small, probably the woman's. Surrounding that, the fine spray of exhaled blood. She was alive when she was here. Still bleeding and still breathing. I looked back toward the bedroom and then down toward the family room. A pair of drag streaks came from the bedroom to this area, and then four streaks led on toward the den. He dragged the man all the way. The woman from here. She walked to this spot. The bullet didn't kill her. She put up a fight but died right here. *God bless you, Mrs. Kushner.*

I moved to the den, where several criminalists continued collecting samples from the mass of flesh and bone that was once the Kushners. The musty smell of blood and death seemed heavier than it had earlier. I needed air.

I retreated into the backyard and walked to where T-Tommy, Scotty, and Sidau stood.

"I just called the department," Scotty said. "They're drawing a blank on the victims. The single thing they have in common is a phone call from the *Huntsville Times.* Seems they just had a subscription drive and called most of the county."

"They called me three times last week," T-Tommy said.

"They'll add the Kushners' data to the soup and see if anything pops up," Scotty said.

"Dub," one of the deputies yelled out the window. "Phone."

"Who is it?"

"Didn't say."

I climbed the three steps to the back door and walked to the kitchen. Who would be calling me on the victims' phone? I picked up the handset, which had a healthy coat of fingerprint powder.

"Hello."

"I see you're hard at work."

I recognized the voice immediately. I motioned to one of the deputies and mouthed, "Get T-Tommy." Then into the phone I said, "You left quite a mess."

"Intentional, I assure you."

"You fucked up this time."

"I don't think so," the calm voice said. "Why don't you tell me about it? What glaring mistake did I make that you so brilliantly recognized?"

"You threatened Ms. McBride."

"I thought that might get your attention."

"I'm your problem, not her."

"Since you're fucking her, I consider you one and the same."

"I'm the one who'll put you away."

He laughed softly. "Pretty sure of yourself, aren't you?"

"Basic character flaw. I've been working on it."

"Good for you. The truth is that I don't think even you can catch me."

"You might be right. You might not make it out of this alive."

"Such talk from a representative of law enforcement. Aren't

there laws against threatening the citizenry?"

"I'm the citizenry, and I'm not threatening you. Merely stating facts."

"As you see them."

"What I see is that I'm your problem. Unless you stop me, I'll find you."

"Like Packwood?"

"Something like that."

"I think you just got lucky on that one."

"Or he got unlucky. Most killers do."

"Good thing I'm not most."

"Good thing I'm lucky."

He laughed. "We'll see." The call disconnected.

"What is it?" T-Tommy asked as he came through the door.

"It was him."

"What'd he say?"

"Mostly gloating. But like I said earlier, the voice on the phone and the crime scenes don't mesh."

Scotty came in from the backyard, his cell phone at his ear. "Thanks," he said. "I'll catch you later." He closed the phone. "He used the same phone. Came through a tower off Governor's Drive, near the Med Center."

Harold Pearce switched off the cell phone and dropped it in his black bag. He then picked up the encrypted cell, called Smithson, and gave him an update.

"Very good," Smithson said. "When's the next event?"

"Tonight or tomorrow. I'm sure Kurtz is infuriated after his meeting with Hublein this morning. I doubt I can hold him down much longer."

"Are the cops getting any closer?"

Pearce sighed. "They're plodding morons. If they don't stumble on the answer soon, I'll dump an anonymous call on them. Even they should be able to figure it out if they have his name."

"Good. Then we can run Kurtz into a corner and set up the final chapter."

"I like the sound of that."

"How much time do we have?" Smithson asked.

"Not more than a few days. He's extremely unstable."

"Excellent."

Pearce punched the END button. He had to admit, all the pieces were coming together perfectly. Brian was falling apart, and Dub was fuming. Time to turn up the heat and then put the two of them together. After that, it would be "Hello, Tahiti."

CHAPTER 52

T-TOMMY STOOD NEAR THE BACK EDGE OF THE YARD, CELL PHONE to his ear. He had been talking for ten minutes when he closed the phone and walked toward me. "That was Luther. You aren't going to believe this." I looked at him but said nothing. "The phone records. I put some guys on them last night, told them to check, recheck, and check again."

"And?"

"It seems that a couple of days ago, a number that called both Allison and Petersen popped up. It belonged to an outfit called Gulf Coast Telemarketing. Since Mike didn't receive a call from there, and since it was a telemarketing company, they considered it a coincidence."

I frowned. "There are no coincidences."

"I know. They dropped in Kushner's data this morning and bang . . . Gulf Coast appeared. They got a list of all of their numbers. Thirty-six lines. Thirty are listed to Gulf Coast, three to Wanda Fisher, the owner, and three to a Mr. Milton Reynard. One of Mr.

Reynard's numbers called Mike."

"How'd this happen? I thought they checked every number. Actually called them."

"So did I. Luther went ballistic, called Wanda Fisher himself. Seems that when she first set up her company, it was on a shoestring. Mr. Reynard, a good friend, loaned her some money. The phone company would allow only three numbers in her name, so . . ."

"Reynard signed off on the other three."

"Exactly. As the company grew, she added more lines in the company name but never changed the original six listings."

"Unbelievable. Where is this place?"

"South. Off the parkway."

"Thank you for seeing us, Ms. Fisher," I said as she welcomed us into her office. An attractive woman, forty or so, trim, fit, and neatly dressed in expensive gray slacks and a pink silk blouse. She had a professional demeanor and a firm, confident handshake.

"Please, sit down," she said. "It's not every day the sheriff calls. What can I do for you?"

After telling her that this wasn't for public consumption, T-Tommy explained the situation. She was obviously shaken. Most people get through their entire lives without ever having to confront the truly ugly side of human nature. It was clear that this blindsided Wanda Fisher.

"What does this mean?" She spread her hands out on her desk as if searching for an anchor. "You think someone here is involved in these murders?"

I shook my head. "Not necessarily. It's just that all the victims received calls from here, nothing more."

"We make thousands of calls each day. Couldn't this be a coincidence?"

"Possibly. But we have to check out every lead."

"I understand." She took a deep, slow breath. "What do you need?"

"Do you maintain a list of calls and who made them?" I asked.

"Sure. That's how we pay our employees. They work on salary plus commissions."

"That's what we need."

"Do you have the names?"

"Carl Petersen, Mike Savage, William Allison, Albert Kushner."

She wrote the names on a notepad and then turned slightly, facing the computer on her desk. We sat for several minutes as she worked, the silence broken only by the soft click of the keyboard. Sitting up straight, she hit a final key and then turned toward the printer on the credenza behind her as it sprang to life. "Here you go." She handed me the pages.

Each page contained a list of the dates, times, and names of the persons who made the calls to each of the victims. Half a dozen to Mike, more to each of the others. Gulf Coast apparently made good use of its call list. Only three names correlated with all the victims: Simon

Baker, Glenda Riordan, and Brian Kurtz. *Brian Kurtz.* The name jumped at me. I handed the pages to T-Tommy and looked at Wanda.

"Looks like Simon Baker, Glenda Riordan, and Brian Kurtz made calls to each of the victims. What can you tell me about them?"

"Glenda and Simon are working today. Brian is no longer with us."

"Why not?" I asked.

She sighed. "Brian is a nice guy, but he has some problems. Been a bit tense lately, and I've had several customer complaints about him being rude. So I had to let him go."

I glanced at T-Tommy.

"At least temporarily," she said. "He's seeing his psychiatrist, and once the doctor says everything is okay, I may let Brian come back. He's a very good worker."

"Anything else you can tell us about him?" T-Tommy asked.

"He got into a fight the other day. Right outside. Some vagrant tried to rob him with a knife. Brian beat him up pretty badly."

"Who's his psychiatrist?" I asked.

"Robert Hublein."

"We'd like to talk with Glenda Riordan and Simon Baker," T-Tommy said.

"Sure." She stood. "Wait right here, and I'll get them."

After she left, I pointed to the page T-Tommy still held. "Brian Kurtz was one of the violent crime files Scotty pulled." T-Tommy raised an eyebrow. "Didn't want to say anything in front of Ms. Fisher."

CHAPTER 53

OUR CHAT WITH GLENDA RIORDAN AND SIMON BAKER TURNED UP little except that both agreed Kurtz was uptight. Simon offered that he was afraid of him. Glenda disagreed but did say Brian seemed stressed lately. I got the impression she might have had a crush on him. We thanked them and Wanda and left.

I called Claire. She and the deputy had searched the area but never saw the kid. Now she was at work, putting together her report. She said she would meet me at Sammy's around seven. After her segment on the six o'clock news.

Before heading back downtown, T-Tommy and I decided to stop by the Memorial Medical Center ER. See if we could chat with the doc who took care of Kurtz and the mugger. T-Tommy badged the receptionist, telling her we needed some information about a patient. She made a quick call to someone named Marcia and then led us back into the treatment area.

Marcia turned out to be the charge nurse Marcia Clark, a pleasant but no-nonsense woman. She wore dark blue surgical scrubs beneath a white coat and had a stethoscope draped around her neck.

"How can I help you?" she asked after we introduced ourselves.

T-Tommy explained why we were there.

"Oh, yes. I remember both the mugger and Mr. Kurtz."

"What do you remember?"

"Let me get Dr. Beck. He took care of them."

She told one of the other nurses to find Dr. Beck and offered us coffee. No thanks. A couple of minutes later a young, handsome man, also wearing the apparent ER uniform of blue surgical scrubs beneath a white coat, came toward us.

"I'm Dr. Beck."

We shook hands.

"I know you," he said, looking at me. "I've read a couple of your books. Loved them."

"That's always good to hear." I looked around the ER. "Is there someplace we can talk in private?"

He led us through the treatment area and into a small office. "Excuse the mess." He sat behind his desk. "What can I do for you?"

"You treated a couple of men several days ago," I said. "Brian Kurtz and a mugger."

I noticed his back stiffen slightly. "Yes."

"Can you tell me about him?"

"That would be a violation of his right to privacy."

"We have reason to believe that Kurtz is involved in a series of crimes. I can't tell you what, but lives are at stake."

"I'm sorry. I can't discuss my patients without their permission."

"We can get a subpoena," T-Tommy said.

Dr. Beck nodded. "When you do, I'll give you their medical records. Until then, I can't." He looked from T-Tommy to me. "You guys know that."

I glanced at T-Tommy, getting a slight nod in return. "Look, Dr. Beck—"

"Please. Call me Charlie."

"Okay, Charlie. This doesn't leave this room. Understand?"

"Sounds sinister." He smiled.

I didn't. "It is."

His smile dissolved. "What is it?"

"We're working on the murders you've no doubt read about in the papers. We're simply following leads, and one has led us to Mr. Kurtz."

"You think he's the killer?"

"Don't know. We do know that the killer massacred a couple last night."

"Jesus."

"It appears his killing spree is escalating. Rapidly. There will be others. Soon."

Charlie sighed and then gazed toward the ceiling, shaking his head. "I knew there was something wrong with him. Not this off-the-wall, but something."

"Tell me about it."

"His attack was way over the top. I've seen trauma, lots of trauma, in my career, but nothing quite like this." He forked his hair back from his forehead. "When the police brought him here just after the altercation, I wrote it off as a heat-of-the-moment sort of thing."

"Wrote what off?"

"His tension. Anger. He was . . . what's the word . . . wrapped too tight. Like he could explode at any minute."

T-Tommy grunted.

"That was right after a fight," Charlie went on. "He was still hyped up. Adrenaline is a powerful drug. Then when he came back, it was different."

"He came back?" I asked. "When?"

"Two days later. Wednesday. Routine wound check."

"I see. What was different?"

"He was calm, even quiet . . . until . . . he started talking about his psychiatrist."

"Dr. Hublein?"

I could see a flash of surprise on his face and the question in his eyes: *How did you know that?* He recovered quickly and said, "Yeah. After he was here the first time, I visited Dr. Hublein to tell him about what had happened with Brian. Brian was angry . . . very angry . . . that I had done that. It was like he went from zero to sixty in a heartbeat. Scared the hell out of Marcia and me."

"What did Dr. Hublein say about him?"

"I guess you know about the research project?" Charlie said.

I shook my head. "What research project?"

"The drug study."

"I'm afraid I don't know what you're talking about."

"Oh. Since you knew about Dr. Hublein, I assumed you knew about that, too."

"We haven't talked with Hublein yet."

Charlie massaged his temples and then told us what he knew of the situation.

"Let me get this straight," I said. "Brian Kurtz is part of some experiment run by Dr. Hublein. You know this because you took care of Kurtz after his mugging and his over-the-top attack on the mugger made you suspicious that something might be wrong with Kurtz. So you met with Hublein, who told you that Kurtz was on an experimental drug, and Kurtz got angry when he found out you had talked with Hublein. Now you think this drug might be part of Kurtz's problems."

Charlie shrugged. "Many drugs, particularly psychotropic ones, have some pretty nasty side effects."

I knew that was true. "What type of drug is it?"

"All Hublein told me is that it's in the benzodiazepine family."

I looked at T-Tommy. "A common class of tranquilizers. Things like Valium, Librium, Xanax. All good meds, but in some people they can cause problems."

"Like anger and aggression?" T-Tommy asked.

"And worse," Charlie said.

CHAPTER 54

T-TOMMY AND I RETURNED TO THE TASK FORCE ROOM AND GATH-ered everything we had on Brian Kurtz. Alice, Luther's assistant, pulled together what she could find on Dr. Robert Hublein. We had talked about going to see Hublein after we left Memorial Medical Center since his office was essentially right around the corner, but we decided to dig a little deeper into Brian Kurtz first. I had the feeling that Hublein just might be on the wrong side of all this, and I wanted more information before talking with him. Don't know why I felt that, but I did. Probably had to do with the term *experimental drug*. It had an old horror movie ring to it.

I flipped open Kurtz's file. "An assault six years ago. Charges dropped. Two others two years ago, just after he left the military. Those were prosecuted. No jail time, but he's on probation now." I turned to the next page. "Now this altercation with a mugger." I read the one-page report again. "Looks like he was attacked outside work. The mugger was hospitalized. Kurtz wasn't charged. Deputies Rodriguez and

Oakley called it self-defense. Looks like the mugger had assaulted others over the past few months."

"Paul Rodriguez is a good man. If he thought it was clean, it probably was." T-Tommy took the report from me. "Says Kurtz is a big guy. Paul wrote down 'approx six feet, two hundred.' That fits who we're looking for."

"Look at this?" I handed him another page from the folder. "Kurtz was referred for psychiatric care after the assaults two years ago. That's how he got sent to Dr. Hublein."

T-Tommy scanned it for a moment. "Part of a plea bargain deal. I see more and more of these. Jails overcrowded, so judges pass the buck to some shrink. Dude remains under the shrink's care until the doc says he's no longer a menace. Then he's free to go whack around some other citizen." He slipped the page back into the folder. "Guess it's time to pay Hublein a visit."

I nodded. "Then stop by and chat with Kurtz."

"Anything new?"

I looked up as Luther walked in. I explained what we had discovered about Brian Kurtz.

"And?"

T-Tommy shrugged. "He fits . . . mostly."

Luther frowned. "I don't like *mostly.*"

"I know," I said. "We got a few things to check out on him, but he's at least a candidate. That's more than we had this morning."

"Make sure he's the guy before you grab him," Luther said. "The media will eat up anyone we bring in, even if it is just for questioning. Keep me in the loop." He left the room.

I buzzed Alice on the com line. She looked up Hublein's number for me. I dialed it, got past his assistant by saying I was with the sheriff's department—amazing how that works—and Hublein came on the line. After explaining to him who I was, what I wanted, and asking if we could drop by, that it would only take twenty minutes tops, he balked.

"I have an important meeting at three. Can this wait until tomorrow?"

"We only need a few minutes, and it's important."

Hesitation. No response.

"If tomorrow morning at the sheriff's department would be more convenient, we can arrange that."

"No. No. Since it's important, please come on over now. I'll push back my meeting if necessary."

Hublein hung up the phone. "We're dead, Mel. That was the sheriff's department. They're on their way here to ask questions about Brian."

"Jesus Christ." Wexlar flopped onto the sofa. "Did they say why? What they wanted?"

"Maybe Brian's been arrested."

"We would have heard from Pearce."

"Where the hell is Pearce, anyway?" Hublein asked.

"Don't know." Wexlar stood and began to pace. "Maybe they're coming here to arrest us."

"They wouldn't call and warn us. Let's wait and see what they have to say."

"We should destroy the files. If they confiscate them, we're dead for sure."

Hublein shook his head. "We talked about this. A few changes to Brian's file and a few of the others and we're okay."

"I hope you're right."

"Better than getting caught shredding files, don't you think?"

CHAPTER 55

DR. ROBERT HUBLEIN WAS A BIG MAN. HIS HANDSHAKE WAS FIRM, his smile genuine if a little strained. He invited us to take a seat, and then asked, "What can I do for you?"

"A couple of questions about one of your patients," I said. "Brian Kurtz."

Hublein smiled. "You know I can't discuss my patients without their permission."

Here we go again. "And you know we can subpoena the records."

His smile never wavered. "No, you can't. The courts frown on opening up doctor-patient records, particularly those of a psychiatrist."

I wanted to swipe the smug look off his face. So I did. "Which you aren't. You're a neurologist. Med school at the University of Wisconsin, residency at Michigan, neuro training at NYU." Always paid to do your homework.

Hublein seemed momentarily flustered. I loved it when people realized you knew a lot more than they thought. Does the soul good.

300

"We're involved in a homicide investigation," T-Tommy said. "Multiple. We'll get what we need one way or the other."

His eyes narrowed. "Are you threatening me?"

T-Tommy leaned forward. "No, Dr. Hublein. We don't want to play hardball, but we're investigating several homicides. So brutal they'd curl your toes. The trail has led us to Brian Kurtz, and his trail has led us here. We know he's on some experimental drug and that you're giving it to him."

To his credit, Hublein didn't waver. Much. Just that quick flash of fear that's so hard to hide.

"Wish I could help you"—he turned his palms up—"but my hands are tied. Without Brian's permission, I can't say a word about his care."

"Mike Savage . . . ex-Sheriff Mike Savage . . . was one of the victims. He was a very close friend of ours." I nodded toward T-Tommy. "Very close. That means that this is personal."

"I fail to see how that is germane to this discussion."

I felt T-Tommy tighten. His voice came out hard. "It means we can dig into the dark corners of your life. Tell you what you had for breakfast last Wednesday if need be. God forbid if you're humping your secretary or hiding money in the Caymans. We can shine a light on your research here. Follow the money trail." He waved a hand around the office. "Quite a palace you've got here. Money like this always has dirt attached."

Hublein's face reddened, and a vein on his forehead seemed to throb an angry rhythm. "I don't take threats and blackmail very well."

Time for the good cop again. "We're just trying to find out who killed Mike Savage and hopefully prevent more killings. We're not even sure being here is the right track, but we have little to go on in this investigation. Sort of grabbing for straws right now. If you could just answer a few questions, we'll be out of here."

Hublein hesitated and then sighed. "What do you want to know?"

That was better. People always have secrets to protect. Hublein was no exception. I suspected he realized throwing us a little info was better than us digging around in his life. Or maybe he just liked me.

"Whatever you can tell us about Mr. Kurtz would be helpful," I said. "We know he came to you about two years ago."

Again a flicker of surprise. "I'm sure all of this is in his police file, but yes, he came to me as part of a plea bargain to keep him out of jail. Brian has had a troubled past. Mostly due to his parents, who were alcoholic and not the most competent of parents. Apparently his maternal grandmother helped raise him. She was the one shining light for Brian, but she died in a home accident." Hublein seemed more relaxed now. "Brian was quite a gifted athlete. Football and wrestling were his sports. There was talk of an athletic scholarship, which would have been his ticket out from under his parents' roof. Might have changed everything for him."

"But?" I said.

"He collided with the goalpost during a football game. Depressed skull fracture, brain injury. In a coma for a week."

"Which ended his football career," I said.

"Exactly. He became increasingly difficult. He did manage to join the military and apparently did well. For a while. Then his behavior did him in. Got an honorable discharge, but I suspect he didn't deserve it. They probably just wanted to get rid of him. After that he had a few problems with the law."

"This is where the experimental drug comes in?" I asked.

Hublein nodded. "I diagnosed him with post-traumatic stress disorder . . . PTSD. This new drug holds great promise."

"Any side effects? Behavioral changes? Anger or aggression?"

"Actually, quite the opposite. The drug has a calming effect. Lessens aggression in males prone to acts of violence. Not just in PTSD, but apparently in anyone with violent tendencies."

I nodded. "I understand it's in the benzodiazepine family?"

Hublein flashed a quick look of surprise, and then his eyes narrowed. "Now I recognize you. I hadn't made the connection. Dub Walker. I've read your books. Can't say I agree with all your theories, but I enjoyed them."

"Thanks."

Hublein smiled. "My own theory is that many violent people actually enjoy the anger, the rush. So each episode reinforces the behavior."

"I happen to agree with that," I said. "In some cases." Hublein seemed pleased that I agreed with him. "Would you say that Brian was one of those types?"

He hesitated as if weighing whether to go into this part of Brian's care and then said, "It's possible." He straightened some papers on his desk. "Brian has progressed well. He's had no problems, no fights or scrapes with the law since starting the medication."

"Until earlier this week?" I said.

Hublein nodded. "That wasn't without provocation."

That was true. "Dr. Beck treated him in the ER. He thinks Brian is angry and unstable."

"Yes, I spoke with Dr. Beck. Seems like a nice guy and a competent and caring physician. It's not often that a treating physician will take the time to visit another doctor. A phone call, sure, but not a face-to-face visit."

"Which might indicate his level of concern?" I said.

"That's why I brought Brian in for a visit."

"And?"

"He was normal in every way. A little embarrassed by the entire ordeal. I checked the level of the drug in his system, and it was in the therapeutic range."

"So you disagree with Dr. Beck's assessment?" I asked.

Hublein gave me a benevolent-appearing smile. "Dr. Beck isn't a psychiatrist." He raised a hand, palm out. "I know. I'm not, either. But I do perform research in the arena of neuropsychiatry, so I'm well versed in the field. I've seen thousands of psychiatric patients in my career."

Maybe we were on the wrong track here. Maybe Kurtz was the proverbial red herring. Maybe the phone calls were a coincidence.

Of course, I didn't believe in coincidences.

"This drug?" I asked. "Are you the only center doing this project?"

"Oh, no. It's an NIH—National Institutes of Health—study. Partially anyway. The manufacturer picks up most of the tab. There are five other centers across the country involved."

"How many patients?"

"Each center enrolled twenty-five subjects."

CHAPTER 56

BRIAN WAS ON THE LAST SET OF BENCH PRESSES IN AN EXHAUST-ing two-hour workout. He hoped it would relieve the anger that rumbled around in his gut. After leaving Hublein's office, he had launched into a rage, driving erratically, screaming at any car that got in his way, before finally reaching the safety of his apartment. Even this haven hadn't dampened his anger. He threw a chair against the door and punched half a dozen new holes in the wall, gypsum dust flying with each blow. Still the fire refused to give way. He stripped to his shorts and began working the iron.

He pressed the 325-pound barbell upward for the fifteenth and final rep, before returning it to its cradle. He wiped sweat from his face and stretched out on the floor to cool down, his inner turmoil finally ebbing.

The phone rang.

He crawled to his desk and picked it up. "Yes."

"Get out."

"What?"

"Get out now. Detective Tortelli and Dub Walker are on the way there."

"Good. It's time to take them on."

"Not yet."

"Why not?"

"You still have things to do. Tonight?"

"Who?"

"McCurdy. Remember him?"

Yes, he remembered. An exceptionally arrogant prick. Had called him names. Screamed at him. Called Wanda and complained that Brian had been rude to him when the truth was the exact opposite. "I remember."

"You want him?"

"Yes. But I want that asshole that has been talking about me, too."

The man laughed. "And so you will. But now is not the time. Trust me on this."

"Why should I?"

"Haven't I been the one to help you through all this? The only one?"

That was true. Brian still didn't know why the man had helped, but he couldn't deny that he had.

"I have a surprise for you later. Something you'll enjoy."

"What?"

"Later. Right now you have to move."

"I have nowhere to go."

"Service station. Corner of Wall Triana and Capshaw. Men's room. There's a cell phone taped to the bottom of the paper towel dispenser. I'll call it in twenty minutes."

"Then what? Where will I go?"

"It's taken care of. Don't worry. Just leave now. Take your gun but nothing else. They'll be there in fifteen minutes tops."

Brian slipped on a pair of jeans and a T-shirt, stuffed a few things in a canvas bag, and looked around. Anything else?

A knock at the door. He froze. Were they there already? He peeked through the curtains. Laranne. He didn't have time for this. He yanked open the door.

"Look, I've got—" he began.

Laranne stumbled past him. Then he saw she had been pushed. Her husband followed her inside.

"I told you to leave my wife alone," Carl said. "I go away, and you two rut like a couple of pigs."

"I have to be somewhere," Brian said. "Right now."

"Too bad." The tendons and blood vessels in Carl's neck stood out like cables. His jaw flexed. "I want to settle this right now."

"Okay," Brian said.

He hit Carl in the face. He went down. Hard. Laranne screamed. He hit her, too. She sprawled to the floor and didn't move.

Carl began rising to his knees. Brian picked up a hand weight. He really didn't have time for this shit.

CHAPTER 57

WE FOUND THE WOODSIDE APARTMENTS A BLOCK OFF HOLMES AV-
enue. A collection of half a dozen tan, wood, two-story eightplexes,
arranged around a central open area. The grass could do with a mowing,
but the buildings seemed to be in good shape. We saw no activity, most
residents probably not home from work yet.

Number 8, Kurtz's apartment, faced the street and was the upper
right unit of the building nearest the parking lot entrance. T-Tommy
and I climbed the stairs. Brian's door stood open.

T-Tommy grabbed my arm and held me back. He pulled his
weapon, a Sig P226, and moved toward the door, stopping just short.
Gun by his shoulder, angled up, he gave a quick look around the
frame. He froze. "Jesus."

Two bodies lay on the floor. A man and a woman. Both with
severe head trauma. A bloody hand weight lay beside the woman.

T-Tommy searched the other rooms while I checked for pulses.
Found none. The bodies were warm, the blood only partially clotted.

Time of death? Ten minutes ago, max. We had just missed him.

The coppery odor of fresh blood mixed with the odor of sweat. A workout bench and several stacks of weights occupied one corner of the living room, a desk and computer the other. A pair of sweaty gym shorts and a towel lay on the floor. I saw several holes punched into the drywall and a mangled chair on the floor near a sofa.

T-Tommy came from the bedroom. "It's clean." He flipped open his cell phone and called for backup and the forensic science crew. I snatched a dish towel from the kitchen and sat down at the desk. Using the towel like a glove, I pulled open each desk drawer. The two to my left were empty, but in the middle drawer I found a notebook and opened it.

There were four pages inside. Each had a name at the top: Carl Petersen, William Allison, Mike Savage, Albert Kushner. *Bingo.*

T-Tommy looked over my shoulder. "He's the guy."

Below each name was the address of each victim's home. Line drawings of the property and the house layout. Hand sketches of the routes of approach and escape. This guy was prepared.

T-Tommy called Luther, told him what we had found, and asked for a BOLO on Kurtz and any vehicles registered to him.

I heard sirens approaching as we stepped back outside. I called Claire. This scoop would earn me a few points.

CHAPTER 58

BRIAN HAD FOUND THE PHONE EXACTLY WHERE THE MAN SAID HE would. It chirped its electronic ring tone before he could even rip it from the envelope. The man gave Brian directions to a "safe house." His words. Brian balked, unsure. Maybe it was a trap.

"If I'd wanted to take you down, I could have done it weeks ago. I'm on your side."

Brian couldn't deny that, so he did as he was told and now stood on the front porch of a nondescript house a couple of blocks off Bob Wallace. He ran his fingers along the top of the door frame and found the key, as the caller said he would. He unlocked the door and stepped inside. Small but neat, it smelled a little musty, but not bad. Better than his apartment. He looked through each room—living area, kitchen, two bedrooms, and a bath. Beer in the fridge. He grabbed one, popped the tab, and took several gulps. That was better.

The cell phone rang. He answered.

"Did you put your car in the garage?"

"Yes."

"It's dead. You can't drive it anymore. The cops are looking for it."

"How do you know?"

"Same way I know everything else. Check the top drawer in the bedroom dresser. I got you some more black pants and shirts, and some fresh gloves."

"You think of everything, don't you?"

"Yes, I do. How was your meeting with Dr. Hublein today?"

"Fine."

"So you don't mind being off the medication?"

"How do you know about that?"

"Let's just say I have access."

"What do you want? Money? I don't have any money."

"I don't need your money. I simply want to help. Is that so hard to understand?"

Why was everyone trying to help him? Hublein? That smart-ass ER doctor? This guy? Why didn't they all just go fuck themselves? But . . . if he could get the drug. "Maybe."

"After all I've done for you, you still doubt me?"

"I don't even know you."

"Haven't I given you what you need? Cleared the path, so to speak?"

"Yes."

"And now I'm going to help you again."

"With what?"

"McCurdy."

"And Hublein. I want him, too."

The man laughed softly. "I wondered when you were going to get around to that."

"If I don't get him and that Walker dude, this is done. I'll walk away."

"You can't. You need the drug, and I'm the only one who can get it for you."

Was he lying? How could he get the drug? Who the hell was he? "When?"

"Tomorrow. Don't you get your injection every Friday?"

How did he know that? "Yeah."

"Relax, Brian. Everything's okay. Take McCurdy, and then I'll arrange everything else."

Brian thought about it for a second. He did want McCurdy. He wanted Hublein and Dub Walker more. But . . . if he could have them all.

"Brian? You still with me?"

"I'm here."

"We'll have to do this one a little differently, so listen carefully. First, don't use this phone for anything except to answer my calls. Clear?"

"Why?"

"Because that's the way it is. Keep it with you at all times. Second, take a peek out the living room window."

Brian pulled back the curtain and looked out toward the street.

"See the car across the street? The gray one?"

"Yes."

"That's the one you'll use. Keys are in the ashtray. No speeding and no joyriding. It's stolen. I switched the plates, but if you get pulled over, the jig is up. Understand?"

"Yes."

"Do exactly as I tell you. Tonight . . ."

Brian's head throbbed. "Tonight? I'm exhausted."

"Yes, tonight. It must be tonight."

"Why?"

"Because the old demon is beginning to chew on you already, isn't it?"

It was true. He could feel it simmering inside. Seemed like it never let up now. Always churning. The caller was right. He couldn't wait. "You know it is."

"Tonight. After ten. Go to the new strip center. The one on Old Highway 431 near Hampton Cove. Where the Italian restaurant is. You know the one?"

"Yes."

"Behind the center are three Dumpsters. An envelope will be taped to the back of the one nearest the east end. You won't need anything but your gun."

"What about the surprise you mentioned earlier?"

"After McCurdy. You'll love it. A little reward for all your hard work."

CHAPTER 59

SAMMY'S WAS CHAOS.

During the week, Sammy went for the more sedate blues of Colin Dogget, but when the weekend rolled around—and Thursday night was considered the kickoff—Sammy brought in more lively entertainment. Bumped up alcohol sales.

Tonight, Jake's Blues Project, a three-piece electric blues band. I'd seen them a couple of times. Fairly new group out of Meridian, Mississippi.

Claire sat at the bar, wineglass in hand, chatting with Sammy. She lifted her purse off the stool she had saved for me, and I sat down. Sammy poured a double shot of Blanton's bourbon and slid the glass toward me. I took a deep pull.

"I imagine you need that about now," Claire said.

Another slug. "You can bet on it. How'd your report go?"

"Great." She tilted her wineglass toward me. "Thanks to you."

"You owe me."

"I'll see what I can do." She ran her hand along my thigh.

I laid my hand on hers and gave it a squeeze. "I'm liking where this is going."

Sammy leaned on the bar. "This Kurtz guy the killer?"

"Yeah."

"And now he's on the run," Claire said. When I nodded she said, "Glad I'm staying with you."

Sammy raised an eyebrow.

"Not a word," I said.

He looked at Claire. His eyebrows gave a couple of bounces. "If you'd rather stay with me, I've got the room."

Claire laughed and poked a finger in my ribs. "If Dub doesn't behave himself, I just might take you up on that."

"Me? You started it."

I felt a hand on my shoulder and turned to see T-Tommy. I told Sammy that we were going out on the patio where we could hear each other talk.

Sammy said he'd send out some pulled-pork sandwiches, adding, "Willie's pushing those tonight. Says it's the best batch he's made in a while." He swiped the bar. "'Course, he says that pretty near every day."

The patio had about two dozen tables. Half were occupied, most people inside taking in the music. We grabbed a three-top along the rail at the far end, away from the other people. Lisa, a waitress who had been with Sammy for years, brought Claire and me a second round, even though I was still working on the first one. She handed

T-Tommy a Corona, saying she would have our food up in no time.

"Anything on Kurtz?" I asked.

"Nothing. Guys are still working his place. No weapon. Took the computer and the techs are digging into it now." He knocked back a slug of beer. "I called Wanda Fisher in case he showed up there. Put a couple of guys on her place. She could be a target after firing him."

"Anyone he called could be, too."

T-Tommy nodded, adjusted his gut, and said, "Yeah, but that's a long list." He looked at Claire. "Good job with your report tonight. Getting his picture out there gives us extra eyes."

"Let's hope something turns up soon. Before—" Claire stopped as Lisa walked up carrying a tray of food.

"Here you go." She placed our plates on the table. "Anything else?"

"Not right now, Lisa," I said.

"I'll check on you later. Enjoy." She headed back inside.

T-Tommy looked at me. "What's wrong?"

"Nothing."

"Come on, Dub. How long've we known each other? I know when something's eatin' you. What is it?"

I drained the last of my first drink and took a sip of the second. "I've been back over everything . . . in my head . . . seems like a thousand times. Keeps circling back to the same place."

"And that would be?"

"There just might be two of them."

"You sure?" Claire asked.

"No matter how I figure it, that's where it lands. The guy on the phone doesn't mesh with the crime scenes. One is rational, the other an over-the-top psycho. Toss in the two sets of shoe prints and the geographic spread of the scenes, and it smells like a tandem deal."

"But?" T-Tommy said.

I took a bite of my sandwich and spoke around it. "This Kurtz guy seems too insane to play well with others. Look at the victims. At what he did to his neighbors. How could anyone trust him? Go into a dicey situation with someone who could go sideways in a heartbeat?"

"Maybe they're both insane," Claire said.

I shook my head. "Not the guy on the phone."

"What about another Manson situation?" she asked.

"You mean one guy sends the other out to kill, like Charlie did with Watson, Atkins, and the others?"

She nodded. "It's possible."

I thought about that for a minute. Could Kurtz simply be a killing machine that was wound up and turned loose on the public? If so, why would he go after people he had called? People who could be traced back to him? "It's possible, I guess." I exhaled a long breath. "Scary scenario."

"This whole deal is scary," Claire said. "The entire city is locked down at night. He's even run me out of my own home."

"That's the only good thing to come out of this."

She smiled. "You just might not get lucky again."

"With my charm?"

"Get real."

"Besides, you owe me."

"Maybe I'll get you a tie or something."

"Funny."

We ate quietly for a minute, and then I said to T-Tommy, "That Hublein guy . . . I got the sense that he was covering something."

"Wouldn't you?" T-Tommy asked. "He's his doctor. Got him on some oddball, newfangled drug. Kurtz beats the hell out of some guy, and then we waltz in asking questions. Tell him we're investigating the worst series of murders in Madison County since Packwood. He sees lawsuit." T-Tommy shrugged. "Makes sense to me."

Made sense to me, too. Almost.

CHAPTER 60

AN HOUR EARLIER, WE HAD SAID OUR GOOD-BYES TO T-TOMMY IN SAM-my's parking lot, and I followed Claire back to my place. While she unpacked her bag—she had decided to bring over some work clothes so she wouldn't have to go by her house again—I opened a bottle of Sapphire Hills Syrah, grabbed two glasses and my guitar, and moved out on the deck. A slight breeze had kicked up, and the night had begun to cool.

Now I sat in a chair on my deck and fingered the fret board of my Martin D-18 through several turnarounds. I was trying to find the right one, an attempt to smooth out the edges of the song I'd been tinkering with for the past month. I kept the rhythm with my bare heel on the hardwood deck. I found that, besides being my fa-vorite way to unwind, sitting with my guitar cleared my thinking. Like the twelve bars of the blues, things often fell into place.

Claire stretched out on a chaise, blanket up to her chin. I think I was keeping her awake.

As I picked and strummed, I thought about doodlebugs. Ugly, caterpillar-like creatures with pincer mouths. Lived in small, round holes in sandy soil throughout the South. As a kid, I had passed many a summer afternoon trying to tease them to the surface. The key was to snap off a stalk of fresh green grass, dribble a bit of spit on the end, and then ease the shaft into the hole. Soon the doodlebug would begin gnawing on it. You could feel its pincers working if you held the grass lightly. Then, timing and luck came into play. If the creature chomped down and if you yanked the grass just right, out he'd fly.

That's what I felt like we had been doing. The TV interviews, the phone calls, everything was supposed to yank the killer out into the open. Like this morning at Claire's. But just as he popped into view, he burrowed back underground again.

I put the guitar down, stood, and walked to the edge of my property. I scrunched the grass with my toes. Nothing on earth felt like that. I looked out over the sleeping city. Only the stream of cars that moved along Memorial Parkway indicated that anyone was awake.

Kurtz was. I was sure of that.

Maybe looking for a new hidey-hole. Like a doodlebug. Maybe seeking out his next target. Maybe he already had one and was simply sitting and watching. Relishing what was to come. Maybe he was at this very moment creating his own special brand of havoc inside one of the thousands of homes I could see.

Yet here I stood. Powerless to do anything about it.

The fact that his murders were coming more frequently and his scenes were growing more violent meant that he was on the verge of cracking. Near full rage. Near going over the falls. A very dangerous phase.

And the other guy? Was there another guy? I didn't want to believe there was, but that possibility kept eating at me. If he had a rational controller, this could get really ugly. Crazies make mistakes. Walk into traps. Don't plan well and get caught. Or get killed in a shoot-out. But . . . if someone was pulling Kurtz's strings, that changed the equation. Kurtz could be confined until his special skills were needed.

I felt Claire come up behind me. She snaked her arms around my waist and pressed her cheek against my back. "You okay?"

"Hublein lied," I said.

"What do you mean?"

I turned toward her. "There's more to this than he admitted."

"He couldn't tell you everything. There are rules about that. Patient privacy. You know that."

"The key to all this is in his office."

"You don't know that."

"Think about it. Kurtz is completely out of control. Hublein has to know that."

"How?"

"He's his doctor. Sees him every week. No way this level of insanity could get by him." She looked at me but said nothing. "Kurtz is on some new drug. Still-in-trials type of drug. His behavior could be from a toxic reaction."

"You're thinking this drug could be responsible for all this?"

"Why do people do violent things?"

"They're crazy. They're mean. They're sociopaths."

"Or they're intoxicated by some drug. Crystal meth and cocaine are notorious for causing anger and rage. Even psychotic breaks."

"There's no evidence that he's doing either of those."

"Those aren't the ones I'm worried about. The drug Kurtz is taking is in the benzodiazepine family. There are numerous cases of people having bad reactions to either taking or withdrawing from these drugs. Remember John Hinckley? Shot Reagan? He was supposedly on Valium."

She nodded slowly. "So, Kurtz could have been pushed over the edge by the drug?"

"Look, Kurtz is the guy. No doubt about that. He's on some drug, and Hublein's giving it to him. There has to be a connection."

"He could just be a plain-vanilla psychotic."

"Sure. Probably is. Statistically that's the best bet. But the scenes? I've never seen anything like them. And I've seen some bad shit. Kurtz didn't just kill these people. He tried to obliterate them. Completely. I can't believe anybody, normal or crazy, could do that, unless something was making him inhuman. Not what I saw at Mike's. The Kushners. Something's pushing him way over the edge. These brain meds can do unexpected things. Maybe buried in Kurtz's chart there are some hints."

I could almost see Claire's mental wheels turning.

"Besides," I said, "if Hublein knew this was possible, we can't let him walk. Maybe he could have prevented what happened to Mike and the others."

"You have no proof of anything like that."

"One way to find out," I said.

"Ask Hublein again? What makes you think he'll tell you?"

"I wasn't planning to ask."

She shook her head. "You are not going to break into Hublein's office."

"Why not?"

"Oh, let's see. It's illegal. It's insane. It's completely moronic. We already know Brian Kurtz is the guy, and he'll be picked up soon. Hard to hide when your face is all over the news. What could you possibly find that would change any of that?"

"Don't know until we see."

"Jesus," Claire said. "Are you trying to get arrested? Breaking into the offices of a respected physician?"

"Now that Kurtz has been identified, if Hublein has been up to something he'll trash the records. If he hasn't already."

CHAPTER 61

PAUL McCURDY RECLINED IN HIS LOUNGE CHAIR, WATCHING THE news and finishing the paperwork that had occupied him for the past two hours. His wife, Diane, dozed on the nearby sofa. The book she had been reading lay on her chest. She stirred, stretched, and then rolled on her side to look at him.

"What time is it?" she asked.

"Nearly eleven."

"Why'd you let me sleep so long?"

"Because you're beautiful when you sleep."

She sat up. "How much longer are you going to be at that?"

"Another half hour max."

"Finish it tomorrow."

"You know Bill's coming by early to pick these up for his meeting in Chicago. He has an eight-thirty flight."

She stood, leaned over, and kissed him. "I'm going to bed. Wake me when you come up."

He rubbed her belly through her nightgown. "I think you're starting to show."

"Not yet. It's only two months."

He cocked his head first one way and then the other, examining her again. "Must be the ice cream, then."

She playfully punched his arm. "It's not ice cream. And it's your fault. You took advantage of me." She mussed his hair. "Don't take too long."

Brian pulled into the half-filled parking area just off Old Highway 431 and parked near the open end of the L-shaped strip mall, away from the busy restaurants and movie theater. Nearby, a group of teenage boys performed stunts on skateboards to a chorus of giggles and shouts from several girls. Busy with their posturing, they paid little attention to him. He screwed the sound suppressor onto the muzzle of the gun and stuffed it beneath the waistband of his pants, covering the grip with his T-shirt. He walked to the end of the building, stepped around the corner, and disappeared into the darkness.

A twenty-foot-wide asphalt alleyway and a six-foot-high cinder-block retaining wall stretched the length of the complex and separated it from a tree-dotted grassy slope. A floral delivery truck and three trash bins sat against the wall. He easily located the heavy-gauge envelope taped to the back of the nearest bin and inside found a coil of yellow ski rope, a small tape recorder, a penlight, and two pieces of paper. Using the light, he read both, one a list of instructions, the other a hand-drawn map, indicating that the direct route to McCurdy's house was up the slope behind him.

The back door to one of the strip mall businesses banged open. He killed the light and peeked around the bin. A young Hispanic man exited the Italian restaurant half-carrying, half-dragging two overstuffed trash bags, and headed straight toward him. Brian sank into the shadows, his hand on the butt of his gun. The man heaved the bags inside the metal bin, each landing with a loud clang. He then retreated into the restaurant, pulling the door closed behind him.

Brian stuffed the recorder, penlight, and rope into his waist pack, the pages into his pants pocket, then scaled the wall and scrambled up the grassy slope. He quickly reached the crest, where he knelt to catch his breath. Fifty yards of open grassy terrain separated him from a quiet street with a handful of houses, most still under construction. McCurdy's was at the near end on the right.

Keeping low, he crossed the field and ducked into the shrubs along McCurdy's driveway. The nearest streetlamp, two houses away, cast a meager light, and a dim door lamp lit the front porch, but little else.

The familiar heat rose in his chest. It amazed him how the rage could rise so quickly. Not that he minded, but he found it curious that he could keep it in check most of the time, only to have it suddenly explode. As if it existed as a pilot light and only at times like this would it burst into full flame. He also knew that once ignited, it consumed everything. Anxiety, fear, pity, rational thought all wilted away.

He thought back to Petersen, the old man. That was the first time he came face-to-face with his rage. Not the low-level anger he had been sensing for several weeks before that night, but the pure fire that he now knew so well. Entering the Russel Erskine, he had been more scared than angry. Yet, something drove him. Something much less than rage, something he could not describe. It drove him up five flights of stairs and down the hallway to Petersen's door. It tugged him through the unlocked door and into the sanctity of Petersen's home.

The first blow he delivered that night had been weak, tentative. When Petersen awoke and tried to rise from bed, panic took over, and he slammed the bat across the old man's raised arms with more force. That seemed to ignite a fury within him, and he flailed at the man with mounting rage.

Afterward, fear and confusion. He couldn't breathe and collapsed to the floor, staring at what he had done. An exhausted calmness settled over him. More peaceful than anything he had ever experienced. In that moment, he pushed all his questions and confusion aside. He reveled in this new feeling of contentment. It was a fire-and-ice thing. The heat of his fury followed by the cool calm that took over once the rage had been extinguished. Both were equally addictive.

Allison, Savage, the Kushners, all had been the same, only more so. Now, crouching in the shrubbery so near McCurdy, the fire whooshed to life. He moved along the side of the house to the last window. It was cracked open, and the room beyond was dark, exactly as the papers in his pocket had indicated. He pulled on his cotton gloves. The window screen, already loosened from its moorings, came away easily. He lifted the window and eased through it into the McCurdys' dining room. Light from the TV danced through the door opposite him and reflected off the glass panels of a china cabinet to his left.

He skirted the dining table and peered around the doorjamb. McCurdy lay on a lounge chair, head flopped to one side, motionless except for the rhythmic rise and fall of his chest. On the large TV screen, the weather report ended and the anchorman reappeared. Brian crept forward, now only five feet from the sleeping McCurdy.

The eleven o'clock news came on. The anchorman appeared. "We have an update on the hunt for the killer that has paralyzed the county. Police have named Brian Kurtz as the primary suspect, and a countywide manhunt for him is ongoing at this time."

Brian saw his own image fill the screen. Oddly, he didn't feel surprise or even fear. He felt . . . nothing. Just an odd sensation that the face on the screen wasn't really him. The anchorman droned on about something, but he couldn't follow what it was. It was as if the man was mumbling nonsense. Two numbers appeared at the bottom of the screen, one for the sheriff's department, the other for the police.

Brian placed the muzzle near McCurdy's temple and squeezed the trigger. The opposite side of McCurdy's head exploded, spraying blood over the adjacent sofa and wall. He directed the weapon toward the TV and snapped two rounds into his own face, ripping holes in the screen, striking something metallic, vital. The screen flickered brightly for a brief moment and then faded to black.

He climbed the stairs, checking each room along the upstairs hallway until he arrived at an open door at the end. Mrs. McCurdy slept on her left side, her back to him. He rounded the bed and stood over her. He yanked the chain on the bedside lamp. Her eyes fluttered open, and she raised one arm to shield the light. She stared at him and blinked, confusion etching her face. Then she focused, and her mouth opened to scream. She never got it out. Brian cracked the gun butt against her temple.

"Shut up. Don't move, don't breathe unless I say so."

Her eyes glazed from the blow, then her pupils dilated like an expanding drop of oil.

He held the gun where she could see it. "Don't try anything, or I'll blow your fucking brains out. Understand?"

She nodded.

"Do exactly as I tell you."

"Who are you? What do you—"

"Shut up." He pressed the muzzle of the gun against her nose. "You don't get to ask questions."

"My husband?"

"He won't ask questions, either. Now, get up."

She swung her legs from beneath the covers and stood. Her legs trembled. She wavered and then collapsed onto the bed. He grasped her arm and yanked her to her feet.

"Please . . ." Tears welled in her eyes.

He clutched her throat and squeezed. "I could kill you right here, right now." He tightened his grip. "Believe me, I will if you say another word. Understand?"

She nodded and he released his grip. She coughed and wheezed, sucking in air.

Taking her by the arm, he dragged her down the hall and the stairs. She stumbled down the last four steps and landed heavily. He never relinquished his grip and yanked her to her feet.

Her eyes widened when she saw her husband. "Oh, my God," she moaned.

"Look at him." He pushed her forward until only inches separated her face from her husband's. "See what happens to assholes."

He released her long enough to grab one of the two oak, ladder-back chairs that sat against the wall. He positioned it in front of her dead husband and bound her to it by winding the nylon rope around her chest and upper arms, tying it tightly.

He placed his lips against her ear. "You're going to do exactly as I say or you'll end up the same way. Understand?"

She nodded through sobs.

He removed the tape recorder from his pack.

Thirty minutes later, Brian retraced his steps to the Dumpster. He slipped the pages and the recorder back into the envelope and dropped it on the asphalt behind the trash container. He had no idea why the man wanted the recording, but since he had delivered McCurdy, it seemed a small request. Maybe he wanted to hear what it was like to be there. Maybe he could only live out his fantasies through Brian.

He liked that idea. The caller had always said that Brian needed him. Maybe it was the other way around. Maybe the caller didn't have the balls to do this himself. Maybe he got off on what Brian was doing. Maybe he needed it even more than Brian did.

When he reached his car, he found it unlocked and another envelope lying in the driver's side floorboard. He looked around. The lot was nearly empty, the skateboarders gone, the restaurant closing up for the night.

He snatched up the envelope and ripped it open, turning so that the car's interior light fell on the page. The first two lines jumped at him:

Want another target tonight?

Want to strike a blow at Dub Walker?

CHAPTER 62

"EXACTLY HOW DO YOU PROPOSE TO GET INSIDE?" CLAIRE ASKED.

I parked the Porsche in a half-filled lot behind the cluster of Memorial Medical Center buildings. The North Alabama Neuropsychiatric Research Institute sat a block away near the intersection of Madison and Saint Clair. "When I was here the other day, I didn't see much security. No cameras. No sign that indicated that they had a security company."

"So this was premeditated?"

"I just notice that kind of stuff."

She shook her head. "Okay, Lone Ranger. Where to?"

"I prefer Bond. James Bond."

"You would."

We crossed Madison and made our way through another lot and then between two buildings. We walked casually as if we belonged. Hiding in plain sight. Behind the buildings, a row of ten-foot hydrangeas embraced a shared lot. We slipped through them and approached the back of the institute. The rear door was locked.

"Gee. They lock up at night," Claire said. "What a concept."

"Don't get cute."

Around the side of the building we found a ramp to the underground parking garage. Only one car. A dark-colored Chevy sedan. I found the door to the stairwell. I knew this because it had STAIRS stenciled on it in large white letters. I'm very clever. Like James Bond.

This door wasn't locked, so I pushed it open. "See."

"You're so proud of yourself."

"Yes, I am."

"This is still a bad idea."

"Probably. Still could answer some questions."

"Or put us in jail."

"Maybe we can share a cell."

We climbed to the fifth floor, where we found that door was also unlocked, and entered a dark hallway. I flipped on my small Maglite. I opened doors as we moved down the hall. Most were offices, one a conference room, and one contained the main server of the computer system. We came to a large room that appeared to be a medical clinic of sorts. We stepped inside. Two exam tables, separated by curtains, several low cabinets, and a door were to the left, while metal shelves, filled with boxes and equipment, lined the right wall. Two long metal tables dominated the center of the room. Probably work areas. At the far end were two deep sinks and an array of three stainless steel refrigerators. I moved to the fridges and pulled them open one by one. Metal racks of blood-filled tubes and medicine vials along with bins of small boxes filled every shelf. The racks and bins were labeled. Things like ABT-454, AN-996, and CB-2322.

"What is all this?" Claire asked.

"Drugs and blood samples for Hublein's studies."

"Wonder which one of these is Kurtz's stuff?"

"Don't know. Maybe after we see the files we can figure it out."

"Must be a file room somewhere," she said.

We headed toward the door, but just as I pulled it open, I heard the ding of the elevator. "We got company." I gently closed the door.

We circled back past the two exam tables. A side door led to a changing room, complete with lockers, a shower, and shelves stacked with scrub outfits. No way out. I led the way back into the main room, but stopped as the entry door began to open. Claire ducked back into the dressing area. I didn't have time, so I flicked off the Maglite and dropped behind one of the exam tables, its curtain offering cover. The overhead lights flickered to life.

I hated it when Claire was right. This was rapidly becoming a bad idea.

Footsteps moved toward the rear of the room. A refrigerator door hissed open, followed by the rattling of glass against glass. I peered over the table and past the edge of the curtain. A man walked to one of the center tables and sat, his back to me. His hair was cropped short, and when he turned his head, his profile revealed a square jaw. At first, I couldn't tell what he was doing, but then he held a syringe up toward the overhead light. It contained an amber liquid. He capped the needle and slipped the syringe into his jacket pocket. He then returned something to the fridge, retraced his steps, turned off the lights, and left.

I waited several minutes before I moved to the door and checked the hallway. Nothing. I walked over and pushed open the door to the dressing area. When Claire came out, I told her what I'd seen.

"One of the lab techs?" she asked. "Working late?"

"Wasn't dressed that way."

"Maybe he forgot something. Came in from home to get it."

"A syringe full of drugs?"

We slipped back into the hallway and continued through the reception area and toward Hublein's office, finding the file room along the way. I swept it with my Maglite. The bad news: it held a gazillion files. The good news: they were arranged by project. The bad news: we didn't know the name of the project. The good news: the thick three-ringed binder on a table near the entrance listed the projects and cross-referenced the drug used in each.

The first three pages indicated that Hublein had twenty-six active projects and three more that would soon start. I scanned the list. Most were acronyms. Only one contained "PTSD" in its title. I found the tab for that one and flipped to that section. Twenty-five subjects, including Brian Kurtz. Bingo. The drug being tested was called RU-1193.

We moved among the rows of files until we came to a section labeled

"PTSD-SAP: PTSD Symptom Attenuation Project." I quickly located Kurtz's file and scanned the twenty or so pages inside.

"Pretty straightforward." I handed the file to Claire. "Just as Hublein said. He's been on the drug for five months. No problems. No side effects. Each blood level in the proper range."

"So, the drug might have nothing to do with this?"

"Maybe not." I saw a copy machine in the corner. "Why don't you copy this while I sniff around a little more."

"That guy we saw might still be around."

"Then hurry."

I heard the copier come on and begin its warm-up sequence as I thumbed through the other files. The first folder was labeled "Project Summary." I took it to Claire. "This one, too."

I then selected a file at random. *Ronald Newsome.* I read through it and then pulled out another one. *Benjamin Hecht.* A third. *Thomas Wilkins.* The names changed, but the story was the same. All had had problems with PTSD, and all were doing well on the drug.

Another thing I hated was when things weren't as I wanted them to be. I wanted to find something out of bounds. Something that would explain Kurtz's obvious psychosis. If what he had done wasn't due to a drug, then it meant he was just evil. That was even scarier.

After Claire copied everything, I put the files back in place, and we left the file room. Left the building. Left the neighborhood.

CHAPTER 63

I WAS WRAPPED IN A DREAM, THE DREAM, THE ONE THAT CAME EVERY night now. Jill struggling to survive. Me failing her. The phone rang, jerking me to wakefulness. Claire rolled toward me, rubbing one eye with the heel of her hand.

I snatched up the phone. "Hello."

"I hope I'm not bothering you."

"What do you want?" I swung my legs off the bed and sat up.

He laughed softly. "Please, call me Brian. After all, we're on a first name basis now, aren't we?"

Time to roll the dice. Take another shot at rattling this guy. "You're not Kurtz."

"Really?"

"You're Kurtz's scout, lookout, controller . . . whatever you are . . . but you're not him."

Nothing for a moment, and then he said, "Believe what you wish." He laughed softly. "I have something you should hear. It

338

might change your mind."

"What might that be?"

"It's a classic. You'll love it. You guys listening in will want your tapes rolling."

I heard the click and hiss of a tape recorder, then:

"Oh, God, no."

A woman's voice, shrieking, terror-filled.

"Shut up."

A man's voice, muffled, away from the recorder.

"Tell my friend what you see."

"My husband, his . . . his . . . head is . . . gone. Help me."

"Look at your husband. See what happens to assholes."

"Why? Oh, God, why?" The woman's voice was frantic, stretched to the breaking point.

"Because he's an arrogant fuck."

The woman sobbed, whimpered, mumbled something I couldn't make out. Then the distinct sound of her retching. *"Please."*

"Shut up." The killer's voice was high-pitched, angry. His demon had taken over. Mr. Hyde was out. My fingers ached from the death grip I had on the phone.

"Please, don't hurt my baby. I'm pregnant."

"Shut up." The man's voice as much a shriek as hers now.

"I'll do anything. Just don't hurt my baby. Anything. I won't tell the police. Please."

The sharp *crack-thud* startled me even though I realized I had expected it. It's what he did, what he needed. The woman screamed, over and over as the blows fell hard against her.

"Leave her alone," I screamed into the phone. Claire was now bolt upright, eyes wide.

The blows and screams continued, the latter weakening second by second. I flinched with each impact as if I was being struck myself. I squeezed my eyes shut, not wanting to listen, unable not to, each blow pushing tears through my tightly closed lids. The screams became whimpers, the whimpers groans and moans, until she fell silent and only sickening thuds could be heard. Then they, too, stopped.

I heard the recorder click off. The calm voice returned. "See. I told you it was a classic."

Stay calm. Keep pressing. "That wasn't you. That was Kurtz."

"Then how did I get this recording?"

"You were there."

"Yes, I was. Alone. Well, the only one alive, anyway." He laughed again.

"You're a sick motherfucker."

"Maybe," he said. "But there's nothing you can do it about it. You couldn't save these people. Just like you couldn't save your sister. Jill, wasn't it?"

Heat rose in my chest, and my throat constricted. *Don't let him do this. Think.* Absolutely nothing entered my mind. Except for Jill's face.

"What's the matter? Your gift of gab's abandoned you?"

"You don't know . . ."

"I could debate what I know and what I don't know all night, but I have more work to do. A very special gift just for you. Talk to you soon."

The line went dead. I dropped the phone in its cradle, and my eyes met Claire's. I pulled her to me, and neither of us spoke for a minute. I just needed to hold her.

"It's bad, isn't it?" she asked finally.

"He beat her to death." I lifted my head from her shoulder and looked into her eyes. "She was pregnant."

"My God."

I took a deep breath and exhaled raggedly. "It's my fault."

"Don't say that. That's not true."

"I baited him, drove him to do this." Tears slid down my cheeks.

Claire kissed them away. "You didn't make him crazy or evil or whatever the hell he is. He did this. Not you."

I wiped my eyes with the bedsheet. "I better call T-Tommy." I reached for the phone, dialed, and when T-Tommy answered I said, "He wasn't lying."

"How bad is it?"

"He killed the man and then tortured the woman. He taped the whole thing."

T-Tommy said nothing, but I could hear his heavy breathing.

"She was pregnant," I said.

"Jesus Christ. This guy has no brakes."

"He's over the edge. Hyde's winning. Wait until you hear the tape. While he was . . . in action . . . his voice was . . . psychotic. High-pitched. Enraged. Not the cold, calm voice of the guy who calls."

"So you're thinking he does have a partner in this?"

"I don't know what to think. He said he was Kurtz. I believe he was lying." I massaged my neck. "It's just hard for me to put the two voices in one person, and yet it's just as hard to imagine this guy with a partner. He's barely hanging on to his sanity. All I know for sure is that we have to get him. Soon."

"We've got everybody on it. Luther pulled guys off just about everything else. I'll find out where the call came from and send some patrols through the area. We might get lucky."

"He said he wasn't finished. Said he has a surprise for me. Maybe he plans to come here."

"I'll put a surveillance team on your block."

"He might spot them."

"Or we just might trap him."

"Let's hope."

I hung up and grabbed my .357 from the nightstand. I walked through the house, checking the doors and windows, peering into the outside darkness. Satisfied, I returned to bed, slipped the gun beneath my pillow, and pulled Claire to me. "I'm so glad you're here."

"Are you okay?"

"Not even close."

CHAPTER 64

"WANT ME TO LOCK UP?" LISA ASKED.

"I'll do it. You get on home." Sammy Lange dunked the last four dirty glasses in the rinse water and aligned them with their mates on the bar.

"See you tomorrow." She waved on the way out the door.

Sammy stood at the front door and watched until Lisa was safely in her car and drove away. He locked the front door, flipped on the neon CLOSED sign, and turned off most of the interior lights. He counted the cash in the register and zipped it in the bank pouch for deposit in the morning. Twenty-two hundred plus credit card receipts. Not a bad night.

He pulled on his Windbreaker and stuffed the bank pouch in one pocket. After locking the back door, he dragged two trash bags to the bin at the side of the building and tossed them in. As he turned, he detected movement in the corner of his eye and by reflex raised his left arm. That deflected the first blow. Not the second. It

343

collided with the right side of his face.

He wavered but somehow kept his balance. A blow to his left temple followed. Bright lights and a searing pain flashed behind his eyes. He staggered, clawed the air for support, and managed to grasp the assailant's arm before he wobbled and fell to his knees. He pulled it to him and bit down, hard. The coppery taste of blood filled his mouth.

The attacker screamed and jerked away. Another blow, this one to his face. Sammy felt his muscles sag, no longer following commands. In slow motion he fell forward until his face kissed the asphalt. Rolling to one side, he looked up at the hulk above him. He couldn't see his face in the dim light, but felt the impacts as the attacker repeatedly kicked his ribs and stomach. Waves of nausea cascaded over him.

The hulk spoke. "This is a message for your buddy Dub Walker. Tell him I said hello."

Sammy started to speak, but a foot slammed into his jaw. The world spun in multicolors, faded to monochromatic gray, and consciousness slipped from his grasp. During his descent, he heard voices, shouting voices, but could not understand what they were saying. The voices, the hulk, the world faded to black.

Brian slammed his foot on the accelerator and held it down until he reached seventy miles per hour.

Don't be stupid.

He eased off, slowing to forty. His arm ached and blood soaked through the T-shirt he had wrapped around the wound. He tugged it more tightly.

How could he be so stupid? Let that old relic get the better of him? Well, not really the better of him, but he did do damage. He balled and relaxed his fist, then rotated his forearm. At least everything worked.

Goddamn it!

Harold Pearce slouched in his car, peering over the steering wheel. He had watched the entire scene unfold. Kurtz's attack. The old man fighting back. The car that pulled into the lot and stopped next to another car. Except for the old man's truck, the only one left in the side lot. Two couples climbed out and laughed and talked. Obviously intoxicated, it appeared that one couple had left their car here while partying elsewhere and had now returned to claim it.

The fight attracted their attention, and the two men ran in that direction, shouting. Kurtz ran behind the building and disappeared into the night. Pearce knew he was headed toward his car, parked a block away.

In minutes, the police and paramedics arrived. After the medics did their thing, they loaded the old man into the ambulance and drove away. The two couples told the deputies what had happened. One officer scribbled on his pad, but appeared bored with the entire situation. Soon, the cops and the Good Samaritans left, and the lot became quiet again.

Pearce flipped open the secure cell phone and called Smithson. He told him about the McCurdys, the tape he had played for Dub Walker, and the assault on Sammy.

"Perfect," Smithson said. "We're nearing the finish line. When will you play the final card?"

"Tonight. It's almost set."

CHAPTER 65

I SAT AT THE KITCHEN TABLE, DRINKING A SECOND CUP OF COFFEE, while Claire finished her share of the eggs and bacon I had made. On the deck, Kramden and Norton squabbled over the bowl of corn Claire had set out for them. I think they were warming to her. Of course, they warmed to anyone who fed them.

"Are we going to dig into the files today?" she asked.

Last night after we got home, I thumbed through the stuff we had lifted from Hublein's office, but was too tired to concentrate. "Yeah." I carried my plate to the kitchen and began to wash it in the sink. "This morning I called Drew Miller, an old med school classmate of mine. He's a researcher at the NIH. If anyone can find out about this drug, Drew can. He's sniffing around. Said he'd get back when he had something."

Claire joined me at the sink. I took her plate and washed it. She poured herself a cup of coffee. "Want more?" she asked.

"Sure."

347

She topped off my cup and then sat at the table again. I grabbed the stack of files and joined her. I went through Kurtz's file first and then moved to the summary folder.

"They'll call soon, won't they?" she asked. "About last night?"

I nodded. "Someone'll discover the bodies, and the whole madness will begin. This is one crime scene I'd rather not see. I heard enough last night."

I read through the list of the twenty-five people in the study, including their addresses and other demographics. "Look at this." I turned the page so she could see it. "The names."

I ran a finger down the row. *Brian Kurtz.*

She nodded. "We knew that."

I continued down the page. *Martin Hankins.* "This guy killed his entire family. Out near Owens Crossroads."

"I remember that story. He had PTSD." She looked at me. "Two people in Hublein's study have committed violent murders?"

"It gets better." Further down. *Gregory Hay.* "The dude who shot up the mall the other day." Further still. *Robert Swenson.* "This charming soul beat his girlfriend to death with a tire iron and is on the run right now."

"Four? Four guys in this study have murdered someone?" She turned the page toward her. "This defies all odds. Hublein and his drug are in this up to their eyeballs."

"Looks that way."

"Could this guy . . . this Swenson character . . . be Brian Kurtz's partner in all this?"

I looked at her.

"I mean, Hankins and Hay are dead. Swenson's not. Is it possible he's the guy on the phone?"

Could that be true? Swenson and Kurtz partners in crime? Both were in the same study, on the same drug. Both had committed violent murder. Both were on the run.

The phone rang.

"And so it begins." I lifted the receiver. "Hello."

"Dub Walker?"

It wasn't T-Tommy as I had expected. "Yes."

"I'm Dr. Sullivan. Do you know Mr. Sammy Lange?"

"Yes. What's this about?"

"He's here at Memorial Medical Center. In the ICU."

"What happened?"

"He was mugged."

"What? When?"

"Last night. Outside his restaurant."

"Why wasn't I called earlier?"

"He was in and out of consciousness and very confused most of the night. Finally cleared his head about a half hour ago and asked that I call you."

"Is he okay?"

"Banged up, but he should do fine."

"I'll be right there." I hung up the phone. "Let's go, Sammy's in the hospital."

Thirty minutes later, a nurse ushered us to Sammy's bedside. His face was swollen and purple, his left eye a narrow slit in a black goose egg. Dark, blood-crusted stitches formed a line along his puffy lower lip.

"Thanks for coming," Sammy said. "You, too, Claire." He offered her a half smile. "You're a sight for sore eyes . . . no pun intended."

She smiled and shook her head. "I see your sense of humor's intact."

"That looks like it hurts a bit," I said.

"Been better, but they tell me I'll live."

"What happened?"

"Somebody jumped me out back of the bar. Big guy. I think he would've killed me if some people hadn't come by and scared him off. I don't remember much."

"Did you get a look at him?"

"Strong's about all I can say for sure. Never saw his face. Too dark. Seemed to have short hair, squarish head. I'd guess six-one or -two." He looked at me. "He's the guy you're looking for."

"Kurtz? I thought you didn't get a good look at him?"

"Didn't. But while he was kicking the shit out of me, he mentioned your name."

Everything came into focus. Kurtz, or whoever had called, had mentioned a surprise, and this was it. Which meant he knew Sammy and I were friends, knew Sammy's routine.

"At least he didn't rob me," Sammy said. "I had twenty-two hundred bucks in my pocket, and they tell me it was still there. Maybe he didn't have time." Sammy winced and clutched his side.

"What's the matter?" Claire asked.

"Broke a couple of ribs. Hurts like a bitch. The doctors tell me I've got a cracked bone beneath the left eye and a bruised lung. Also peed a little blood."

"Doesn't sound like you're okay to me," she said.

"Bruises and cracks, nothing more sinister."

"I'm sorry, Sammy," I said. "I never suspected you might get dragged into this."

"Not your fault that the world's full of lunatics. I was unlucky. So was he. I took a pretty good bite out of his arm."

"You did?" I asked. "Which one?"

"Left. I think."

The nurse returned. "I'll have to ask you to leave now. The tech is here to do an EEG, then he needs to rest."

"Dub," Sammy said with concern in his eyes. "Be careful. This is one bad dude."

"I know."

"Anything I can do for you?" Claire asked.

"A sponge bath would be nice."

"He didn't beat the smart-ass out of you, either."

"It'd take more than this," Sammy laughed and then winced and grabbed his ribs.

On the way out, we stopped at the nurses' station, where one of the nurses looked up from the chart she held. "Can I help you?"

She had dark hair, showing a few streaks of silver. A blue name tag attached to the pocket of her crisp white uniform indicated she was "B. Hawkins, RN, Charge Nurse."

"I'm Dub Walker, a friend of Mr. Lange's. If any change in his condition occurs, could you contact me?"

"Of course."

"I'll give you my cell number." I wrote it on the scrap of paper she handed me. I pulled out my iPhone to make a different call. No signal.

She looked at me. "They rarely work in here. Too much electrical stuff. Here." She lifted a phone, placed it on the counter, picked up a chart, and headed toward one of the patient cubicles.

An answer came after the first ring. "Tortelli."

"T-Tommy?"

"Dub. I just tried to call you at home and on your cell. Where are you?"

"I'm at the hospital. Apparently cells don't work in here." I gave him a quick rundown on Sammy's attack and then asked, "What's happening on your end?"

"Last night's victims. Paul and Diane McCurdy. McCurdy's business partner came by to pick up some papers and found them."

My dream images reformed in my mind, but I pushed them

away. "Give me the address. I'll meet you there." I scribbled the location on a piece of paper. "One other thing. Sammy says he took a bite out of the guy's left arm. Contact the local hospitals, and see if anybody came in for treatment."

CHAPTER 66

BY THE TIME WE ARRIVED AT MCCURDY'S HOUSE, THE FULL ZOO HAD assembled. A half dozen deputies and a perimeter of crime scene tape held nearly thirty gawkers at bay. A man stood on a red plastic bucket, filming the house. I guess the bucket gave him a better angle. A middle-aged couple handed out coffee and doughnuts like it was a church social. Two young boys wrestled on a neighbor's lawn while a young girl danced pirouettes in the street. My fellow humans can be bewildering.

"Look at them. Where do they think they are? At a goddamn picnic?"

"People are strange," Claire said. "Makes my job a lot more interesting."

"I should take some of these clowns inside and show them the really gruesome stuff. Most of them would faint. I've seen it a hundred times, and I still get queasy." I let out a long breath. "They don't have a clue. They think this is a just a TV show."

The only death most people ever see is on TV, where the corpse is pretty, at times even sexy. Hair perfect, makeup perfect, and there is

354

always perfectly poignant background music. The fair maiden corpse appears to be asleep, as if a kiss from Prince Charming would awaken her. Real death is a different story. It's ugly. Pale and blue and smelly and sad.

The Channel 8 truck Claire had called for came up the street and pulled to the opposite curb. She headed that way. I walked into the house. The musty odor of blood and death greeted me. In the family room I found Paul McCurdy. Draped over one arm of a recliner. Dried blood rendered his pale blue pajama bottoms and white T-shirt the color of black cherries. Blood from his head wound had cascaded to the floor and produced a dark circular stain on the carpet. A much larger stain surrounded the body of Diane McCurdy. Mr. McCurdy had died quickly, too quickly to bleed much. His wife hadn't been so lucky.

A yellow nylon rope bound her body to a shattered wooden chair, which had toppled on its side. She and the chair appeared to float on a sanguineous sea. Sprays of spattered blood spread in every direction from her battered body and peppered the floor, the furniture, everything. Several long cast-off streaks painted the ceiling, just as I had seen at Petersen's. She was battered to an unrecognizable mass, and a fireplace poker stood erect from the side of her chest. Kurtz seemed to have a thing for fireplace tools.

The sound of Diane McCurdy's screams and the *thud* of the blows echoed in my head.

"This guy takes evil to a new level."

I turned to see T-Tommy enter the room, Sidau Yamaguchi in tow.

"Satan himself couldn't have dreamed this guy up," I said. "How'd it go down?"

"He came through an open window in the dining room," T-Tommy said. "Removed the screen, similar to Kushner's." He nodded toward the dead man. "One shot to the head. The bullet embedded in the wall near the sofa. Looks like a nine."

Again, the woman's screams rose in my head. "Mrs. McCurdy?"

"Not so lucky . . . as you know," Sidau said. "Can't be sure until Drummond does the autopsy, but my guess is that most of her injuries are premortem. I suspect the head wounds occurred after death. Too bad they weren't first."

I turned to T-Tommy. "I need to talk to you. Outside."

We went through the kitchen and out into the backyard. It was large and open, trees lining the far end.

"We need to turn Dr. Hublein inside out," I said.

"How so?"

"You know Kurtz was in some drug study of Hublein's." T-Tommy nodded. "So were Martin Hankins, Gregory Hay, and Robert Swenson."

"You're kidding."

"Wish I was."

"You know this how?"

"You don't want to know." He frowned. I went on. "Swenson's still out there. He could be as crazy as Kurtz." Now his jaw tightened. "They could be working together."

"Maybe the guy who's been calling you?"

"Possible."

My iPhone rang. It was Wendell Volek out at NASA. He said, "You want to take a look at what I found on the video you gave me?"

CHAPTER 67

BRIAN HAD HAD A RESTLESS NIGHT. TOO WIRED TO SLEEP. TOO angry with himself for losing control of that old geezer. He had paced, crawled into bed, tossed and turned, paced, drank a half dozen beers, did hundreds of sit-ups and push-ups, but nothing worked. Finally, as the sky began to lighten, he stretched out on the sofa at the safe house, closed his eyes, and concentrated on taking long, slow breaths. One of the calming techniques Hublein had taught him. It rarely worked.

He didn't realize that he had drifted to sleep until an electronic tone jerked him awake. Momentarily confused, he sat up. He glanced at his wrist. No watch. He'd left it on the nightstand when he fled from his apartment. The cell phone chirped again, and he picked it up from the floor, where he had tossed it.

"Hello."

"I have what you need."

"Now?"

358

"Relax," the caller said. "Didn't I tell you I'd have it today?"

Brian was now fully awake. "When?"

"Tonight."

"You're coming here?"

"No. At the institute. Say, seven thirty."

"At Dr. Hublein's office?"

"In the underground parking area. It'll be quiet, no prying eyes."

"You'll have the drug with you?"

"Of course. Besides, it's time we met. And tied up a few loose ends."

"Dr. Hublein?"

"And Wexlar. After you get what you need, they'll be yours. It's all arranged."

"How?"

"I'll explain it tonight."

"And Walker?"

"Him, too. I told you. It's all set up."

Pearce disconnected the call and glanced at his watch. Not much longer. He leaned back in his chair and massaged his neck.

For him, waiting was a love-hate thing. It sapped your strength, made you soft, weakened your resolve, yet required discipline, patience, self-control, the qualities that separated him from others. A few hours? No sweat. He had once squatted in a hole in the Iraqi desert for five days to take out a Republican Guard general. Sitting in this claustrophobic office was like R and R.

Besides, the end was near. Of course, he didn't trust Smithson, didn't trust anyone, but what choice did he have? Smithson had pulled his bacon from the fire. Otherwise he'd be an errand boy at the Pentagon. Or worse.

He did have a grudging admiration for the man, however. Neither his focus and determination nor his plotting and planning abilities could be denied. What truly amazed Pearce was Smithson's immediate access to information. He seemed able to accumulate data in a heartbeat. His research on Kurtz, Hublein, Wexlar, each of the victims, even Dub Walker, had been exact and complete. Every inquiry Pearce sent was fulfilled within hours, if not minutes.

He knew Smithson had a doctorate in chemistry. He had also been a more or less lifer in the army. Made full colonel. Then left for civilian life and a much bigger paycheck. Now CEO of Danko-Meyer Pharmaceuticals, he was in some kind of pissing contest with Spellman Pharmaceuticals. Each trying to be the first to put out a new drug for PTSD. A huge and growing problem, which meant big bucks to whoever won the race. Hublein was tied in with Spellman's new drug through the PTSD-SAP project. Smithson wanted to trash the study and their new drug.

Enter Harold Pearce.

After Smithson rescued him from his dead-end military career, he somehow maneuvered this job with Spellman. Pearce had no idea how he pulled that off but suspected that Smithson had a handful of his own people inside Spellman. The only thing Pearce knew for sure was that Spellman had hired him as a project security manager and had assigned him to this project. To prevent competitor espionage. To protect the secrecy of Spellman's new drug. Talk about the fox in the henhouse. The irony was that Spellman was actually paying him a hefty salary and was totally unaware that Pearce was the enemy. Got to love Smithson's nerve.

Once Pearce got him all the data on the trial, Smithson selected Brian Kurtz and a few other members of the study as the pigeons. Now they were only hours away from blowing the whole thing up. Once the police discovered that Hankins and Hay and Swenson and Kurtz were all on the same drug, a drug that was known to make people violent in higher doses, the shit would fly. Spellman would fall. Smithson would win the prize.

He opened the soft black pouch, removed the vial, held it up to the light, and examined its rich amber color. It looked like the others, but he knew it was different.

All twenty-five members of the study had been receiving the same dose of the drug. That's what the protocol called for. But for the past three months, Pearce had substituted the vials designated for the four chosen subjects with ones that looked identical yet contained a triple dose of the drug. Hublein had faithfully injected these into the four men each week, just as the protocol dictated.

The swap had been easy, as had the exchange of their blood for "cleaner" samples. Ones that contained the expected concentration of the drug, not the toxic level that had run through all of them and that now ran through Brian Kurtz's veins. Hublein, for all his smarts, didn't have a clue.

Hankins and Hay had gone postal and gotten themselves killed by the police. Too bad, but Pearce never felt good about those two. Swenson looked better for the final stage, but he went off the reservation, and Pearce had had to terminate him. He smiled, thinking about the cops still looking for him, when he was in the ground far from where anyone would look.

Brian Kurtz had turned out to be the perfect subject.

Pearce rotated the vial back and forth between his thumb and forefinger. This final dose contained not only a massive amount of the drug, but also a hefty dose of amphetamines. Guaranteed to send Brian over the edge. Pearce had only to give him the injection, sic him on Hublein and Wexlar, drop a dime to Walker, and let the games begin.

When confronted with an enraged Brian, the two good doctors and Walker wouldn't stand a chance. The police would ride in and do what they always did. Shoot first and plant a weapon later. Hublein's files and Brian's autopsy would expose the entire project, bring Hublein and Spellman down, and Smithson would make a killing. And fill Pearce's pockets.

He could almost smell the clean ocean air of Tahiti.

CHAPTER 68

T-TOMMY AND I MADE OUR WAY THROUGH THE SECURITY checks at the Redstone Arsenal and were again escorted to NASA headquarters. We met Dr. Wendell Volek in the same conference room as before.

Volek got right to it. He tapped a couple of keystrokes on his Mac laptop and a video appeared on the large screen that covered one wall. It was the video I had seen when last here, only now cleaner and brighter. The ceiling-mounted camera angled on the ornate central stairway at the Russel Erskine. A man moved into the frame, took the stairs two at a time, and disappeared as the stairs zigged to the right. Volek let the video run a few cycles and then worked the keyboard again. Now the same man came down the stairs and moved out of frame. Again, he let it repeat half a dozen times. A few more keyboard taps and a series of still images, mostly close-ups of the man's head, appeared. In the final one, a partial profile could be seen as the man neared the bottom of the stairs. Volek left that one up.

"Here's the raw image. Cleaned up a bit. This frame gives us the only look at part of his face. Not great, but that's the best we have." The keyboard clicked under his fingers. "After a few manipulations, this is what we have."

The picture snapped to amazing clarity. The facial features were now sharp-edged and brighter. Kurtz. No doubt. The shape of the jaw, the nose, the narrow lips. Just like the mug shots of him I had seen. I glanced at T-Tommy.

"That's him," T-Tommy said. "Brian Kurtz. Our primary suspect."

"The time on the first clip, as best I can reconstruct, is five after one. Give or take a couple of minutes. He came back down about thirty minutes later. Thirty-two to be exact." He tapped the keyboard again. "This was forty-five minutes earlier. Around twelve twenty."

Another man, smaller, also in a jacket and cap, hurried up the stairs. Took them three at a time. Definitely not one of the residents.

"And then six minutes later."

The same man descended the stairs and moved out of frame. He kept his head down and one hand at the side of his face, blocking the camera.

"He knew there was a security camera," I said. "And exactly where it was."

"Son of a bitch," T-Tommy said. "Kurtz does have a helper."

I looked at T-Tommy. "This guy's connected to Hublein."

"What do you mean?"

Time to 'fess up. "I took a look at Hublein's lab. Claire and I. Last night."

"That's how you knew about the others? Hankins and Hays and Swenson?"

I nodded. "This guy . . . the one on the video here . . . he was there. At least I think it was this guy. Same size, same walk. Came in and took something from the refrigerator. Looked like a syringe filled with a yellowish liquid."

"For Kurtz?"

"That'd be my bet."

"Why?"

That one I didn't have an answer for.

Volek tapped up several stills of the man's head. None showed any of his face. "Sorry. Not a single frame gave me anything to work with."

CHAPTER 69

"WHAT THE HELL HAVE YOU GOTTEN YOURSELF INTO?"

It was Drew Miller. The call I'd been waiting for. "What do you mean?"

"This RU-1193 is heady stuff."

I felt the hair on the back of my neck snap to attention. I looked across the table at Claire and T-Tommy. Claire had pretaped her report. She did that some nights and others went live. We had watched it just a few minutes earlier while we finished a dinner of pizza and beer on my back deck. T-Tommy was waiting for word from Judge Feigler on a search warrant for Hublein's office. He had a team ready to move, but needed the warrant.

"Tell me."

"It's being studied in six centers. The one you have down there and five others. LA, Chicago, Dallas, Miami, and Boston. Twenty-five subjects in each locale. Been going on about a year. All approved by the NIH and cofunded by Spellman Pharmaceuticals."

"I understand it's a benzodiazepine, and the studies are on PTSD patients."

"Exactly. It and another drug manufactured by Danko-Meyer seem promising. They're in a race to see who gets to the market first. Whoever wins will have the first real drug for PTSD."

"That's worth millions."

"Actually billions. PTSD is a big problem. And growing. Not only with Iraq vets but with people in all sorts of stressful situations."

"So, what's the problem?"

"RU-1193 is a derivative of a drug studied many years ago by the US Army. It was designated RU-1186. Also for PTSD, but didn't exactly pan out."

I massaged one temple. "This is the part I'm not going to like, isn't it?"

"Who said you weren't perceptive? Both are synthetic drugs. The army began research on RU-1186 in the early 1990s. By the time the studies moved from rats to baboons, things went sideways. After several months, the baboons became hostile, territorial, ripped each other to shreds, even killed a lab worker. They shut down the project."

"Obviously that's not the end of the story," I said.

"Several years ago RU-1186 went through several modifications, and the Pentagon conducted human studies on military prisoners. Using the modified drug in lower doses. The results were better. At first. The subjects showed improvement in their PTSD symptoms. Less headaches, insomnia, restlessness, depression, that sort of thing.

Apparently, five months into the study the men became extremely combative and hostile. One of them killed two others with a mop handle."

"And?" I asked.

"Back to lab, a few more molecular tweaks, and RU-1193 was born. It fared better in animal trials and the initial human studies. Now this phase-three study is under way."

"Are you aware of any problems at any of the other centers?"

"Such as?"

"Violent behavior."

"Is that what you're dealing with there?"

I gave him a quick thumbnail of the murders. He listened quietly and then said, "The major problem with both of these drugs is dosing. They tend to accumulate in the system, and when the blood levels rise, so do the side effects. One of which is violent tendencies."

"What else?"

"Paranoia, rage, anger, headaches, insomnia, the usual."

"So as far as you know, there've been no problems at any of the other centers?"

"Haven't seen anything on that, but I didn't specifically look. I can make a couple of calls and see what I can find out."

"Don't get yourself out on a limb over this."

"You know me. I live out there."

I thanked Drew for his help and said I'd let him know if I found out anything. He said he'd do the same. I hung up and then told T-Tommy and Claire what Drew had said.

T-Tommy shoved his fingers through his hair. "So Kurtz has been on this drug for several months. He goes bonkers and kills Mike and the others. So did the other three guys. And apparently there are nearly two dozen other Kurtzes out there."

"That about sums it up," I said.

T-Tommy stood. "Fuck the warrant. I think it's time to pay Hublein another visit."

CHAPTER 70

THIRTY MINUTES EARLIER HAROLD PEARCE HAD CALLED HUBLEIN at home, telling him that he and Wexlar needed to shred the files immediately, that the police knew where Brian was, and that his arrest was imminent. Hublein freaked. Perfect.

Now, he stood in the shadows of the institute's parking garage and sucked down the remains of a bottle of water. Tossing the empty plastic aside, he strapped his Sykes-Fairbairn commando knife against his left calf and nestled his 9 mm Beretta against his back, beneath the waistband of his pants.

The gray sedan came down the ramp and turned into a parking space across from where Pearce stood. Dressed in black pants and T-shirt, chest and arm muscles straining against the shirt's thin material, Brian stepped out and looked around.

Pearce eased from the shadows and stood beneath an overhead light. "Hello, Brian."

Brian stopped, stared at him for a moment, and then walked

toward him.

Pearce unzipped the leather pouch, slid the syringe out, and held it up. "Is this what you need?"

"I still want to know who you are."

"The one who can supply this." He spun the syringe between his thumb and forefinger. "The one who can deliver Walker. Hublein and Wexlar, too. After all, they're the ones responsible. The rage that lives inside you. You know Hublein put it there."

"What if I like the power it gives me?"

Pearce nodded. "Anger can be very powerful. Vital. Addictive. But what about when it spins out of control? What about when you lose control?"

"Maybe I like that, too."

The man laughed softly. "I know you do. But you've been used. By Hublein and Wexlar. I can help you make it right."

"The only person I see using me is you. Why do you care what I do? What's your payoff?"

"Why does there have to be a payoff?"

"There always is." Brian rotated his neck as if relieving a knot.

Pearce smiled. "True."

"So? What do you want?"

"We agree that I've helped you. Right?" He didn't wait for Brian to respond. "I've covered your back. The gun. The un-locked doors and opened windows. All the information and maps and . . . well . . . everything. I've made your work easy. Now I want you to take care of something for me. Something you'll enjoy immensely."

"What?"

"I want Hublein and Wexlar gone as badly as you do. Maybe more so."

"Why?"

"That's not important, but if you do this . . . take care of them . . . you'll have an endless supply of this." Again, he lifted the syringe toward the overhead light.

"How do I know I can trust you? I don't even know you."

"Because I've helped you. Can you say the same for Hublein? Didn't he pull the plug on you?"

Brian's jaw tightened. Pearce could almost feel the heat radiating from him.

"How do I know you can get the drug? Maybe that's all you have."

"I told you . . . I have connections."

"What connections?"

"The same ones that allow me to know so much. To help you." He held up the syringe. "Ready?"

Brian tugged down the elastic waistband of his pants and turned a hip toward Pearce. Pearce jabbed the needle deeply into the muscle and depressed the plunger.

Brian pulled up his pants and turned back to face him. He started to say something but acted as if the words were lodged in his throat. His pupils dilated, consuming the blue of his eyes. His chest heaved, sweat erupted on his face, and the muscles of his jaw contracted. He screamed and clutched his head. "What did you give me?"

Pearce backpedaled, too slow. Brian charged, slammed both palms into Pearce's chest, propelling him to the floor. Pearce rolled to his feet only to be met by a fist to his jaw. Pearce reached for the 9 mm but as he cleared the weapon, Brian hammered his arm across Pearce's forearm, dislodging the gun. It clanged against the concrete floor.

Pearce struck Brian beneath the chin with the heel of his hand, snapping his head back, cracking his teeth together. Brian fell to his knees, clutching at Pearce, who spun away and slammed a foot into Brian's ribs. He danced away, and then spun back, aiming his heel at Brian's head. Brian partially deflected the kick, and it bounced off his right ear. He grasped Pearce's ankle and with a maniacal scream pushed it toward the ceiling. Pearce toppled to the floor.

Brian was on him and crashed his fists into Pearce's face. Right, left, right. Pearce blocked most of the blows and then snapped Brian's head back with three quick strikes to his chin and a final one to his throat. Brian recoiled, clutching his throat, sucking in wheezing breaths.

Pearce grabbed a fistful of Brian's hair, yanking him to the left as he rolled to his right and sprang free of Brian's grasp. He clutched the handle of the commando knife, the carbon steel giving off a twanging sound as he yanked it from its scabbard.

Brian stood, his face a mask of rage. "I'm going to kill you."

"I'm not the enemy."

Brian charged, but Pearce sidestepped his attack and swiped the knife toward Brian's midsection. Brian deflected the blow, grabbed

Pearce's forearm, and twisted it.

Pearce felt his arm resist, then snap, sending a shock of pain through him as he collapsed to the floor. Brian fell on him, fingers locked around Pearce's throat. Pearce rained blows on his face, but Brian ignored them.

Brian now had the knife in his other hand. He drove the blade into Pearce's chest, raised it, and thrust it into his abdomen, burrowing it deep. He grabbed Pearce by the hair and pulled his face close to his. "Who the fuck are you?"

"Nobody," Pearce grunted.

"Don't fuck with me. Who are you?"

Pearce felt the knife grind deeper into his gut. "Fuck you!"

Brian withdrew the knife and shoved it to the hilt beneath Pearce's ribs.

Pearce coughed, blood foaming from his mouth. Pain surged into his chest as Brian worked the knife deeper.

"You're dead anyway," Brian said. "Tell me why you're here."

Pearce's breaths bubbled through the red foam that flowed from his mouth. Harold Pearce was dying, and he knew it. But he was a soldier. That's what he was, all he was. He had carried out dozens of missions in which he could have lost his life. That risk was part of the job, and he accepted it as any good soldier would. He would not die without completing this mission. Sending Brian after Hublein would expose everything. Exactly as Smithson had contracted him to do.

Sir. Mission completed, sir.

"Hublein," Pearce gurgled. "Wexlar . . . they're the ones you want." Pearce coughed, spraying blood over his chest. "They're . . . upstairs . . . right now." He coughed again, pain racking him. "Trying to . . . cover up . . . what they've done."

Brian jumped to his feet. He screamed and kicked the knife that still protruded from Pearce's abdomen. It skittered across the floor. Pearce groaned and sputtered, struggling to draw air into his lungs. Brian slammed his heel onto Pearce's face and stormed through the nearby stairwell door.

Nine-one-one. Nine-one-one. Pearce mentally repeated the numbers. One last piece of the mission. He pulled the cell phone from his pocket, struggled to see the dial pad, finally managing to punch in the number. He shivered as a damp coldness settled over him.

"Nine-one-one operator. What's the nature of your emergency?"

"Hublein." He coughed, pain raging through his chest. "Dr. Robert . . . Hublein's office."

"Could you speak up? I can barely hear you."

Pearce mustered what strength he could. "Dr. Hublein's . . . office . . . Send police."

The lights dimmed, and Harold Pearce drifted into darkness.

CHAPTER 71

IN THE HEADLIGHTS, I SAW THE MAN STRETCHED OUT ON THE FLOOR of the parking garage. Blood splayed across the concrete. I jerked the Porsche into a parking slot and jumped out, telling Claire to stay put. T-Tommy swung in next to me.

I knelt beside the man. Forty or so, square jaw, short-cropped hair, solid build. The guy I had seen in the lab last night. And on the video today. I felt his neck, the pulse weak, his breathing a coarse rasp.

"Hey, buddy." I squeezed his shoulder. No response. I pulled my iPhone from my jacket pocket and punched 911. An operator answered, I identified myself, and requested an ambulance, giving her the address.

"We just got a call from there," the woman said. "The police and medics are on the way."

"What?"

"I think the line to the caller is still open." I heard her ask someone named Martha if she still had the call online. Then back to

376

me, "Yeah, we still got it. It's a cell phone."

I looked around, saw a phone wedged beneath the guy. I pulled it free and spoke into it. Martha was on the line. "Okay, we're here on scene. What's the ETA of the ambulance?"

"Should be any second now. They've been rolling for four minutes."

I could hear the faint sound of sirens, closing in. I punched the END button on both phones, stuffed mine in my pocket, and dropped the other one beside the man.

I ripped the man's bloody shirt off, wadded it into a ball, and pressed it against his abdomen. "I'm sorry, but I have to slow the bleeding." The man grimaced, breathing in gasps.

T-Tommy's cell rang. He answered and listened for a minute, and then snapped it closed. "That was Abe. The killer's phone just called nine-one-one. From around here."

I nodded toward the cell on the floor. "That's it."

"You sure?"

"Yeah."

T-Tommy pointed to the floor. "What the hell is that?"

"Looks like the syringe I saw last night," I said. "And this is the guy I saw in the lab." I bent close to the man. "What's your name?"

"Pearce." He barely got it out. Blood foamed from his mouth, and he coughed, wincing. "Work here."

"What happened?"

"Kurtz . . . Brian . . . Kurtz."

"Where is he?"

"Up . . . stairs . . . Hublein . . . kill Hublein."

I looked toward the stairwell entrance, now seeing the blood drops leading that way, and more blood smeared on the door. Two patrol cars and an ambulance rushed down the ramp and squealed to a stop.

CHAPTER 72

As Brian entered the outer office, voices and an intermittent machinery sound spilled through the door from Hublein's office. He pulled his gun—no silencer, no need here since no one was around. He stopped near the doorway and listened.

"You sure we have everything copied onto discs?" he heard Hublein ask.

"Absolutely," Wexlar said. "So does Spellman."

"Then let's get this finished and get the hell out of here."

Brian stepped into the door. They didn't even notice, too busy destroying evidence. Evidence of what they had done to him. Hublein stood by his desk, near three stacks of paper. He handed several pages at a time to Wexlar, who fed them into a shredder.

"Wonder what's keeping Pearce," Hublein said. "He should be here by now."

"He won't be coming," Brian said.

Hublein and Wexlar whirled around, their eyes widening

379

in shock.

"Brian . . . what are you doing here?" Hublein stammered.

"Surprised to see me?"

"No . . . uh . . ."

"Pearce fucked up. He's dead." His pulse hammered in his temples.

Hublein recoiled. "How? Why?"

"I got lucky, he didn't." Brian raised the gun, directing the muzzle at Hublein's chest. "And neither did you."

"Brian . . . I . . ."

"Shut up," he screamed.

Wexlar stepped toward him. "Listen, Brian—"

The gun exploded three times with deafening roars, which reverberated endlessly in the room. The first bullet struck Wexlar in the middle of the chest. The second penetrated the dying man just inches left of the first. The third cut into his face as he toppled onto the shredder, knocking it to the floor.

"Any other comments?" He stared at Hublein through the blue fog that hung between them.

Hublein raised his hands for protection. "Brian . . . I'm—"

Three more shots in quick succession, each bullet striking Hublein in the chest. His massive frame absorbed the first two, but with the third he staggered backward and toppled onto the desk. A brass desk lamp crashed to the floor, and papers cascaded onto Wexlar's lifeless form.

I pushed open the fifth-floor stairwell door, noticing a smear of blood on the handle. This time I remembered to bring my .357. I tugged it from my jacket pocket and moved down the poorly lit hallway where Claire and I had tiptoed last night. I crossed through the reception foyer and continued down the opposite hall toward Hublein's office. The door stood open, light falling through it on the floor. The odor of burned gunpowder hung in the air. Nothing else on earth smells like that.

T-Tommy and I took positions at either side, and I peeked around the jamb into Hublein's assistant's office. It was brightly lit but empty. We crossed to the open door that led into Hublein's private office, and again I peered around the jamb.

"Jesus."

Hublein's blood-soaked body reclined across his desk. The body of a smaller man lay stretched over a pile of papers and file folders. I checked them, both dead. As I stood and turned, I saw Kurtz in the doorway behind T-Tommy, gun leveled.

"Get down!"

Everything seemed to move in slow motion. The gun jerked. An explosive flare. A cloud of smoke. T-Tommy dropped to the floor. The bullet whizzed past my head and hit the wall behind me with a dull thud. The gun jerked again. This time the noise seemed louder and things moved faster. I fired twice, but Kurtz had disappeared. One bullet splintered the doorjamb. I had no idea where the other one went.

T-Tommy got up, a hand clamped over one ear, blood between his fingers. "Son of a bitch shot me." He pulled his hand away. "Let's go."

We moved through the outer office and into the hall, just in time to see Kurtz moving away fast, down the hallway, toward the foyer. He turned and fired, the bullet striking the ceiling above us. He pulled the trigger again. *Click.* He threw the gun at us, turned, and disappeared across the foyer.

CHAPTER 73

As I approached the stairwell door at the end of the hall, I heard Kurtz's footsteps, headed down. I pushed open the door and listened. Nothing. No footsteps. We moved down the stairs to the next landing, "4ᵀᴴ Floor" stenciled on the door.

"I'll take this one," I said. "You get three."

I slipped through the door, and pressed my back against the wall, the .357 directed down the dark hallway that ran the length of the building. Faint light from the streetlamps along Saint Clair filtered through windows along the right side, revealing several doors along the opposite wall.

"Brian?" My voice echoed in the empty corridor, followed by silence, leaving only my own coarse breathing and the pulsing of blood in my ears. "Brian? I don't want to hurt you. I know what's been going on. It's not your fault."

Was that true? For days all I could think about was planting this guy, keeping my promise to Mike, taking the sick son of a bitch out.

But Kurtz really was sick. He wasn't merely another sociopath with a head full of snakes, a head that couldn't be tweaked. Kurtz had been tampered with. Kurtz could be fixed.

Or could he?

After Mike, the Kushners, the McCurdys, after all he had done, could Kurtz ever come back? Could his brain be rewired? Did that really matter? Did he deserve that chance?

"A ton of cops are going to be up here in a couple of minutes. You can't get away. Just give up, and we can sort this out."

Nothing. I moved along the hall to the first door and twisted the handle. Locked. The second door opened to a dark room. I flipped the wall switch and banks of overhead fluorescents flickered to life, revealing an office with a desk and bookcases, but little else. I killed the lights, waited for my eyes to readjust, and then continued down the hall.

"Brian, please listen to—"

The blow struck the back of my head, spinning me sideways. The .357 thudded to the floor. A second blow caught my jaw. I staggered, but managed to remain upright, and raised my fists as he came at me. I snapped a right hand against the side of his head. It did nothing to slow the assault. A fist slammed into my gut, sending a paralytic shock everywhere. Multicolored balls of light danced before my eyes.

Jesus. This kid is strong.

I hit him with three shots to the face. He didn't seem to notice. My knuckles burned. I caught another heavy blow high on the left side of my head. I seemed to move in slow motion, arms heavy, legs heavier, unable to fend off the blows that followed. Right cheek, left temple, right eye, point of my chin, and then I found myself down on my hands and knees, gasping for air.

He leaped on me and in a single motion lassoed something around my neck, pulling it tight. I clawed at the ligature. It was thick and leathery. A belt. I couldn't wedge a single finger beneath it. My lungs fought for air, convulsing against the constriction.

My left arm, now supporting us both, quavered. I knew that if I collapsed to a prone position, I would have no leverage and would be finished. Where was T-Tommy?

I attempted to twist and buck against him, but his strength proved to be too much. The pressure in my head seemed to push my eyes from their sockets. The room spun, and the window above me seemed to twist, flex, and melt. For some odd reason it reminded me of a Dali painting. My arm gave way and I collapsed forward, forehead striking the floor. Supported only by my knees and forehead, I fought to remain conscious.

"Have a nice death, Dub." He pulled on the belt.

I searched for some way out. I needed T-Tommy, I needed the cavalry. I twisted and turned but couldn't break free. My lungs burned, my vision dimmed, and my forehead and knees screamed for relief.

Do something.

I slipped my left hand into my jacket pocket and yanked out the small bottle of Tabasco, spinning the cap off with my thumb. I shook a generous amount into my cupped right hand.

Brian leaned forward and pressed his lips close to my ear. "Good-bye, asshole."

I jerked my left shoulder up, against his chin. He recoiled slightly. I gave another hard twist of my shoulder and managed to turn just enough so that I could slam my right palm into his face. The fiery liquid splashed into his eyes, up his nose.

Kurtz screamed and leapt to his feet, clawing at his face.

I rose to all fours, tugged the belt loose, and gulped air. Getting my feet under me, I lunged at him with all the strength I could muster, driving my shoulder into his chest, knocking him backward.

He staggered, arms flailing, and crashed into the window behind him. The glass shattered and the aluminum frame groaned, then collapsed under the impact of his weight. He toppled through the window, screaming as he fell.

CHAPTER 74

I STOOD WITH CLAIRE, TWENTY OR SO FEET FROM WHERE Kurtz's body lay. Dead, he seemed ordinary, not the enraged beast he had been just minutes earlier. Not the monster Hublein had created. I hugged Claire tightly. I never wanted to let her go. A near-death experience will do that to you.

T-Tommy walked up and clapped a hand on my shoulder. "You okay?"

My voice was barely a whisper. "I'm fine. You?"

"Scratch."

"Dub," Luther said as he approached. "Good work. Claire filled me in on this whole operation. Just when you think you've seen everything, something like this happens."

"Sounds like you have a couple dozen more Kurtzes to find."

"Scotty and the guys are on it. They're up in Hublein's office packaging up the remaining files."

"What about Pearce?" I asked.

387

Luther shook his head. "Didn't make it."

"He was Kurtz's partner in this."

"Why do you think that?"

"The cell phone. Pearce had it. Used it to call nine-one-one. It's the same phone he used to call me."

Luther rubbed his forehead, shook his head. "So Pearce was Kurtz's controller. The rational voice."

"Looks that way."

"Who exactly was Pearce?" T-Tommy asked.

I shrugged. "Not sure, but I'd check out a drug company called Danko-Meyer. They were in a serious competition with Spellman to develop a new drug for PTSD. Spellman made the drug Kurtz and the others were taking."

"Why do think that?"

"Got it from an old med school classmate. He's a researcher up at the NIH now."

"A drug competition? Is that worth all this?"

I nodded. "Billions, Luther. It's worth billions."

Luther shook his head. "Don't it always come down to money?"

I looked at T-Tommy. "Let's go by the hospital and get your ear looked at."

"Just a scratch."

"Humor me."

The Channel 8 truck rolled up. "Time to work," Claire said.

"I'll go over to the ER with T-Tommy," I said. "Have them drop you there when you're done."

"Will do."

"Then you can take me home and put me to bed."

"That's the best offer I've had all day." She slapped my butt.

CHAPTER 75

IT WAS A FUNERAL KIND OF DAY. DRIZZLE FELL FROM A HAMMERED pewter sky and a cool breeze pushed in from the north. Didn't feel like July.

Over a hundred HPD and sheriff's department officers attended Mike Savage's graveside service in Maple Hill Cemetery. Raincoats covered their uniforms and fat raindrops tapped the umbrellas that sprouted above their heads. Several of the guys who had worked with Mike over the years spoke, including T-Tommy and Luther. And me. Wasn't easy. Wasn't nearly enough.

After the crowd began to head for the shelter of their cars, I stood at the edge of the rectangular pit and stared at the gray-metallic casket. "We got the bastards, buddy. For what it's worth, we got them." I walked toward the car where T-Tommy and Claire stood talking beneath an umbrella.

"You okay?" Claire asked.

"Been better." I glanced back toward the grave. Two workers

were shoveling dirt into the hole. I looked away. Didn't want to see that. I looked at T-Tommy. "Anything new?"

"We've located all the other subjects. Except for Robert Swenson. Still a murder warrant out on him."

"Kurtz's tox report? Anything on that yet?" We had couriered samples up to NMS in Pennsylvania Saturday morning. They agreed to rush the work. Helped that they knew what to look for.

T-Tommy nodded. "They called a couple of hours ago. Right before I headed over here. Kurtz had toxic levels of that drug in his system. Toxicologist said that his blood, liver, and muscle tissues were saturated with it. Said that to reach those levels he must have been given a series of very large doses over several weeks. Maybe longer. Looks like Pearce had been tampering with the dosing and with the lab results. The syringe you guys found at the scene contained a large concentration of the drug and a hefty amount of methamphetamine."

"Why would Pearce do that? What was the payoff?"

"Scotty did some digging into Harold Pearce's background. Had to use some of my DC sources. Ex-marine intel. Ex-CIA. Lot of wet work. Iraq, Iran, Bosnia, North Africa, even Russia. Didn't play well with others, though. A handful of reprimands in his file. Punched out a general once. Ended up leaving the military and hooked up with a guy named Lawrence Smithson."

"And he is?"

"CEO of Danko-Meyer."

"So this Smithson guy hired Pearce to sabotage his competitor,"

I said, more a statement than a question.

T-Tommy nodded. "Don't have it all nailed down, but it sure smells that way."

Claire shrugged. "Money trumps all."

Ain't it so.

CHAPTER 76

I DON'T KNOW HOW I ENDED UP HERE.

After Claire and I left Maple Hill, I drove up over the mountain, intending to head home. Instead I drove past my street and back down the hill. I was too restless. Didn't want to be confined. I felt as if the case had been solved, yet not. As if it had been neatly wrapped, yet a corner had worked loose. As if something inside me needed to get out. To Claire's credit, she seemed to sense that I needed to be lost inside myself and said nothing, letting me zigzag all over the city.

I drove north, and then south, and then found myself on I-65 south, toward Birmingham. Then I was at the UAB Medical Center. Where I had spent nearly four hard years. I drove past the buildings and hospital wings that had been my life so many years ago. My entire life. Seemed as though I rarely ventured beyond those walls.

I drove past the ER. The new one. It had been moved out of the Old Hillman Building, where it had been when I was there, and into the new North Pavilion. The move didn't change things much,

393

though. The receiving ramp was busy. It was always busy. Like it had been that night twelve years ago. Now three ambulances sat there, having disgorged the ill and injured.

I continued farther down Fifth Avenue and turned into a parking lot. *The* parking lot. The one where Jill had waited for me. The one where someone besides me met her. Took her. I pulled up next to the exact space where my car had sat that night. It was empty.

I left the engine running and got out of the car. I ignored the light rain and stared at the space. Slicked with rain and oil stains, it looked like a black hole. It looked like a grave.

"I'm so sorry, Jill." I sniffed. "I always will be."

I stood for a few minutes and then wiped tears from my eyes and got back into the car.

"Are you okay?" Claire asked.

"No." I would never be okay. I pulled from the lot.

One More Moment

A CATCH IN TIME

DALIA RODDY

In one moment, with no explanation, six billion humans fall unconscious. For three minutes, minds collide with truths hidden beyond the physical realm.

During those decisive minutes, every conceivable accident transpires. People reawaken to a world that has changed, drastically and horrifically, with decimated populations and gutted social order. And no one seems to remember the truth that has been revealed.

But Laura remembers—most of it, anyway. Yet even she doesn't know why all post-Blackout births are mutations, and what is so wrong with some of the survivors.

ISBN# 978-160542103-2

Mass Market Paperback / Horror

US $7.95 / CDN $8.95

AVAILABLE NOW

THE JAKE HELMAN FILES

PERSONAL DEMONS

BY GREGORY LAMBERSON

Jake Helman, an elite member of the New York Special Homicide Task Force, faces what every cop dreads—an elusive serial killer. While investigating a series of bloodletting sacrifice rituals executed by an ominous perpetrator known as The Cipher, Jake refuses to submit to a drug test and resigns from the police department. Tower International, a controversial genetic engineering company, employs him as their director of security.

While battling an addiction to cocaine, Jake enters his new high-pressure position in the private sector. What he encounters behind the closed doors of this sinister operation is beyond the realm of human imagination. Too horrible to contemplate, the experimentation is pure madness, the outcome a hell where only pain and terror reside. Nicholas Tower is not the hero flaunted on the cover of Time magazine. Beneath the polished exterior of this frontiersman on the cutting edge of science is a corporate executive surrounded by the creations of his deranged mind.

As Jake delves deeper into the hidden sphere of this frightening laboratory, his discoveries elicit more than condemnation for unethical practices performed for the good of mankind. Sequestered in rooms veiled in secrecy is the worst crime the world will ever see—the theft of the human soul.

ISBN# 978-160542072-1
Mass Market Paperback / Horror
US $7.95 / CDN $8.95

AVAILABLE NOW
www.slimeguy.com

Dawn Schiller

The Road Through Wonderland is Dawn Schiller's chilling account of the childhood that molded her so perfectly to fall for the seduction of "the king of porn," John Holmes, and the bizarre twist of fate that brought them together. With painstaking honesty, Dawn uncovers the truth of her relationship with John, her father figure-turned-forbidden lover who hid her away from his porn movie world and welcomed her into his family along with his wife.

Within these pages, Dawn reveals the perilous road John led her down—from drugs and addiction to beatings, arrests, forced prostitution, and being sold to the drug underworld. Surviving the horrific Wonderland murders, this young innocent entered protective custody, ran from the FBI, endured a heart-wrenching escape from John, and ultimately turned him in to the police.

This is the true story of one of the most infamous of public figures and a young girl's struggle to survive unthinkable abuse. Readers will be left shaken but clutching to real hope at the end of this dark journey on *The Road Through Wonderland*.

Also check out the movie Wonderland (Lions Gate Entertainment, 2003) for a look into the past of Dawn Schiller and the Wonderland Murders.

ISBN# 978-160542083-7
Trade Paperback / Autobiography
US $15.95 / CDN $17.95
AUGUST 2010
www.dawn-schiller.com

WILLIAM JABL★NSKY

Karl Gruber wasn't an ordinary German clockmaker. And it wasn't an ordinary night in 1893 when his unique creation, a sweet spirit name Ernst, came into the world. Fashioned of cogs and wheels and nickel, this inanimate object had no beating heart. He ticked . . . like a clock. Yet somehow Karl gave his fantastic man the gift of life.

On the amazing pages of a diary, Ernst records the events of his time-keeping existence. With mortal sensitivity, he lives with enthusiasm and passion, feeling, thinking . . . even loving. This piece of clockwork is alive. Some might call him a piece of work with his shimmering blue eyes. Within his mechanical soul is a sterling personality that far exceeds the average human being.

Then a dire series of events puts this automated man out of action for over one hundred years, plunging him into a dormant state of despair. He wakes in the twenty-first century, facing a dangerous, unfamiliar civilization. Ernst has a new purpose. He cannot stand by and watch as innocent people are intimidated, endangered, and harmed. The Clockwork Man does not comprehend apathy. Apathy is a human frailty.

As long as Ernst can rewind, he will live in the shadows of the city, shunning materialistic society and avoiding the capture that threatens to reduce him to a museum-quality piece of machinery. Another urban legend has been born . . .

ISBN# 978-160542099-8

Trade Paperback / Steampunk

US $15.95 / CDN $17.95

SEPTEMBER 2010

THE FRENZY WAY

GREGORY LAMBERSON

In every hardened cop's worst dreams there lurks a nightmare waiting to become reality. Captain Mace has encountered his. When a string of raped and dismembered corpses appears throughout New York, the investigation draws Mace into an interactive plot that plays like a horror movie. Taking the lead role in this chilling story may be the challenge of his career, testing his skills and his stamina, but even a superhero would find the series of terrifying crime scenarios daunting.

Unlike anything Mace has experienced, every blood-spattered scene filled with body parts and partially eaten human remains looks like an animal's dining room strewn with rotting leftovers. Only Satanic legends and tales from the dark side of spiritual oblivion resemble the mayhem this beast has created in his frenzy. In the wake of each attack is the haunting premonition of another murdering onslaught.

As Mace follows this crimson trail of madness, he must accept the inevitable conclusion. Whoever—or whatever—is responsible for this terror does not intend to stop, and it's up to him to put an end to the chaotic reign of a perpetrator whom, until now, he's met only in the annals of mythology. The mere mention of the word would send New York into a panic: *werewolf.*

ISBN# 978-160542099-8

Mass Market Paperback / Horror

US $7.95 / CDN $8.95

JUNE 2010

www.slimeguy.com

HEIRS OF CAIN

TOM WALLACE

Fallen angels.

The last words of a dying man. To the local cops, the words are meaningless. But legendary assassin Cain knows exactly what they mean.

A hit is in the works.

And the target is big.

In 1971, five U.S. soldiers trained as assassins landed in North Vietnam to complete a deadly mission under the watchful eye of Cain, a man feared by the Vietnamese on both sides of the DMZ. Today, joining forces with his old boss General Lucas White, Cain soon learns that Seneca, a former ally, has been hired to kill the president of the United States and three top leaders in the Middle East.

Against a ticking clock, Cain must hunt down his former ally. But an even deadlier betrayal could sabotage his mission—and cost him his life.

From the dark jungles of Vietnam to the midnight shadows of Central Park, *Heirs of Cain* takes its readers on a thrilling ride they won't soon forget.

ISBN# 978-160542102-5

Mass Market Paperback / Thriller

US $7.95 / CDN $8.95

MAY 2010

wormfood

jeff jacobson

Arch Stanton has a bad job that's about to get a hell of a lot worse.

He's sixteen, scrawny, and dirt poor. He has an almost supernatural ability with firearms, but it may not be enough to survive the weekend.

Welcome to Whitewood, California, an isolated small town in northern California, a place full of bad manners and even worse hygiene. Money is tight, jobs are scarce, and bitter rivalries have simmered just under the surface for years.

Fat Ernst runs the local bar and grill. He'd stomp on his own mother for a chance at easy money, and when he forces Arch to do some truly dirty work, all hell breaks loose.

Fat Ernst's customers find themselves being infected by vicious, wormlike parasites and dying in unspeakable agony. As events spiral out of control, decades of hatred boil over into three days of rapidly escalating carnage. Will anyone in this town escape . . . before they're eaten alive?

ISBN# 978-160542101-8

Trade Paperback / Horrible Horror

US $15.95 / CDN $17.95

JULY 2010

Theater of Illusion
Kathy Steffen

Children of an abusive father who spiraled into madness and murder, Sarah and Tobias Perkins survived by holding to each other.

As adults, the siblings live and work on the Spirit of the River, the riverboat that saved their mother from their father's wrath. Yearning to pilot the riverboat herself, Sarah is forced by custom to stand by as her childhood rival, Jeremy Smith, becomes not only pilot but first officer. It is 1910, and the River Board has specific opinions about where a woman belongs—and it is not behind the wheel of a riverboat.

Tragedy strikes when Théâtre d'Illusion—a traveling theater extravaganza—comes aboard to entertain passengers during the journey downriver. One of the performers vanishes, and then one by one, the passengers and crewmembers on board the Spirit of the River fall victim to a mysterious and deadly illness.

Plagued by the voice of his murderous father, Tobias finds peace only during overnight drinking binges. But when he awakes each day to a trail of death and destruction, he begins to fear his father's spirit has possessed him. As the sins of the past threaten to destroy the future, Sarah races against time to stop a vengeful killer. Will she bring the Spirit of the River and the surviving passengers home, or is all hope of escape an illusion?

ISBN# 978-160542086-8
Trade Paperback / Historical Fiction
US $15.95 / CDN $17.95

AUGUST 2010
www.kathysteffen.com

FORTY-EIGHT X

THE LEMURIA PROJECT

BARRY POLLACK

A colonel with a shadowy past . . .

A new kind of war and warrior . . .

A military science experiment out of control . . .

On the tropical island of Diego Garcia in the middle of the Indian Ocean, the United States has gathered together its most talented scientists to conduct top secret experiments. Their goal—to create a revolutionary new warrior. A warrior so strong, so valiant, so expendable that the age of "casualties of war" becomes only a sad and distant memory. And so, the Lemuria Project is brought to life—by a Nobel laureate in genetics and a three-star general seeking redemption in a long-lost and forgotten metaphysical civilization.

Haunted by a dark and dangerous past, Colonel Link McGraw is the officer chosen to train and lead these special "soldiers." In the course of battles to renew his tattered reputation, he, above all, knows what constitutes the perfect soldier. It's simple: Follow orders, command decisively, make no excuses, and have no regrets.

When Egyptian beauty Fala al-Shohada and Israeli Joshua Krantz, romantically paired archaeologists, stumble across the top secret project, they are determined to uncover its true nature and pursue their quest to the island of Diego Garcia. Science and politics clash, as do Krantz and McGraw, who vie for Fala's affection. When they discover they aren't the only ones on the island competing for her attention, shocking truths are revealed.

The future of the entire human race comes to a crossroads on Lemuria. Will humanity find there its loftier spirit or become a lesser species in earth's evolution?

ISBN# 978-193475502-0
Hardcover / Thriller
US $24.95 / CDN $27.95

AVAILABLE NOW
www.barrypollack.net

SHAMROCK ALLEY

⊹ ≕✦≔ ⊹ A NOVEL ⊹ ≕✦≔ ⊹

RONALD DAMIEN MALFI

Secret Service agent John Mavio infiltrates the infamous Hell's Kitchen in New York to shut down a ring of organized crime leaders involved in an elaborate counterfeit money operation, perhaps the worst in history. Based on a true story, the Irish villains of Mickey O'Shay and Jimmy Kahn are real. These violent criminals, once known as the West Side Boys, terrorized the community and inflicted grue-some deaths on numerous victims by bludgeoning, stabbing, shooting, and cutting into pieces the bodies of those who got in their way or refused to cooperate with their treacherous schemes.

Mavio is the courageous agent who risked his life to stop what may have been the most sinister operation this country has ever endured—a hero based on Ronald Damien Malfi's own father. Every step closer to the drugs, the booze, and the blood brings him one step closer to his own demise, a risk he takes to save innocent citizens from ongoing torture. His life undercover is a gory, dangerous world far removed from his personal reality—his pregnant wife, Katie, and his terminally ill father wait for him to return from each threatening encounter alive.

Then one day . . . these two worlds meet. Mavio must implement every skill he has painfully learned to save himself and the people of New York. He cannot fail, for failure would mean the end of everything honorable, just, and right. And, above all, justice must prevail.

ISBN# 978-193383688-1

Hardcover / Thriller

US $24.95 / CDN $27.95

AVAILABLE NOW

www.ronmalfi.com

MEDALLION

P R E S S

Want to know what's going on with
your favorite author or what new releases
are coming from Medallion Press?

Now you can receive breaking news,
updates, and more from Medallion Press
straight to your cell phone, e-mail, instant
messenger, or Facebook!

Sign up now at www.twitter.com/
MedallionPress to stay on top of all the
happenings in and
around Medallion Press.

For more information
about other great titles from
Medallion Press, visit

m e d a l l i o n p r e s s . c o m